One
in
the Gravy

Also by Delia Rosen

A BRISKET A CASKET

One Foot in the Gravy

Delia Rosen

KENSINGTON PUBLISHING CORP.
http://www.kensingtonbooks.com

KENSINGTON BOOKS are published by

Kensington Publishing Corp.
119 West 40th Street
New York, NY 10018

All Kensington Titles, Imprints, and Distributed Lines are available at special quantity discounts for bulk purchases for sales promotions, premiums, fund-raising, and educational or institutional use.

Special book excerpts or customized printings can also be created to fit specific needs. For details, write or phone the office of the Kensington special sales manager: Kensington Publishing Corp., 119 West 40th Street, New York, NY 10018, attn: Special Sales Department, Phone: 1-800-221-2647.

Kensington and the K logo Reg. U.S. Pat. & TM Off.

ISBN-13: 978-0-7582-4171-9
ISBN-10: 0-7582-4171-2

First Mass Market Printing: October 2011

10 9 8 7 6 5 4 3 2 1

Printed in the United States of America

Chapter 1

"The Creeping Leeches?" Thomasina said as she approached the van. "Lawfy, what kinda sick, disgustin' name is that?"

I folded a stick of gum in my mouth as I eyed the logo painted emphatically on the side. Although Thom's reading of it wasn't entirely correct, her reaction was understandable. I had worries of my own that the realistic painted leeches forming the letters might kill people's appetites. But transportation was transportation and we couldn't afford to be choosy.

Thom should have known making a fuss wouldn't help. Then again, when had knowing better ever stopped her from complaining? Under *any* circumstances?

Luke frowned down at her from the driver's seat. Moments earlier, he'd swung into the alley between my restaurant and the country-western nightclub next door, braking loudly in front of the service entrance. An unlit cigarette hung from his mouth—

he was trying to gratify his oral fixation while once-and-for-all, no-I-really-mean-it quitting the habit cold-turkey—and his orphan's don't-give-me-crap attitude hung from his brow.

I'd been waiting there on a somewhat muggy afternoon with my manager for about fifteen minutes. We were both a little grumpy.

"Before you criticize, Thom, you oughta try 'n read it right," Luke said through his lowered passenger window. "Ain't no 'the' in it. And it's writ *CreepLeeches*—one word—for a reason."

"And what might that reason be?" she demanded, turning away.

"Reason's the rockabilly group that owns the van ought to know how they want their name spelled. And you're lookin' at their official tour vehicle."

"I'm all a-tingle."

"You should be," Luke said. "And stickin' to the point, you should show some respect. A name's a name's a name. Like mine's Luke. Like yours is Thomasina Jackson. And like Nash here's, well, y'know . . ."

Luke scratched under his ear, realizing I wasn't the best example he could have chosen. See, it's a little tricky. Nash is short for Nashville Katz, my full nickname. The "Nashville" part refers to the location of my restaurant—Murray's—which happens to be the first and only Jewish deli in Music City. The "Katz" comes from my *real* name, Gwen Katz. And the whole thing is a play on the title of an old Lovin' Spoonful song that without question could have been written about my late Uncle Murray, from whom I'd inherited the place right before my messy, humiliating New York divorce from the Pied Piper of Stripper-land was finalized.

Told you it was tricky, didn't I?

"Okay, forget Nash," Luke said. He was still looking at Thom. "I want to hear where you figure we'd be if the *CreepLeeches* hadn't loaned us their ride."

"Inside, where we belong, preparin' for dinner," she said, still looking away. "And if you don't stop repeatin' that godawful name, I'm gonna puke! I didn't sign up to be no deliverywoman for some rich old crackpot."

I checked my watch and decided it was time to interrupt. As much as they enjoyed squabbling with each other, we had to get cracking. "Easy, Thom, that's unfair," I said. "Lolo Baker's a good customer."

Thom "phewed." "Glad you didn't say 'nice lady,'" she said. "'Cause she's a snob, one who's got nothin' better to do with her nights than playact with her friends. God, I wish I had the time to be eccentric and stuff."

"Don't change the subject. We were talking about her dinner party—"

"*Murder* party," Thom interrupted. "You can at least be truthful about what it is while tryin' to persuade me she ain't batty."

"Okay, fine. If you stop being so obnoxious," I said.

Thom's brow furrowed under her bob of silver hair. "How'm I being obnoxious?"

I sighed. "Because it's ridiculous for us to argue about this. First and foremost, it's a paying gig. Second, audience-participation dinner shows are mega-popular everywhere. Third, Lolo's into reading murder mysteries. I don't see a problem here."

"I think throwing a mystery-themed dinner is a fun idea," Luke tossed in.

Thomasina shot him a sneer, saw the logo again, and looked away. "Well, I think it's silly. She can get half-naked men in Spartacus costumes to serve her food for all I care."

"Then—I'm not getting what your problem is," I told her.

"It's since when are *we* in the caterin' business?"

I shrugged. "Since Lolo offered to pay us big-time."

"Then you admit this is about her havin' oodles of money."

"Who cares? Did I ever tell you it hurt? You know how much we're taking in for the party. Businesses have to grow—"

"Says who?" Thom frowned disapprovingly. "In all the years he owned the deli, Murray never mentioned a word about growin'—"

"Maybe that's true," I said. "But things change."

"How, why, and who said so? Why should *any*thing be different besides you bein' in charge nowadays? Oh, and because of that fact, your boyfriend Royce Sinclair wantin' to buy us out."

I looked at her. "That isn't fair. It's been six months since Royce approached us. And he isn't my boyfriend."

"Oh, no?" Her tone went from critical to knowing as smooth—and cutting—as a meat slicer. "Then what you gonna call him, sugar?"

The phrase *unstoppable turbocharged sex dynamo* jumped into my head, but I wasn't sure that would help make my case. I was starting to feel woozy. Maybe it was yet another debate with my staff. Or maybe it was the van's gas fumes pooling in the alley. Whatever, it was time to break this up.

"Listen, if you want to argue, count me out," I replied. "I shouldn't have to remind you, but I will, that our insurance premiums doubled after the flood. We can use some added revenue. And special events planning is just an extension of what we already do. It's honorable. It's *smart.*"

"Smart," Thom repeated. She stood there scowling at me a few seconds. Then she nodded back toward the van. "Might I ask how rollin' up to Belle Meade in that eyesore's gonna make us look? Or you really think Lolo's a fan 'a the Slime Bugs?"

"*CreepLeeches!*" Luke shouted. "I suggest you get that straight, because the band's got itself a huge followin'."

"Yeah? In what *swamp*?"

"You ain't the slightest bit funny." Luke shook his head. "People do us a favor, we ought to be grateful. My cousin Zach and his boys were even kind enough to remove their instruments—"

"Your *cousin*? The one with the wishbone nose ring? He's a Creeping Leech?"

"*CreepLeeches!* Yes, the son of the aunt and uncle who raised me, and who was kind enough to clear

the van—except for a drum kit and some cables—
so we'd have plenty of room for food."

"Speaking of which," I said, tapping my watch,
"we'd better get ready to roll."

Thom looked at me. "So you really intend to go
through with this deal, batty biddy, bloodsucking
bugs, and all?"

"Right you are, Thom. We're professionals, and
whatever you might think, this job's important to
us. It'll open doors. I have absolutely no intention
of blowing it."

She opened her mouth to answer, then seemed
to change her mind. It was almost two o'clock on
a Saturday afternoon and the murder mystery
dinner was set for seven p.m. Moreover, we'd
booked it several weeks before. Her grumbling
aside, Thomasina really was as professional as they
came. She would have never backed out—or
expected *me* to back out—at this late stage. Complaining was just her way of venting. She hadn't
made it the fine art my own family had, but then
her folks weren't Old World.

Losing the sour puss was another story, of course,
and I got a serious eyeful of it from her when the
service door swung open and twenty-two-year-old
college dropout Newt—that's short for Newton
Trout, nothing complicated there—poked his head
into the alley. He was wearing his cook's cap and
apron and had wrapped his bushy brown whiskers
in a beard net.

"Hope ya'll are good 'n' ready," he said. "Everything's about set to go."

I faced him and started ticking off items on my mental checklist. "The turkey—?"

"Carved."

"The corned beef and pastrami?"

"Laid out on platters."

"The goulash?"

"Packed in a hot food carrier," Newt said. "Same for the stuffed cabbage and meatballs."

"Knishes, kugel, latkes, kasha, varnishkes . . ."

"Got them too. Plus plenty of supper rolls."

"Pickles?"

"Sours, half-sours, you name it."

"And the sides?"

"I just got the lid down on a six-pound tub of coleslaw. It was so chock full, I practically had to stomp it shut with my foot."

"Let's make sure to tell that to Lolo," Thomasina said.

"Jimmy crammed another one with potato salad and we got a smaller one for some of your uncle's special bean stew."

"What about the garlic eggplant canapés? The ones we're supposed to serve to just one guest?"

"Present and accounted for."

"Do we know who that is yet?" Thom asked.

"No," I told her. "Lolo will let us know. She said there will be other instructions and not to worry about them now."

I was feeling pretty good when panic struck. "The Sterno! Oh, *crap,* I forgot to order the—"

"Watch your foul mouth!" Thomasina interrupted. "Girl, when you gonna learn better'n to be *vulgar?*"

"Right, sorry, let's try this again," I said. "Oh *Lawfy,* Newt, this is a real bitch-stinker of a screwup. What in goddamned *hell* are we going to do *now?*"

I deliberately avoided looking in Thom's direction. But I could feel her disapproval wash over me like the heat of an open oven on broil.

"Don't fret," Newt said heroically. "A.J. stopped by our wholesaler on her way into work, bought a whole carton of Canned Heat."

"Goin' up the country . . ." Luke sang foolishly, entertaining only himself.

"Has anyone seen her yet?" I asked.

"She's waitin' in that fancy new convertible of hers." Newt jerked his chin toward the outdoor parking lot at our rear. "Oh, and I asked one of the busboys to dig the warmin' trays outta the storeroom. He's gonna put them in her backseat so she can drive them over to the party."

Relieved, I exhaled through my mouth, my gum almost shooting from it like a dart from a blowgun. "What about Medina and Vernon?"

"They already started out in Vern's rust bucket."

I nodded. That would leave us seriously undermanned at the restaurant and force Raylene Sue Chappell, one of my best waitresses, to work the cash register. But I didn't see an alternative. Lolo was plugged in to Nashville high society in a major way, and some of the city's most influential people would be among her guests that night. If word of mouth on our first catering gig was positive, there would be many more. If not, we'd be deader than the fake corpse at her soiree.

"All right, Newt, I think we've covered everything," I said. "As long as you're okay holding the fort tonight. . . ."

"Don't you worry," he said. "We'll be fi—"

He broke off all at once, gawking at the van with his mouth wide open. I realized he had just noticed the logo on its side.

"Whoa! Is it my imagination or are those letters supposed to look like slugs?"

"Worms," Thomasina said.

"Leeches!" Luke moaned. His arm was hanging out the window and he slapped the door in frustration. "Can't any of you folks *read*?"

Newt stared at him, his brow crinkling in disgust. "I stand corrected," he said. "I mean, leeches. They're gonna look a lot less nauseatin' when they roll in with our food, now won't they?"

Luke made a bulldog face. It was time to go.

Four hours later, Thom and I were in the immense dining hall of Lola Baker's restored antebellum plantation house, giving our buffet tables a final inspection. All pillars, porticoes, porches, gables and hanging eaves, the estate was set on three acres of farmland that had been in Lola's family for generations—well, technically, in her late husband Colton's family for generations. It had been years, if not decades, since crops had grown in its fields, but Lola didn't need their production in order to stay rolling in ripe green stacks of moolah. Thanks to Colton making some successful high-yield investments back in the freewheeling 1990s, she could afford to sit back and let the value of her financial shares grow . . . and grow and grow and grow. No watering, fertilizer, or plows required. As a retired accountant, I appreciated his foresight almost as much as she did.

"Well, now, it seems to me everybody's here," Thom said, looking up from a tray of beef goulash. The room's mahogany pocket doors had been slid back into the wall, giving us a wide-open view of the parlor where Lola's guests were having cocktails and hors d'oeuvres. "Another few minutes and they can come fill their faces before the stupidity begins . . . though I suspect some of the men might stay behind to get better acquainted with A.J.'s bra."

I didn't say anything. Once we'd hit the road, Thom had gone from griping about the party itself to the outfits we'd worn. I had prepared my defense in advance, figuring I was bound to hear her squawk about it at some point on the way out to Belle Meade. And same as when I'd seen the band logo on the van, I frankly understood her exasperation—although I wasn't about to let her know that.

Uncle Murray had wanted the atmosphere at the deli to be what he'd always called Western casual.

As long as the staff dressed neatly, he was satisfied. But it was easy to distinguish diners from servers in a restaurant, where the customers stayed put at tables while the waiters and waitresses came around and took their orders. At special events, it was different. Because partygoers moved around and circulated, they had to be able to identify the servers in a crowd. That meant uniforms.

I'd opted for basic black. Shirts and trousers for the guys, skirts and blouses for Thom, A.J., and me, pairing them respectively with honey gold silk neckties and feminine scarves of the same color and material. I told everybody they were free to choose their own footwear and tweak their outfits with whatever jazzy personal touches they chose, as long as they didn't stray from the color combo.

It still didn't go over well with the staff. Forget what I said about personal touches. They'd responded like I was forcing them into Sunday school outfits. And I admit their unhappiness surprised me. I didn't see what was wrong with wearing black. In fact, I thought it was kind of cool. Johnny Cash wore it. The E Street Band. Angelina Jolie in *Lara Croft: Tomb Raider*.

Anyway, after seeing how disgruntled they were, I'd decided to set a positive leadership model in catering couture. Besides adding a wide retro patent-leather belt to my getup, I'd squeezed into a pair of black sky-high heels that made my feet look sexy, my legs longer and my hips swingier . . . not to mention adding four or five sylphlike inches to my height. So what if they bunched my toes together and left them swollen red radishes? I'd had confidence in my ability to keep from screaming in pain till I got home and took them off. And bear in mind, I *was* trying to prevent a full-scale staff mutiny.

Unfortunately, A.J. had pushed—or maybe I ought to say pushed *up*—the bounds of professional attire a little too far south of the modesty line, wearing her blouse half unbuttoned from the top, getting plenty of lift from the alluded-to bra, and guiding the eye down the Major Cleavage Expressway with a string tie straight out of a Dallas Cowgirl pinup.

One thing, though. With the party barely under way, my tootsies were already sore from rubbing together. And since that probably *wasn't* true of A.J.'s twin peaks, I felt it was just plain stupid of me to stand in judgment of their exposure level. Or even to stand, period.

I looked through the entry into the wainscoted parlor, where A.J. was offering hors d'oeuvres to the guests, including a short, roly-poly man who was taking in a choice view of her personal scenery.

"The girl doesn't watch herself, she's gonna spill out into his food," Thom said. "That's *got* to violate some health code or other, Nash. Don'tcha think?"

I kept quiet. At first, it was because I didn't want to spur her on. But then I realized I knew the man.

"Hey," I said. "That guy over there's Hoppy!"

"Sure does seem to be," Thomasina said.

"Could a fella take any more time reachin' for his weenie-wrap?"

I frowned. Being the perennial church bakeoff queen of Nashville—I kid you not—Thom knew everybody's wife and mother and was consequently as plugged into the city's social scene as anybody. "Quit playing dumb. You know as well as I do it's Hoppy who owns the chocolate shop over on Charlotte Avenue."

"Uh-huh. And so what?"

"I just wouldn't have expected Lola to invite him," I said, lowering my voice to a hush. "I'm not saying she's a snob. But most of her other guests *are* kind of upper-crusty."

"And what makes you think he ain't?"

I opened my mouth, then closed it, at a loss for words. Hoppy was a well-known penny squeezer. He would give away chocolates if it helped him socially, but that was it. He wouldn't part with an extra shopping bag if a customer begged and pleaded for one, it didn't matter that you were walking around his store with chocolates spilling from your arms and containers of dipped strawberries balanced on your head. I shouldn't have needed a reminder that the world was full of rich, cheap jerks. As a former forensic accountant on Wall Street, I'd specialized in following the money trail of financial hotshots who were cooking their books on the way to their second or third or fourth billion.

I looked at Thom. "Okay," I said. "What's Hoppy's story?"

"Hapford's, you mean. His full name's Hapford Hopewell Jr. The inventor of Hopewell's chocolate patties."

The ice cream treat that looked like frozen cow patties. They were a local sensation, especially among teens . . . or anybody with a juvenile sense of humor. "Wow, no *sh*—"

"Mind your cussin' tongue." Thom speared me with a reproachful glance, forget that I'd been speaking in a whisper.

"Sugar," I said. "Wow, no sugar!"

Thom went on. "Downtown rents and overheads bein' what they are, ain't no way Hoppy could make ends meet without sellin' a lot of them."

"I thought there was a family fortune—"

"I heard that too." Thom nodded, squaring her jaw. "That would explain how come he thinks he can treat customers the way he does. It's the same to him if he gets one or a hundred walking through the door every day."

"Sounds like you've had some run-ins?"

"I take my nieces in there for chocolate lollies, only place you can get 'em. He looks at us like we only carried Canadian money. He's an a-hole, to put it bluntly."

I have no patience for someone who's entitled *and* arrogant, but I let it stand. Who knows what goes on inside anyone's skull, even your own? Meanwhile, I wasn't too sure that *I* could go on standing much longer. My toes had cramped up like I'd just run the River Kwai Half-Marathon.

Thom noticed me shifting uncomfortably. "What's the matter?" she said. "You got quiet all of a sudden."

"So?"

"So quiet ain't your regular M.O."

I shrugged. Couldn't argue. "It's my feet. They're killing me."

She stared down at them. "Wah-wah. I could've told you wearin' stripper shoes was a bad idea."

"Strip—Thom, these are dress pumps, *not . . .*"

She chopped her hand through the air to cut me off again, wiggling her foot to showcase her square-toed orthopedic flats. "Stop with the whiny excuses. Whatever happened to people takin' responsibility for themselves?"

I raised my eyes from the black bricks she was passing off as shoes and looked her in the eye. "Same thing that happened to taking pride in their appearance."

"Oooh, snap. I should've expected that'd be your attitude," she snorted. "Well, I worked hard my entire life. After thirty years in the restaurant business, I know what to put on my hush puppies. I'd rather *be* professional than just look the part."

I kept looking at her, caught by surprise. She seemed really aggravated and upset, as opposed to being just her usual intentional pain in the neck. "Thom, what's wrong?"

"Forget it," she said. "I just don't appreciate

people gettin' all judgmental about my choices or my footwear."

"Hang on . . . that's unfair," I said. "You're putting words in my mouth."

"You want to stick a label on me so you can feel superior, go right ahead and knock yourself out."

"I wasn't—"

Since there probably isn't much chance our squabble would have devolved into an out-and-out catfight, I won't exaggerate and claim we were saved by the bell. But we *were* interrupted by a glassy little tinkle from the parlor.

I turned toward the sound and saw Lolo Baker holding a glass dinner bell on the other side of the entryway. A slender, silver-haired woman in charcoal trousers and a paler-than-pale pink silk blouse, the mystery bash's hostess sported a pearl necklace with an appropriately Sherlock Holmes-ish magnifying glass pendant, and stood ringing the bell amid a lively crowd of guests.

"Excuse me, friends!" She beamed a smile. When she didn't immediately get everyone's attention, the eyes narrowed thin as threats and the smile became a shrill piccolo trumpet. "Your attention *please*!" That did it. "Dinner will be served in ten minutes . . . and then our criminal mischief begins!"

Delighted murmurs swarmed around Lolo as Thom returned her attention to the goulash. She gave it a stir with her spoon, closed the lid, checked the burning Sterno underneath it, then sidled over to the tray of mushroom-and-carrot-stuffed flank steak.

A moment later, she cocked her head at an angle, scrunched up her face like a puzzled bulldog, and began looking around the buffet table for something.

"What's the matter?" I asked.

"The gravy terrine," she said. "I don't see it anyplace."

I didn't either. But I did remember Luke carrying the gravy from our borrowed *CreepLeeches* van in its insulated container and promising he'd fill the terrine with it. "Hang on, I'll be back in a jiff," I said, and turned toward a hall off the dining room.

"Where you going?"

"The kitchen." We'd pulled our vehicles up around one side of the house to its entrance and lugged everything inside. "Bet you the gravy's still there."

"All ri-i-ighteeo!" The faintly familiar, drawling male voice, as well as the lip-smacking that went along with it, had come from right behind me. "I do so love to have nice, thick, piping-hot gravy with my steak."

Hoppy, I thought, facing him unhappily. It hadn't been more than ninety seconds since Lolo's ten-minute dinner alert. But there he was with his strong, craggy face, eager eyes, thick lips, and the word "Hoppy" embroidered on the handkerchief tucked in his blazer. At least it wasn't accompanied by a rabbit or a picture of a cowboy.

"We're just finishing our preparations," I said,

and struck my best professional pose. "Give us a few minutes and we'll have everything ready for you . . . and the rest of the guests."

I'd hoped Hoppy might take those last words as an unsubtle hint to scram. Instead, he leaned forward to study the flank steak, then straightened with a cringe-worthy wink. "No tastes? For a good neighbor in the downtown business community?"

I stared at him. Putting aside that he'd never offered me a professional discount at his shop, it was the first time Hoppy had let on that he knew me from a hole in the wall. "How about I give you the same kind you give me?" I said.

Hoppy's mouth twisted in thought. "Well, now, I can't quite recall—"

"Exactly," I said, swinging into the hallway.

The gourmet kitchen was at the end of the hall past a door to a storage or linen closet. I heard guitar-playing from inside as I rushed closer, and then saw Luke, dressed in a black Western shirt and matching skintight slacks, strumming away on his Gibson acoustic beyond the entrance.

"You mind if I ask what you're doing?" I said, stepping through.

He looked at me from where he stood beside a countertop. "I'm workin' out tonight's theme song, Nash."

"Theme song?" I hesitated. "News flash! This is a catered party. It is *not* one of your nightclub gigs."

I wasn't nearly old enough to be Luke's mom. But his baby-blue eyes always brought out my maternal instincts. He smiled, all innocence. "I just figured that if we're gonna do these parties as a regular thing from now on, I could provide some special musical touches. Here, let me show you."

"Wait a sec, Luke. I need to find the—"

Too late. He was already plucking out a chord. And singing along to it. *"It's a deadly deli mystery, killer could be you, victim could be me. Time will tell, we'll have to see, what happens when the clock strikes three . . ."*

I held up a hand like a traffic cop. "Luke, please. Do me a favor and hit the pause button a sec."

He blinked a little woundedly and aborted the tune. "Sorry. I figured you'd love it."

"That day may come," I said. "I mean, I think it's really good." Talk about feeling guilt-tripped. "But it's way past three o'clock . . ."

"Right. That's how come I was smoothin' the kinks in here. I need a different word to rhyme with 'see.'"

I cleared my throat. "Maybe we ought to discuss this later," I said. "At the moment, I'm looking for the flank steak gravy. Have you seen it?"

Luke nodded and swung the guitar strap from his shoulders. He stood the instrument up against the counter and went over to a large stainless-steel sauce pot on the range.

"I was warming it while I composed," he said. "Ought to be about ready."

Ready or not, it was going out to the dining

room. I spotted our terrine on the central kitchen island, hurried over to get it, ladled it full, and carried it toward the entryway, declining Luke's offer to take it himself. I was in too much of a hurry to fuss around.

That was when my foot seriously cramped up again. It was like a sadistic gorilla had my toes in its fist.

"Ouccchhhh!" I blurted out unbecomingly.

"Nash, you all right . . . ?"

"Yeah, don't worry. Just put away your guitar and come help us in the dining room *pronto*."

I limped through the entry without waiting for his arm. At least six or seven minutes must've passed since Lolo had waved her dinner bell high in the air, leaving me with no time to waste.

I'd barely gotten into the hallway when I heard a loud crash over my head. And I mean loud enough to halt me dead in my tracks.

I looked up, the terrine in my hands. There was more crashing and pounding in what seemed to be the room directly above me. And whatever was causing it had made the ceiling visibly shake.

"What's *that* about?" Luke said. He'd raced to my side from the kitchen. "Sounds like some wild ol' orangutan's jumping around upstairs."

I glanced over at him. It was a banner day for primate similes, I guessed. I was tempted to ask if it might be the same one that had mashed my foot.

I never got the chance to ask that or anything else. Before I could get out a word, or even react, we heard the loudest, most violent crash yet. And then the ceiling came down in front of us, breaking up into a dusty shower of plaster and lath and whatever else might've gone into two-hundred-year-old ceilings.

"Sand?" he blurted out.

Luke was right. That was the last thing pouring out. I later learned it was stuffed up there to put out fires, in case the flames burned through.

I recoiled in shock and surprise, the terrine tumbling from my fingers, gravy spilling from it, splashing everywhere on the parquet floor.

I suppose only an instant passed between the collapse event, as Deputy Chief Whitman would call it later on, and the grisly arrival of Hoppy Hopewell through the hole above us. At the time, I barely realized what was happening. I saw a big, wide, ridiculously limp body falling through the ragged hole, wondered in stunned confusion whether it actually might *be* an ape, and then recognized Hoppy as he reached the end of his downward plunge with a hard meaty thump, his arms and legs bent at impossible angles, a coating of white dust on his person, one foot in a spreading brown puddle of gravy.

"Jeez," Luke said in a horrified voice. "Who's *he*?"

I stood looking down at the dead, broken body, dimly aware that the hallway had suddenly gotten crammed with partygoers. Most of those who hadn't fainted or withdrawn for fear of additional falling objects were screaming like—well, chimps.

After a while, I managed to pry my attention from Hoppy and meet Luke's horrified gaze with my own.

"Guess it's pretty safe to say he's the victim," I replied at last.

Chapter 2

According to the Constitution—and I haven't read it since sixth-grade civics, so I may be off a word or two here—everyone's supposed to get equal treatment under the law. But the truth is, rich people have good friends where it counts, so they get better treatment.

No one left the party. I guess no one wanted to look guilty, or else they didn't want to miss a second of whatever was going to happen. The police were called, a patrol car arrived in less than ten minutes, and Deputy Chief W. W. Whitman Jr. was there less than five minutes after that.

But all that was still a few minutes away. From the moment "Hindenburg" Hoppy crashed to his demise—and one of the guests, Dr. Curt Festus, a podiatrist, did press two fingers to his neck to make sure he was deceased—everyone milled around like wind-up toys, moving in another direction with no purpose other than to avoid looking at the body. Most of them hovered near

Lolo, who sat in a thick-cushioned antebellum side chair in the parlor.

"I still think we should cover that boy up," Thom said, wrinkling her nose.

She had just returned to the kitchen where Luke and I had gone to—well, sit, since my feet were a flaming agony and Luke felt the need to cradle his guitar. My manager had continued serving, since dinner was obviously not going to be served, and came back with an empty tray. She checked the spinach puffs that were reheating in the oven.

"You're not s'posed to touch a crime scene," Luke said.

"Oh, and how do you *know* it's a crime scene?" Thom asked. She didn't bother with tongs, but pulled the little pastries out with her fingers. "Old house, fat guy—all kinds o' possibilities there."

"Do we have to talk about this?" I asked.

"No," Thom said. "We can talk about how we're not going to get paid for this."

"We got the deposit," I reminded her. "That'll cover most of our costs."

"'Most,'" Thom huffed.

"So stop serving stuff," Luke said, playing split chords that made the night seem like this was a Greek tragedy.

"Hey, I'm tryin' to salvage some good will from all this," Thom said. "Otherwise, we're gonna be known as the providers who were providin' when Hoppy Hopewell swan-dived through the roof. You want that juju?"

"Were you talking to me?" I asked.

It took a second for Thom to get it. She laughed and shook her head and disappeared with the full tray. Luke was still trying to figure out what was so funny when the squad car arrived, followed by Deputy Chief Whitman.

Lolo lived in the upscale Belle Meade neighborhood, which had its own small police force. That was why Whitman was here. Personally, I was glad Detective Grant Daniels of the Nashville PD was not involved. This isn't how I wanted my loverboy to see me, all aching feet and imploded catering dreams. I felt the disappointment was all over me like a big, popped Bazooka bubble.

Whitman was a wee one, about five-six, bald with a brushy mustache and gray eyes. He was in his early forties, I guessed, and built like a little cannonball. He squatted carefully beside the body, looked this way and that, up and around, examined the edge of a fallen chunk of plaster, then got out of the way so the photographer could take his pictures.

A cop came in and asked us to leave the kitchen. That was where the forensics team was going to spread out. I shut the oven as I left and told him to help himself to whatever hors d'oeuvres were left. At this point, good will was all the nosh was going to get me.

Another cop helped us negotiate the "collapse event" and gravy. We were shown to the parlor where everyone was being gathered. Lolo was tucked in a corner, just to the side of a full-length portrait of her husband.

"You were right there, weren't you?" someone said beside me. I looked over. It was Mrs. Letty Kurtz, wife of Nashville parks commissioner Sperling Kurtz. The wispy, white-haired lady was a former member of the Cozy Foxes, Lolo's luncheon group that gathered regularly at the deli to talk about the latest mysteries they'd read, watched, or listened to—as in old-time radio recordings. She lost interest in mysteries, she said, when they became too predictable.

"One step slower and I would've been wearing him," I said with inappropriate levity.

Mrs. Kurtz didn't seem to think so. "You might have been killed too," she said with a true mystery lover's awareness of the fun to be found in death. "Flattened flat."

I smiled and edged away politely. Pausing just long enough to take off my shoes, I weaved through the crowd to where Lolo was sitting. Her blue eyes were open and staring, her expression numb. The magnifying glass around her neck was catching the light of the small chandelier; if this were one of her beloved old mystery movies, I'd tap her on the shoulder and discover she'd hypnotized herself with it.

It wasn't and she hadn't. People were standing a respectful distance from their hostess, and mine was the only hand near to her. She clutched it without breaking her stare.

"Did you know him?" she asked.

"Not well," I told her. I could tell she was stressed.

Lolo was originally from Georgia and whenever she was stressed or excited, her thick accent returned.

"I noticed you talking to him as though you knew him," she said.

"I didn't, no. Not really. He wanted to sample the steak."

Her eyes turned to me slowly, like little machines. "He did like to eat, but not chocolate—isn't that *just* so strange?"

"I'd say it was more ironic," I replied, not sure it mattered what I said. Her eyes went back to staring. Lolo looked like she was in a daze.

There was a bit of a commotion in the hallway as Deputy Chief Whitman started pulling the guests, one at a time, into the great room. That was where the dinner table had been set up. I stood on my crushed toes so I could look over the crowd. I saw two officers seated at opposite ends of the table. They had digital recorders before them and would be starting to take statements. I lowered myself gingerly back onto my heels.

"What a terrible thing," Lolo said. Her expression was starting to crack. It looked like she might cry. I couldn't blame her.

"You're going to get through this," I assured her.

"My husband died in this house too," she said. "Not the same way, of course. He had an aneurysm."

"Lolo, why don't you try to think about something else," I suggested. Sometimes death *wasn't* funny, even to mystery readers.

"I'll have to have the hole repaired."

"Don't think about that," I suggested. "Think

about the Cozy Foxes, something you want to read. Tell me about a movie I should see. Anything you recommend?"

"Become a recluse like my Uncle Jonah," she said. "I believe it is a far easier way to live."

I was one of the last people asked to provide a statement.

By the time it was my turn in the not-so-hot seat, the little big lug himself had moved over to Lolo's neighborhood. He had pulled over his own ball and claw chair and there the two of them sat, cozily facing each other like a pair of centaur-lions. The expression on the Deputy Chief's melon face was still flat and unfathomable, like a latke. Lolo had not given in to tears, but had rallied like the society trouper she is, presenting a formal, admirably dignified customer for Whitman.

I was asked over by a beanpole in his late twenties, his voice lacking emotion or more than a hint of a local accent. Since moving here, I'd noticed a lot of the young didn't sound like they were from the South; one of the few benefits of growing up watching unbroken hours of TV.

He watched me come over, watched me sit down, then just watched me. It was a curious kind of by-the-book questioning. Since nearly everyone had been in plain sight of someone else, no one missing for more than a bathroom run—except for Lolo, when she briefly went upstairs to get her little dinner bell, which she kept to gently and occasionally summon her housekeeper to her mystery-reading second-floor library—there was not a lot to ask. I'd eavesdropped the last two interviewees, and the basic narrative was pretty much the same from person to person. We heard a crack, there was a boom, and Hoppy went smash.

"Did you know the deceased?" asked the cop—Officer Clampett, whose parents, I hoped, had gotten some sleep before settling on a first name.

I told him.

"Did you have any exchanges with the deceased tonight?"

I told him.

"Did you hear anyone say anything disparaging about the deceased?"

I told him no. Thom was still in the parlor. Enough people had gone home so that she could hear everything being said. And the narrowed eyes told me she was listening.

"I heard nothing," I replied.

Officer Clampett looked at me in a way that suggested he was seeing me for the first time. It wasn't lustful or anything; I get those glances now and then, I'm pleased to say, though unless I noticed the guy first, they're probably not worth acknowledging. It was more like he was formulating his first fresh question.

"Do you always work in your stocking feet?" he asked.

"No," I told him. I explained about the shoes. I had set them beside Lolo's chair and pointed them out.

"Were you barefoot when Mr. Hopewell approached you?"

"I was not." Though I *was* curious about where this was going.

"Might he have been attracted to you, looking the way you did?" Officer Clampett inquired.

"I'm sorry. 'The way'?"

"Well, those *are* stripper shoes."

I could feel Thom laughing at my back. I told Clampett that where I come from they are considered somewhat chic, and that, in any case, Hoppy seemed genuinely more interested in food, especially free food.

"Why?" I asked suddenly. A kid like Clampett didn't just come up with a question like that. "Did Hoppy have a reputation?"

The officer seemed uncomfortable being on the receiving end, and didn't answer. I was told I could go home but waited for Thom and Luke to finish so we could get our stuff from the kitchen.

"*Strip-puh* shoes," Thom said with a triumphant little dance.

"I guess so," I said. "If we finish up quick, I'll do my pole dance on the lamppost."

I couldn't tell from Thom's expression whether that intrigued or shocked her.

It seemed strange to not seem strange that we were working where a man had died a little more than an hour before. But then, it no longer looked like a crime scene. The coroner's team had arrived early in the questioning. Save for the occasional burst of a camera flash, you wouldn't have known they were there. At about the same time I sat down for my interview, they escorted Hoppy Hopewell out the side door, leaving behind the puddle of gravy with its dusty white coat and now-congealed heel-print.

"That's almost as disgustin' as blood," Thom remarked as we scanned the kitchen to see if we'd missed anything.

"It doesn't look like they show in the cartoons," Luke said.

I admitted to him I had no idea what he was talking about.

"The hole," Luke said, jerking a thumb toward the ceiling. "It's not his outline. It's just—a hole."

Thom snorted. "That's *exactly* the man's outline. Like I said before, he was an a-hole."

"Well, he got what he deserved," Luke said. "A bonbon voyage."

I scowled and hushed them both. There were still cops in the house, downstairs, upstairs, and on the grounds.

"That was a joke," Luke protested.

"I don't think the police would see it that way," I said. "Mr. Whitman will be under a lot of pressure to find a person of interest right-quick. We don't want it to be you."

Luke made a motion of zipping his mouth as he grabbed his guitar from a corner and did a vintage Prince-move pirouette out the door.

I decided not to brave the inconstant blue line to say good night to Lolo. She probably wouldn't remember whether I did or didn't. She still looked proper and all, only now it had the added appearance of being in a stupor. Which brings me back to what I said before about the rich getting better treatment. The Deputy Chief had poured her tea and sent Officer Clampett—whose name, as it turned out, unfortunately *was* Jed—to get her a shawl from the hall closet. Even if Lolo herself had beaten Hoppy to death with a hammer, in front of thirty-six witnesses, she still would have gotten the white-glove treatment. In Nashville, while individual Bakers might turn out to be embarrassments, the Baker name was inviolable. Smearing that was like peeing on the holy red brick of Ryman Auditorium, the former house of worship that once housed the Grand Old Opry. It just wasn't done.

"There is one saving grace in all this," Thom said as our little band of cater-waiter warriors clopped along the stone steps to the driveway.

Luke and I both waited for the pearl to come, the observation that would chase away the gummy aftertaste of death, lying cartoons, and Jed Clampett.

"Having leeches on the side of the van didn't matter worth a damn," she said.

I smiled.

For once, we all agreed.

Chapter 3

I slept pretty well for someone who had witnessed a man's death and the grim launch of her own catering business. The alarm was set for seven, but I beat it by ten minutes thanks to the bright Nashville sunshine pushing through a crack in the drapes. I bopped the switch off, showered—still unused to the hard water here and the extra soap and shampoo it took to get clean—then hobbled into my work clothes and shoes. Now my feet weren't just sore, they were swollen; I opted for loosely laced tennis shoes instead of my regular black swivel shoes, since my toes really needed to breathe.

While I waited for my mail-ordered-from-New-York coffee to brew—McNulty Chocolate Cherry, something I was not about to give up, especially for the mass-produced mud preferred by the deli crowd—I searched Hapford Hopewell Jr. on the Web. After getting the basics—His Entitledness graduated with a master's in business from the University of Virginia, he was forty-eight years old, twice married, with no children—I went right to the images, since a picture is worth ten thousand columnist words. The deceased may have been cheap, but he liked the good life. Most of the photos showed the big happy Hoppy squiring this lady or that to this event or that, mostly paid for by someone else. The women tended to be older than he, probably because they had access to the kinds of parties he liked to attend. A few photos showed him welcoming Music Town celebrities to his shop. My first pass didn't reveal anything except that, socially and professionally, he knew a lot of people. On paper, Thomasina still had the best reason for killing him.

Assuming he was murdered, I told myself.

And that was my second search: the morning online papers. I looked at what they had to say even before I checked to make sure they got my display ads right.

"Right now this is being classified as an unfortunate accident," the *Nashville National* quoted Deputy Chief Whitman as saying. "The house is 150 years old, and we've got a structural engineer going over there this morning to check the floorboards."

"That'll buy you a couple more hours to investigate," I said.

Whitman added that he was awaiting an autopsy report, and would have more to say later in the day. Obviously, if it turned out that Hoppy was dead before he hit the ground, that would change the "unfortunate accident" status. I hoped to God they didn't find out he choked to death on one of our wieners. Grant Daniels would have access to that information. Maybe I'd call him later for a how-do-you-do-hot-stuff and oh-yeah-what-killed-Hoppy-Hopewell?

I washed down my multivitamin with orange juice and poured a deep cup of coffee. I picked at an everything bagel as I leaned against the counter wondering if there were any way it *could* have been an accident, and if not, who had access to wherever Hoppy was when he fell. Now that I had the chance to think about it, I wondered what Hoppy was doing upstairs at all when the party, the kitchen, the coat room, the bathroom, and the guests were all downstairs. If he wasn't exploring— and he didn't seem the curious type—maybe he'd been there before? Or maybe someone he snuck off with had been there before?

I heard my father's voice in my head, not my own, asking, *"Why are you wasting time with this when you have a business to run?"*

I wasn't still wondering that when I drove to the deli. I knew the answer: because you're basically, inherently, unrepentedly curious, like when a column of numbers doesn't make sense or a line item entry doesn't have a tag. That's what made me such a top-notch forensic accountant, the fear of Madoff wannabes and old Bernie himself. My brain just acts up. I decided to not go right to work but to stop by and visit Lolo—or rather, the house— under the pretense of having forgotten something important there the night before. All I had with me was my purse, so it would have to be my wallet I forgot.

I called Thom to let her know I'd be late.

"Lawfy, how's this any of your bus'ness?" the manager said.

"It did more or less drop in my lap," I said.

"Girl, customer once tipped a corned beef omelet in mine. I cleaned it up and forgot about it."

"Wait—Luke told me about that. Didn't you hit the guy?"

"We're talkin' 'bout the omelet," she said, "not cranky old Mr. Brown, who had it comin' and never complained about nuthin' again after that. This is a mess, but it ain't your mess."

"And I'm not trying to clean it up," I insisted. "But Lolo is a loyal regular. I want her to know she's not alone."

Thom hung up with a "whatever" and said she had to get ready for the morning rush.

I actually believed what I told her, a little. Mostly, though, this was the Nashville equivalent of being a New York neighbor. Whenever you heard the sounds of arguing or sex coming from another apartment, you listened discreetly outside the door. It was expected. It may actually be *instinctive,* racial memory from a generation when tenement dwellers actually looked after each other.

I hadn't been in Tennessee very long, but my first impression driving through the neighborhood of Belle Meade was that it was "Old South." Not just in look but in attitude. I don't mean that in a bad way, all Confederate flags and political incorrectness, but as an example of a stately, genteel way of life. The main thoroughfare is fronted by majestic equine statues and lined with pillared mansions that have big lawns and great shade trees. The names on many of the properties haven't changed since the 19th century, and Baker is one of them.

I was surprised not to find police at the property. The long, curved driveway had only the Baker Bentley, the Camry of the housekeeper—parked discreetly in the back, near the kitchen entrance—and a van that said "Better Reconstruction." The humor of the name, whether intentional or not, was priceless. I parked my Lexus so it was facing the street. I always liked to be prepared.

Lizzie Renoir, the housekeeper, was a severe, bony woman in her sixties. I had learned from Thom that she had worked for the Bakers since she was a bony woman in her thirties. She had the previous night off so that no one would make tired jokes during the murder game about the butler having done it, even though she was a housekeeper. She certainly would have been my first choice, judging from her looks: mouth in a perpetual scowl, eyes suspicious, nostrils with chronic flare.

"I think I left my wallet last night," I told the *dybbuk punim* that greeted me. Lizzie swung aside like a second door. "Thanks," I said graciously. Charm is a trait I acquired doing audits, to put people at ease. It does not come naturally to my family, who, after all, came from the Ukraine where they had no reason to trust or show gratitude to anyone. It's also served me well at the deli, especially when Thom is in what she calls one of her "black-eye moods." Meaning, like the omelet-tilter, you cross her and you're apt to get a shiner.

I went to the kitchen before Lizzie could arrive. I made my way around two workmen taking measurements in the hallway and "found" my wallet beside the oven.

"I didn't see zat zer before," Lizzie said when she arrived, a French accent still clinging proudly to ze tongue.

"It was under a dish towel," I explained, patting one that was already hanging neatly on the oven door. "Is Lolo awake?"

Lizzie nodded. "Zeze men, zey are not very quiet." She indicated the workers with a cock of her skull-head. One of them was standing on a high ladder with a digital tape measure, the other was iPad-ing the information he called down.

"May I see her?" I asked.

"Go ahead," Lizzie said.

That surprised me. "You don't need to ask?"

"She already told me that whoever came could go to ze mystery library. You know ze madam. Zis brings ze attention and she likes to receive."

There was a certain dark charm to that, and I smiled and went to the stairs. As I passed the workmen I asked the one on the ladder, "Termites? Is that what did this?"

"Not unless they had a power drill."

"Really?"

"There are some thread marks and fresh shavings in the old beams," he said. "Could be from some recent wiring, but I don't see any cables. Maybe they were planning on doing something."

I looked at Lizzie. "The madam wanted HDMI cables in her bedroom for CSI in zee *haute definition.* Zey were putting zem in yesterday morning. Zey did not finish. Zey will be back."

"That would explain it," the worker said.

I figured the police were on top of that, but filed it away.

I knew my way around from having checked the venue out two days before the party. Back through the hallway, past the parlor and great room, and up the grand staircase.

Something occurred to me and I stopped, turning to Lizzie as she came back that way. I'd half-expected she would; she had smelled strongly of fabric softener and the laundry room was in the servants' wing on the other side of the staircase.

"Lizzie, is there another way upstairs?" I asked.

She looked at me with a hint of puzzlement. "Why? You are already halfway up."

"Not for me, I mean . . . I'm just curious."

"Only on ze outside," she said. "Stairs to the terrace outside ze madam's bedroom."

"Ah. Very Shakespearean," I offered.

Lizzie clearly didn't care what it was and continued on her way. I walked back down a few steps. The corridor beside the staircase ended in a pair of ornate wooden patio doors that opened onto the pool area. The passageway was dark, with just a single light in the center. Someone could have slipped away from the party without making an ostentatious exit. That might have been how Hoppy went upstairs.

I continued on my way. This was all terra incognita now. Before I went to the library, which was to the right, I went to my left. To the area above the workmen. The section of collapsed flooring was in a cozy media room with a large HD TV, audio equipment, and a satellite console. A toolbox sat discreetly in the corner. The cable upgrade made sense. The big hole in the center of the floor still did not. If beams were weak anywhere, it would be under the enormous cabinet that held all the equipment.

"Lizzie, is that you?"

I dashed back into the hallway to the steps, and headed to the library. "No, Lolo. It's me, Gwen Katz."

"Oh. I thought I heard someone coming up the stairs."

The steps were marble and pretty quiet. She must have heard the voices.

I entered the library, which, like the media room, was what you'd expect from a second-floor room: small and comfortable. There were two windows on the longer far wall, both of them shuttered. This was the room where she kept all her mystery novels, of which there had to be about four thousand. She was sitting in a love seat, wearing her robe, slippers, and a pallor. Her entire appearance suggested someone who had the flu but refused to let it beat her. There was a standing lamp by her head, throwing a cone of white light that was a few watts shy of the third degree.

Lolo folded the book closed after carefully laying in a fabric bookmark. She set it on a table that was part of the lamp.

"So nice of you to visit," Lolo said. Her voice was nasal.

She even sounded sick. She'd probably been crying—but about what had happened to Hoppy? Or that this had happened to her on the night of her big party?

"I was worried about you," I said. "How *are* you?"

"Just heartsick," she said. "Such a terrible thing. . . ."

"Yes. But you'll get through it."

"One must."

"Have the police been treating you well?" I asked.

"Oh, very. They stayed quite late, asking questions—well, you saw."

"Yes. Tell me, did they come up here?"

"They went *everywhere*!" Lolo said. "They had questions about the floors, the rug—"

"Rug?"

"The bearskin rug in the media room," she said. "Not very fashionable, but Mr. Baker loved it."

"What about it?"

"It fell partway through the hole when Hoppy . . . when he. . . ."

"Of course. Why would they be interested in that?"

"The location," Lolo said. She had begun sniffling when she talked about the rug. I handed her a paper napkin, which was all I had in my coat. She didn't seem to notice as she dabbed her nose. "I explained that I usually have it near the sofa to keep my feet warm, but it was on the other side of the room last night."

"Why?"

"To cover the hideous hole the electrician made," Lolo said.

"I don't understand why they made such a *big* hole, though," I pressed.

"The electrician lifted the hardwood strips in sections in order not to damage them. That was my idea—he's just a boy. New at this, but recommended. They are over a century old, you see, those floor planks. Quite irreplaceable. I suppose that's how . . . how. . . ."

Hoppy didn't see the hole, I thought. "What was he doing up here anyway?"

"Such a silly thing," she said. "There was a game last night. The Cavaliers? His alma mater? I think that was it."

"He came upstairs to watch TV?"

"To check the score, I think. He was always a big . . . big . . ."

"Athletic supporter," I said, though my brain said, *"Jerk."*

Lolo nodded tearfully.

"You told that to the police?"

She nodded again.

That would explain why Deputy Chief Whitman was willing to call it an accident. The scenario made sense. "What are you reading?" I asked affably.

"*Murder of a Scoundrel,* a roman à clef about the mysterious death of Serge Rubinstein, the infamous swindler and blackmailer. Do you know it?"

"I know of him," I said. I had read about his exploits when I was at NYU, a womanizer and con man who was found strangled in 1955 in his magnificent Manhattan pad. They never found who did it, though as one investigator put it, *"We've narrowed the list of suspects to about a thousand."*

I hoped the choice of reading material was purely coincidental. If not, this wasn't the time to ask.

Since I was there, Lolo insisted on paying me the full amount for our services the night before. She went to the master suite further down the hall and returned with a check. I tried to decline—okay, not *too* forcefully—not wishing her to think that was why I had come.

"I know that isn't why you're here," Lolo said. "You were concerned about me and I appreciate that so very much. You're so like your uncle that way. He was a very compassionate man."

There were a number of misconceptions in that statement—for one, Uncle Murray wasn't a compassionate man, he was a just a bad composer who thought the next sob story would inspire his first gold record, so he listened to them all—but I let it stand. Lolo said she and the Cozy Foxes would be back later in the week, as usual, as soon as she found out when the funeral for Hoppy Hopewell was.

"I don't even know who's arranging it," she said.

"I'm sure someone will come forward," I said. "After all, I understand there's a small fortune involved."

Lolo smiléd crookedly—like when you say, "She's such a nice woman" to someone who thinks that woman is a bitch—but I left that alone as well. The information was like a Passover seder, a lot of food that needed time to digest. It wasn't time to go hunting for the afikomen.

I hugged Lolo, who had returned to her book even before I was out the library door. I hurried down the staircase, mercifully missing Lizzie, who I noticed moving about in the far wing with armfuls of laundry.

Five minutes later I was driving back past the brass horses on my way to the deli. Part of me was satisfied and part of me was disappointed. I was sort of glad the story made sense, however comical it was that Hoppy had fallen through a bear rug while looking for the remote to turn on the TV. But a corner of my brain wasn't buying it, not yet. People could check scores on a cell phone. Why would a social gadfly, especially a hungry one, leave a party chockablock with wealthy divorcées and widows—just before dinner was about to be served?

That was something my dad might have done, but he was long-married and loved the New York

Yankees and had no sense of social finesse. But Hapford Hopewell Jr.?

This was one of those situations where while the numbers seemed to add up, my gut told me there was a second set of books.

Chapter 4

I reached the deli at 9:40, just in time to miss the bulk of the morning rush. For us, that meant coffee and bagels with shmear. Though they didn't call it shmear in Nashville. They called it cream cheese. It was one of the traits that made the celebrated town so quaint.

Thom gave me a look as I arrived. I gave her one back. I was usually there, apron on, helping whoever needed it. It's not like I was sleeping in or goofing off.

I got pleasant hellos from the customers who knew me. I wasn't used to "pleasant." In New York, a person was either ignored or greeted like a wealthy relative, looked down on or sucked up to. Nashville was the sane center of New York extremes. I'd only been here seven months and the culture shock of the people, the sounds, even little things like the lack of street smells, was still strong. I wondered if Dad and Uncle Murray had ever acclimated. I knew one person who hadn't.

My father lived in Nashville for twenty-five years. He had only been here once, on a mustering-out layover at Berry Field Air National Guard Base on his return from Germany, but he liked the weather and the slower pace of things. Being an impulsive man, he decided to open a deli here with my mother and his brother Murray. Dad worked for his father-in-law's company, Royal Woven, which made the labels that went in the back of shirts. He oversaw the shipments that came from South Carolina looms and he hated it. Uncle Murray was a borderline-unsuccessful jingle writer who thought he'd have better luck selling real songs where songs were being bought. They were being bought in New York too, but he had competition there from guys with names like Bacharach and Diamond. He didn't do any better in Nashville, but the deli enjoyed a novelty success at first, and then just became a local fixture.

Why did Dad choose a deli instead of, say, a clothing store, which was something he at least knew a little about? I couldn't say for sure, but I think it was rooted in the old Jewish idea that if you were a baker or a butcher your family would never go hungry. Or maybe he was running from the past he loathed. Probably a little of both.

After a few weeks, Mom decided not to stay. She missed her family, she didn't want me growing up in the South, and—call her a prima donna—she didn't like smelling of pastrami and grease day after day. She never divorced my father, but they never lived together again. I think they knew that would happen and just let events take their course. Dad wasn't happy working for her father in the garment district, and she wasn't happy with a husband who was willing to give up a sure thing for something so risky.

P.S. Her dad went bust when the shmatta business migrated to Taiwan and India in the 1970s, and we ended up moving in with him and *bubbe* in Queens to help pay the bills. My mother worked as a department manager for Gimbels, also not a smart move. They went bust in 1987. After that, it was all pickup jobs at store after store. It was like a Western where someone kept shooting horses out from under her. My father helped when he could; sending us money was one reason he never had the cash to expand or diversify. The big urban tornado of 1998 was another reason. The storm tore up the Nashville business district, including the deli. Insurance covered some of it, but Dad and Uncle Murray decided it was time to upgrade the electrical and the appliances. That was all out-of-pocket.

My mom died in 1999, shortly after her parents. Dad died later the same year, stressed all to hell by rebuilding in the aftermath of the tornado. I was in school by then, working hard not to be them. My folks had been so cocked up by finance in one form or another that I decided to make it my career. I wanted to understand what they never could: how people and companies went broke. I swore that would never happen to me. If anything, I was going to be the one who sent other people to the poorhouse. The revenge of the Katz family was at hand. The financial rapture. Gweninator: Judgment Day.

Cut to inheriting the deli when my Uncle Murray passed. By that time I was thirtysomething, unhappily married, and a little bored with theory. I had spent years studying what other people did wrong, and right, and the shortcuts they took to make things work. I wanted to try that myself. And, like Dad, I wanted to be away from my significant other. In this case, though, Phil Silver, my husband, was equally happy to be rid of me. I took my cats, I took my original name, I resigned from the accounting firm of Schneider & Stempel, and I moved into the forty-year-old colonial my father and his brother shared on the unfortunately named Bonerwood Drive. I had just enough money to gut the two bedroom place and make it habitable for a non-man-slob.

I didn't see my father a lot over the years—he was big on letter-writing, a holdover from the Air Force, and I saved them all—and when I did visit I didn't get to see much of Nashville. Still, I noticed that the city had changed a lot between then and now. It was no longer a few blocks long and all about twangy country music, the Hank Williamses and Roger Millers and even the Glen Campbells. It was sprawling and taller and it was about all music and entertainment. People from New York and Los Angeles and Chicago and Philadelphia had relocated here. They had changed the dynamic, making it more cosmopolitan. That influx was also what kept my father going. He gave them a taste of home. They gave him a living he enjoyed. It was what my *bubbe* used to call *chochem*—being a genius due to luck.

I don't have quite his passion for this business, but I do love *business*. As long as I have Thomasina to handle the deli—and I do, since one of the stipulations of my inheritance was that I retain her until she wanted to leave—I'm pretty content.

Especially when I have something like the Hoppy death to add some kosher salt to the week.

I walked in as Newt, on the grill, was saying to Thom, on the register, "What kind of a name is Lolo anyway?" He saw me walk in and repeated the question.

"You askin' a girl nicknamed 'Nashville' to explain a name?" Thom laughed.

"It's short for her maiden name, Lollobrigida," I told him. "She's a distant relative of the Italian movie star."

"Never heard of her," Newt said. "Was she hot?"

"She defined the term," old Mr. Crowley said from his seat at the counter. "She had what we called 'bosoms.'"

"We call them that too," Thom pointed out.

"We do?" Newt said, his face ruddy from the heat lamps.

"In this restaurant we do," Thom said with an edge of menace. "How is the grand dame?"

Thom said it like it's spelled, possibly being ironic, possibly because she didn't know any better.

"She's fine," I said and slapped the check on the cash register as I walked toward the back room.

"Hoooo-eee!" Thom shouted.

"Any tips?" Newt asked hopefully as I passed.

"Buy low, sell high," I said. Ordinarily I don't swing at the easy ones but, as I suspected, the country boy had never heard that. And didn't get it when he did.

I closed the door to my small office and sat on the worn vinyl cushion on the precarious old swivel chair. One day I'd have to get over the sentimental value and replace it. It had belonged to my father and was one of two chairs crammed in the room. The other one, on the back end of the desk—where the Good Luck Troll and framed photos of various Jackson kin resided—belonged to Thom, who had run the place while Murray tried to write and sell music. It was in much better shape since Uncle Murray was rarely in it.

I moved aside an empty plate; I'd been gloomy about my love life the night before and had eaten a sliver of cheesecake. I didn't do either often— brood or indulge—but sometimes I felt a little lonely down here. That feeling came back as I flipped open my cell phone and looked at it for a moment. Did I really want to call Grant Daniels? The detective and I had enjoyed a torrid little fling that threatened to become more. Both of us had just ended relationships, and neither of us particularly wanted another. But when you start calling each other pet names, it's time to get serious or cool it.

We chilled. But I really wanted to know what the autopsy—

My phone buzzed. It was Grant. Well, howdie-do.

"Danny Boy," I said.

"Kazakhstan," he replied.

Yeah, those were the names. I admit mine wasn't very inspired, while his had kind of hot, geopolitical appeal.

"How've you been?" I asked.

"Busy," he said, which was an explanation and a false-front apology all in one neat word. "You?"

"Busy," I replied in kind. "Lolo?" I asked.

"Lolo," he replied.

"What's your involvement?" I asked.

"Local swells are involved, so the mayor asked me to stay in the loop."

"'Involved' as in suspects?"

"I didn't say that."

"You didn't say they're not."

"You were there," Grant said. "Any impressions?"

"You read my report?"

"Oh yeah. 'Hoppy tried to shnorr,'" Grant quoted. "'I think he was a shnorrer.' Christ, Kaz. What does that even mean?"

"Officer Jed Clampett didn't seem to have a problem with my report."

"He didn't realize this was his first murder."

That sat me upright and caused the chair to squeak. "You got the autopsy report?"

"Right here on my laptop," Grant said. "Want to tell me about last night?"

Well played, thought I. "No, but I'll tell you about this morning."

"What happened this morning?"

I told him about my return trip to Belle Meade and my observations about the hole in the floor, Hoppy's visit to the media room, and the parts that didn't sit right.

"His leaving just then doesn't make sense," Grant agreed.

Something in his voice made me ask, "Why do you say 'just then'?"

"Rhonda Shays had just arrived," he said.

Once again my back straightened and the chair made like Mickey Mouse. "Rhonda Shays? Royce's ex?"

"They were reportedly an item," Grant told me.

That was a kick in the *kishkes*. I must have missed her in the crowd, and then when I was in the kitchen. Or maybe my block-wealthy-snobs program was running. Royce Sinclair is a wealthy real estate developer who had visions of turning our block into an entertainment complex. His only impediment: the deli. He tried to buy it, wooed me, won me, lost me, tried to steal it—it was a mess. Especially for Mrs. Sinclair, who accused me of being all kinds of slut even though she was rumored to be having multiple affairs herself. Not that she'd ever said that to my face. We moved in different social circles; all my intel was secondhand. Of course, she had breeding and I had none. Rhonda's world was like a Thoroughbred stud farm where that kind of behavior was tragic in its absence. She was entitled to roam. Her husband was supposed to be jealous and fight for her, not wander off himself. She divorced him and pulled a "me," taking back her distinguished maiden name.

"How did you find that out?" I asked.

"Lolo."

"Makes sense," I said. "Rhonda isn't a member of her literary group, the Cozy Foxes."

"I don't follow. Why does that make sense?"

"If you're not there, everyone guns for you."

"I see."

"But Rhonda's a little younger than his usual consort."

"How do you know *that*?" Grant asked.

"Thom."

"How does *she* know that?"

"Restaurant workers are invisible," I told him. "People talk. Then Thom talks, sometimes to herself, but I overhear."

"Well, I hear Hoppy was creative with melted chocolate—"

"Shays fondue? I'm shocked."

"—or so his saleswoman Victoria Bundy told us. Seems he used to practice on little white chocolate women in the kitchen."

I told him I got the picture. I did, though it occurred to me that white chocolate women would melt under heated chocolate. Maybe that was all a metaphor for how he saw himself. Men approaching fifty have weird issues.

"So he was killed and he was seeing Rhonda," I said. "*How* was he killed?"

"Someone drilled him."

"Really? Wouldn't we have heard a shot?"

"No, Gwen. Someone drilled him. With a drill. Up the nose, into his brain. Then they let him fall through the hole in the floor."

I tasted bagel high in my throat. "Jesus."

"Now, everyone claims that everyone else was pretty much there all the time and no one saw Hoppy leave. So whatever happened was quick."

"He could have gone out the back," I said.

"How?"

I explained the layout. I was still thinking about a drill bit being rammed up his nose. Someone would have to be awfully close and intimate to pull that off.

"So he may have slipped out the back and gone upstairs for a private rendezvous—"

"Under the pretense of checking a ball game," I added. "But why bother explaining? Why not just disappear?"

"Because—and I'm just spitballing here—Rhonda might not have been the only one he was chocolate-coating."

"Ecch. Don't."

"Since when are you so priggish?" She could picture Grant smirking, his handsome lips curled to one side, his strong jaw showing just the hint of manly five o'clock shadow, his gray eyes soft and . . . reading an email while he talked to her.

Pop!

"I have been known to eat a *Mars Bar* or *Hershey's Kiss* from time to time," I told him. "I don't want to think of Hoppy and Rhonda when I'm feeling indulgent. But getting back to his harem, do you have any idea who else might be in it?"

"That's one reason I'm calling," Grant said. "The other being how the hell are you?"

"We already covered that," I reminded him.

"No, I mean really."

"I'm *really* busy. Trying to grow the business. Last night didn't help."

"I can see where it wouldn't," Grant said. "Like selling the house from *The Amityville Horror*."

"God, DB, it's not *that* bad," I protested. "I mean, we survived a van with leeches painted on the sides."

"Come again?"

"Never mind," I said. My brain had moved on. "Other women, other women . . . I don't know, but let me ask Thom and the waitstaff."

"Thanks. Obviously, it would be women who were at the party last night and within earshot of his proclamation. Deputy Chief Whitman makes that to be Hildy Endicott, Mollie Baldwin, Helen Russell, and of course Lolo."

"Hildy and Mollie are members of the Foxes," I said. "Helen I don't know."

"Sister of John Warden Russell, founder of the—"

"H3 Group," I took a wild guess. "The venture capitalists."

"None other. She's the majority shareholder."

"I'll talk to you later," I said. "And thanks."

"What for?"

"For the image of a power tool being stuffed up Hoppy's nose," I said. "You know, there was a box of tools in the corner of that room."

"We know. The drill was in there—forensics found blood samples belonging to the victim—but no fingerprints except those of the electrician, and those were smudged."

"Wiped clean or was the perp wearing gloves?"

"We don't know," Grant said. "But that's a good get: Deputy Chief Whitman noted that Ms. Endicott was wearing gloves and that they were smudged. She claimed it happened when the roof came down and she was covered with dirt. It's possible. She was nearby."

I thanked Grant again—this time for real—and hung up. There was a lot to think about and a lot I didn't want to think about ever again. First, though, I had a call to make. One that might point me in the right direction.

Chapter 5

According to the morning paper—or rather, the morning online paper, which isn't a paper—the Hopewell funeral was being handled by the most upscale place in town, the Hubbard Eternal Rest Home. It might just as well have said "Bluebloods Only" on the big, carved wooden sign on the lawn. No one else could afford them. My father and uncle had been buried by Chan's, the same Asian family that provided us with our whitefish.

That raised the question of who was paying for this. It was obviously coming from Hoppy's estate, but I needed to find the executor. I could probably find that out from the courts, but I had always wanted to check out Hubbard and this was a good excuse.

I drove over to the old mini-plantation house on Church Street, which was literally around the corner from the deli, which was on Fourth Avenue N. I pulled into the U-shaped drive that ran in front of the mansion. The outside smelled lightly of the rose bushes that lined the facade. Inside, not only did the intensity of the light plunge from sun to real candles, it smelled of vanilla from those candles.

I stood in the foyer while my eyes adjusted to the relative darkness. A surprisingly round, jolly fellow all in black seemed to materialize in front of me, like a returned bowling ball. The three holes were his face and two hands.

"How may I direct you?" he asked.

"I wanted to find out about the Hopewell memorial," I told him.

"The service is tomorrow at ten a.m."

"Will family be present?" I asked.

"I really couldn't—"

"Oh, I'm not asking you to break any confidences. It's just I didn't really know the deceased except as a fellow merchant and I'd like to know who I'll be addressing."

"I was *about* to say that I really couldn't tell you because I do not possess that information," the man informed me with the same conviviality. I realized he was probably trained to be cheerful no matter what grief walked through the door. "You would have to inquire at the law office of Mr. Solomon Granger, who made the arrangements."

Ah, good old Solly. A transplanted WASP from New Hampshire who had chased an ambulance to Nashville and stayed. He came down about the same time as my father. He was one of the attorneys who had been helping to put together the Royce deal. Big windfall for him if it went through.

He didn't care for the sight of me, and made no effort to pretend when I walked into his office.

"If you've come to make peace, take your pipe and—"

"I haven't," I assured him as his receptionist shut the door behind me. "It's about Hoppy Hopewell."

His long, pinched face became only slightly less pinched beneath his close-cropped white hair. "What about him?"

"He nearly fell on me yesterday night."

"That would be a claim for Mrs. Parker's—"

"I'm not here to make claims or sue or apologize or any other wrong guess you're apt to make," I told him. "I just want to know the disposition of the chocolate shop."

Okay, I pulled that one out of my fundament. But it was the only way I could think of to get the information I wanted.

"Ah," Solly said, with a trace less hostility than he had displayed heretofore, though the pinched expression was fixed. "Would you care to sit?"

I wouldn't, but did. Accepting any form of hospitality from this *shlang*, this viper, boiled my derma.

"The shop has been left to someone," Solly said.

"I figured that. Are we going to play twenty questions?"

He smiled humorlessly. "I'm not permitted to say who the new owner is. As for selling it, I was going to place an advertisement in the Sunday press, but I see no reason why I can't share this information with you. Pending pro forma probate of the will, I have been instructed by the individual in question to field offers. These are to be made through an attorney, in writing, with a decision to follow by August 24th."

"That's four months from now—"

"Correct."

I counted quickly. "And three days. Significance?"

"None that I'm aware of. None that is relevant to a potential purchaser. That's what I was told."

I thought, *If I told you to jump off the Brooklyn Bridge. . . .*

"Are you interested?"

"That will depend on the price."

"That I cannot yet divulge. Are you still represented by Mr. Dag Stoltenberg?"

I nodded. His great-great someone-or-other had left the textile industry before the Civil War to become the first in a long line of lawyers. Those were all the credentials my father needed to retain him. He had history, like an apprentice in the old country.

"Excellent." Solly almost smiled. "If you are still interested after Sunday, I'll expect to hear from him. Not you."

"Suits me. You got a ballpark for me?"

"To buy?" He chuckled.

I didn't chuckle back. And people thought my jokes were bad.

"As I said, that number will be in the public notice," Solly replied.

"Fine, one more thing. When's probate?"

"Friday." His smile was genuine now. "Whatever information you're looking for, for whatever prurient reason you want it, will not be available to you for another three days."

He rolled the "r" in the "three." It made me shudder. I got out of there as quickly as my sore feet would allow.

I had *bupkis* from my morning adventure, nothing actionable except for a date: August 24. The good news was, the date was so unrelated to anything logical that it had to be significant.

I went back to the deli and went online. The family histories of all the ladies were listed in the Greater Nashville Social Diary. None of them had a birthday on August 24. None of them had a child born on August 24. One of them probably had an anniversary with Hoppy Hopewell on August 24.

Which left me with nothing I didn't know before: that someone who stood to gain from Hoppy Hopewell's death may or may not have been at Lolo's party, and that there was a chance August 24 was connected to whoever was the beneficiary of Hoppy's largesse. Which may or may not have been someone at the party.

The scope of what I didn't know made my head hurt. It figured, though. Of all the things that could give a former accountant *shpilkes*, it had to be a number.

By now it was lunchtime and I went to help. That meant working the counter, since my feet were too achy to waddle between tables. Fortunately—

or maybe it was God looking out for me—Hildy Endicott had a craving for tongue. I was certain now that God had cooked this one up for me. She was the biggest *yenta* of Lolo's group,

Hildy—short for Hildegardebeth, a cruelty with no sane explanation—was a fifty-year-old divorcée. Shortly before my arrival in Nashville, her sixty-two-year-old husband had left her for a younger man. But there were no hard feelings. Dwight Endicott had also left her with half the family fortune, made in magazine publishing when magazines were still being published. She was actually quite friendly with Dwight and his boytoy Gavin. She was, in fact, a pussycat, as far as I could tell. Even so, dogs knew enough to circle wide around them.

I braved the thickening crowd clustered around twenty wooden tables to bring Hildy's Deluxe and a Coke to her booth.

"Gwen," she said, patting the back of my hand and gazing up with Pound Puppy eyes as though we were old friends sharing a bitter new reality. "How are you doing?"

"Devastated," I lied.

"I know. Can you set a minute?"

I *sat.* The South and their vocabulary. I actually missed people who *aksed* me a question or said *sí* when they meant *yes.*

"Sure, honey pie," I replied. I could be Southern-charming too. I slid into the seat opposite her. Hildy adjusted the plate so it was a micrometer nearer. I don't understand why diners do that. "This must be awful for you," I said. "I barely knew poor Hoppy, but you. . . ." I let the statement hang there, like an apple waiting to be picked.

"Yes, me. I never got to set that rat's plaster."

"Right," I said, trying to conceal my surprise. This pussycat had issues!

She looked down at her coleslaw. "I know the other ladies talked about it when they came in here. I don't blame them. They warned me."

No need to ask if whatever she was talking about happened on August 24. It didn't sound as though Hoppy left anything for her except grief. Still, I wondered if she knew how to use a power drill.

"You know, Hildy, we all do silly, impetuous things," I said. *Coax, coax.*

"But I was supposed to *know* better," she said, her voice cracking.

I pushed the Coke toward her. She sipped it by leaning her mouth over it. Maybe she never went to finishing school, or just skipped lunch there. "Well, you know now," I said. I was beginning to think it would be possible to have an entire conversation without knowing what she was talking about.

"Do you know, my dear, it's much more difficult being a divorcée than a wife," she said with icy indignation.

My dear meant she was going to discourse. I had to get her back on track. At least, the track that was closer to where I wanted to go.

"It's just difficult being a *woman,*" I suggested, and clasped the hand that was still on mine.

That made her melt. *"Yes!"* she gushed.

"No woman, married, divorced, or widowed, should have to deal with the likes of Hoppy Hopewell. The dog."

Hildy discovered her sandwich and her appetite. She began to eat. "It's not that I am above speculation," she said around a tongue that wasn't hers. "But he said he was going to use the money to expand and that I would be a silent partner."

"Men like women who are silent."

"Oh, *yes they do,*" she said, showing teeth. "*This is a growing market, Hildy.*' '*I need to hire more help, Hildy.*' '*I need a woman's counsel, Hildy.*' All lies, all rubbish. What he wanted was to buy into another business, one to which he did not wish his name attached."

That was something. I leaned forward, whispered conspiratorially, "I hadn't heard about that!"

"I only just found out myself." She sipped more Coke.

"There's a straw," I said, helpfully pointing to the one sticking from the other side.

"I never use them," she said. "In *The Matter of the Black Wasp,* a lothario poisoned his women with arsenic pellets concealed inside straws. It terrified me as a child. Young girls are so impressionable."

"Aren't they," I said. *Oy.* I shouldn't have distracted her. "This business of Hoppy's," I said. "Weren't there mobsters involved?" I thought, if anyone was going to shove a drill up a man's nose it was *La Cosa Nostra*.

"Were there?" she said with horror.

"I thought so," I said. "You know, that business—"

"Importing exotic vegetables?"

I stared at her blankly. I wondered if I looked less dumbstruck than I felt. I cast off any pretense of knowing what the hell I was talking about.

"I'm confused. Why didn't he want his name attached to that?"

"He was afraid that if people found out he was importing healthful foods it would be a tacit admission that chocolate was *un*healthy," she said.

"Is that really a news flash?" I asked.

"I don't know. You hear all these conflicting reports, don't you?"

Not about a product loaded with sugar and fat, but I let it pass. "Go on," I told her. "About the new business."

"It was highly, highly risky," she said. "There were problems with customs, an unreliable work force, global warming. That's why he didn't want to put his own money into it. African Horned Cucumber, Jelly Melons, Adzuki Beans—I would never have invested in something so . . . so *foreign*."

"How did you find out?" I asked.

"By purest happenstance," she said. "An attorney for McDonald's sent a letter saying we couldn't use the name *Hoppy Meals* for our enterprise. I had my attorney, Solomon Granger, look into the matter. *That* was how I found out! I wanted to confront my *partner* the night of the party but he avoided me. By dying."

The way she spat out the word *"partner"* made me pretty sure she hadn't been the one who put a drill bit in his frontal lobe. The woman was still nursing way too much unreleased anger.

I slumped from the effort of pulling all that out, then rallied and excused myself. I paused before standing.

"What do you know about power drills?" I asked. For another hour or so, only the police, myself, and the killer would know it was the murder weapon. I watched carefully to see if she flinched.

Her eyes grew sad. "Dear, I cannot possibly discuss another investment opportunity," she said. "Not now."

I smiled and stood and returned to the counter. I did look back, though, as Hildy finally picked up her Coke glass—with a paper napkin wrapped around it. I wondered whether she was protecting her delicate skin from the cold or making scrupulously, paranoiacally certain she didn't leave fingerprints.

I didn't know. For now, the worst I could say about Hildy was that she was one *meshugena* lady.

Chapter 6

The afternoon crowd was abuzz with the news, which we had all seen on the TV that hung silently in a corner behind the counter.

"It has been determined that Mr. Hapford Hopewell, Jr., late of Forest Hills, expired as a result of cerebral distress caused by the introduction of a sharp, metal object. . . ."

That was as respectful a way to put tool-up-the-nose as I could have imagined. I wondered if the police had staff writers who came up with this stuff, or if they had a file of euphemisms the way comedians kept index cards filled with jokes. In any case, it caused a lot of talk about what exactly that meant—since Deputy Chief Whitman declined to take any questions from reporters—and who might have done it.

Grant called after the announcement. I took the call outside. I smelled like chopped liver and it was time for the afternoon airing-out.

"So it's out there," I said. "Are you watching the airports and highways?"

"Nothing so dramatic," he said. "We'll be doing follow-up interviews, and if anyone tries to skip we'll find them."

"You can probably cross Mrs. Endicott off your list," I said and told him about our chat. I also told him about my meeting with Solly.

"He's a pip," Grant said.

There were very few people who could make that word sound like a natural part of his vocabulary. The Nashville born-and-raised Grant Daniels was one of them.

"What about you?" I asked. "Anything new?"

"Warren Whitman sent someone over to talk to the housekeeper, Ms. Renoir. She wasn't there that night but she had access."

"And?"

"We can't arrest someone for being a crab."

"I'm guessing she didn't hold anything back?"

"Hated Hoppy and said so. Called him rude and arrogant."

"Based on?"

"He gave hand-dipping classes to the ladies at Lolo's house."

"By that you mean?"

"Fruit. Strawberries, apricot slices, and his specialty—"

"Let me guess. The banana."

"The banana," Grant said. "Covered in chocolate and ground nuts."

"Who attended these classes?"

"All the Foxes—Lolo, Mollie, Helen, and Hildy. Plus one other gal, Ms. Pinky Donovan."

"Who is—?"

"The new assistant manager of Hoppy's shop."

"Talk to her yet?"

"That very night," Grant said. "She was home watching TV."

"How'd she take it?"

"Like someone being told she'd have to look for a new job."

"So there was no personal connection."

"Not that she let on," Grant said.

I snickered. "Gotcha. I assume the shop is open?"

"My guess is yes, and there will be a lot of transactions that don't end up in the cash register," Grant said.

"Discount for cash," I said. "Of course. I'll let you know what I find out."

"You're a peach."

"Dipped in the finest chocolate," I said. That was another word that seemed to fit his golden Tennessean tongue just so.

I hung up and went to the bathroom to wash my face and hands and apply a little lotion. A careful application of lanolin can hide even the most stubborn deli meats.

Sweet Hoppy's was located on Charlotte Avenue in the Capitol Hill area. The rent was high but the traffic was good. His distinctive dark brown bags and glittery boxes were a common sight around the fountain. Gift baskets were always moving here and there as state officials rewarded workers or lobbyists thanked secretaries.

As I parked a few doors down, it only just occurred to me—*Sweet Hoppy's. Hoppy Meals.* The "Hoppy" handkerchief in his pocket. The deceased was nothing if not a world-class narcissist. To some, like yours truly, that could be a killing offense. Though it made me wonder something; maybe Pinky would have some insights if I could get her to share.

There were two workers in the shop, no customers. One of them was a slender blond girl, about twenty-one, twenty-two, with a tattoo of a harp on her neck. The other was a healthy-looking girl about the same age with blue hair streaked bright pink and a silver nose ring. Both were carefully removing white chocolate-covered potato chips from a baking tray.

There were no customers in the shop. That seemed unusual for the tail end of lunch hour on a pleasant afternoon. I would have thought the gawkers would be out. Then again, maybe the politicians, hearing murder, decided to stay far, far away. Blood had a way of splattering even the innocent. It probably would have bruised Hoppy's ego to learn that his last and biggest social activity had been a colossal bust.

"Can I help you?" the skinnier girl asked with a lilting, almost musical accent.

"I'm here to see Pinky," I said.

"I'm Pinky."

Naturally. The blonde. "Hi, I'm Gwen Katz—owner of Murray's, the deli."

"Hi," she said taking a stab at bonhomie. Either it was foreign to her, or she was in mourning. "What can I do for you?"

"I would like to place a special order for a catering job," I said. I was becoming very, very impressed with my ability to extemporize.

"What and when?" she asked.

"Truffles for Friday," I told her.

She made a shifty little face. "I, uh—have you heard about the owner? Like, what happened last night?"

"Yes," I said with as much gravitas as I could manage. "It's terrible. But I assume the shop will continue to operate. There must be provisions—"

"We don't know," the other girl said.

Pinky sighed. "It's unclear."

"But you're both here. . . ."

"I got a call from Mr. H's attorney, who told me to, like, open as usual," she said.

"Solomon Granger."

Pinky brightened, like someone had thrown her a life preserver. "You know him? You got any info?"

"I do know him. In fact, we were discussing the place this morning."

"What did he tell you?"

"That there was a new owner," I said. Then I lied. "I naturally assumed it would be you."

Pinky shook her head. "I don't know who it is, but I'm not it."

"Did you hear anything else?" the other girl asked.

"No," I said, deciding not to tell her about the pending sale. Solly might try to sue me for interference with commerce or some baloney.

"So, look," Pinky said. "I can, like, take your order and a deposit and assume it will be business-as-usual . . . but who knows? Do you want to do that?"

I hesitated. I didn't want to have to order truffles and this was a good out. "Maybe I'll just come in Friday and buy whatever's in stock."

Pinky nodded. "Good plan."

"It's too bad about Hoppy," I went on reflectively. "I wanted to take his dipping class, but it conflicted with Pilates."

"You didn't miss much," Pinky said. "Before I worked here, I shopped here. He wasn't a very good chocolatier."

"No? What about all this?" I gestured grandly.

"*This* is from some do-it-yourself DVDs I once caught him watching in the back," she told me. She noted my surprised expression. "He thought I'd gone home, didn't see me picking up sprinkles behind the big showcase. I think he kept them in the safe. He took them home after I busted him."

"What about the cow patties?" I asked. *The famed ice cream turds that were the rage of Tennessee State University.*

Pinky laughed.

"What?" I asked.

"His older sister Melanie surprised him one day, came in with her grandkids in tow. While he, like, gave them chocolate lollipops and a little attention, she talked to us, which I thought was, like, pretty nice. I don't remember how it came up, but one of us said something about the shop being popular, and she said she was surprised because her brother knew as much about the kitchen as she knew about flying the space shuttle. Mr. H got all protesty and puffed up and pointed to the frozen display case with the patties. That's when she said, 'Oh, right. You probably pulled *them* out of someone else's ass.' Which I thought was pretty funny. So did the rugrats."

"Hello!" the other girl said. "PG-13!"

"How did her brother take that?" I asked.

"He got real red. He reminded her that he had studied in Europe after she had left the house."

"Left for—?"

"I don't remember," Pinky said.

"Someplace, South Carolina," the other girl told me. "She married some rich hotel guy, said that whoever invented them, she was glad she didn't have to slave over hot bubbling vats of fake cow dung like her brother."

"Wait—I thought the Hopewells had money."

"Well, *she* did," the girl said. "I don't know about Mr. H."

"Yeah, he didn't really talk to us about his private life and personal finances," Pinky said. "To him, we were just wage slaves."

"Eye candy for the state senators."

Pinky air-high-fived the other girl—who, by this time, I was tired of thinking of as 'the other girl.' I shifted a little so I could see her name tag: Jennifer.

"Yeah, those were, like, the kind of people he talked to," Pinky went on. "Big shot politicians. Whenever they came in he was, like, really supernice. He told us that we should be too."

With the form-hugging shirts they were wearing—white with brown sequins that spelled "Hoppy" across their chests—I didn't imagine it mattered how nice they were. But I was glad for the opening: that was what I'd been intending to ask when I first arrived.

"Do you think he had political aspirations?" I asked.

Pinky didn't express an opinion, and deferred with another glance at Jennifer, who raised a shoulder and let it drop.

"The only things I ever saw him show any interest in was women and money," Jennifer said.

"In that order?" I asked.

"In that combination," Jennifer replied, beyond her years.

Pinky was still standing there. Her forearms were resting on the top of the display case. She was looking at a wall. "He definitely struck me as a wannabe," she said, apparently still thinking about my question and, by association, her late boss. "Why else would someone pay high rent to be near the capitol and look at a statue of some old-days dude on a horse?"

The "guy" was Andrew Jackson, but I decided not to give them a history lesson. They'd given me a lot to think about, and I took it all in while I glanced around the shop. Now that she'd mentioned it, the place lacked any love, any real inspiration. An interior decorator had probably done the dark chocolate walls and swirly, white chocolate drizzle wainscoting. The display cases, stands, trays, even the rug were strictly catalogue.

I thanked the young ladies for their time.

"By the way," I asked Pinky, "how'd you get your nickname?" It wasn't important, but I always have time to scratch a brain itch.

"From the way I hold this finger when I play harp," she said, holding up the little finger of her right hand like a crook. "It's, like, kind of my trademark."

"Nice hobby," I said.

"I play at gigs, if you're ever catering one with music," she offered.

"I'll remember that," I promised. And I would. I was a soft touch for kids who follow a dream.

I left with a hollow tinkle—even the bell over the door was bottom-of-the-line mail order—and the sense that while I hadn't uncovered much except a treasure chest of "likes," I knew Hoppy a little better. I had a theory. Not a unified theory, more like an impression. He made a decent amount of money from this shop and used that, and his own fortune, so he could be around people of influence. Not just movers and shakers on the hill here, but also in society. Whether he pursued women to pursue women, or pursued women to pursue access, I had no idea. But it was something worth investigating.

Chapter 7

I decided to go home. I didn't want to be distracted while I re-Googled the dead man. Now that he was a victim of homicide, all the top searches would be about that. I wanted stuff I *didn't* know.

I word-searched *Hapford Hopewell Melanie*.

Duh. That still gave me his death and the next-of-kin. I added the word *fortune*. That gave me a biography in the *Dessert Professional* online magazine. I skimmed.

"Hapford Hopewell, Jr. Born 1963, father was—aha. Father was the founder of the Checkers Sugar Corporation of Greenville, South Carolina. So he probably gets—*got*—his raw material at cost. Father died in 1998, mother committed suicide a month later—*that's* love or debt—and Hopewell spent two years traveling the world—oh, this is rich—studying chocolate-making techniques while preparing to open his shop."

I brought up online *Battleship,* a habit I acquired during my accounting days to get my mind off numbers. I played while I considered that.

"Hoppy lied about his interest in chocolate. He probably went around the world blowing his inheritance. But sister—"

I minimized the game, looked up Melanie Hopewell. I added the word *nuptials* so I wouldn't get more "survived by" references. There was an announcement in the Charleston *Post and Courier* from May 1981. I had to register with the website to read it—and remember to uncheck the box that would have sent me free offers—but it was worth it.

"Melanie Hopewell married Dollarama Motel founder Waldo Tidyman in a ceremony . . . blah blah . . . daughter of. . . ."

And there it was. Her mother's name in blue. I clicked on it and was taken to an article about her death, which was still eighteen years off. The temporal magic of the Internet! I scanned it:

"Barbara Cox Hopewell was found dead from an overdose of prescription barbiturates by her chauffeur . . . alerted by the barking dog . . . said to be depressed over financial woes revealed during a proxy battle following the death of her husband Hapford Sr."

Hello Ruth Madoff! Hubby crashes and you find out you're in the hole?

I looked up Checkers Sugar, found out that the Agriculture Undersecretary investigated them in 1996 for driving up prices of cane and beet sugar by purchasing and shutting down domestic refiners in the United States to make their monopoly on raw Brazilian imports more desirable. The investigation caused stock prices to plummet, and sent Checkers into a borrowing frenzy. The three-year loans were personally guaranteed by Mr. Hopewell.

"Oh, my."

So Hoppy Jr. only had the money on his back. He probably was on a round-the-world jaunt when he got the news, and decided to stay out of the country so he wouldn't be dragged into it. According to another article, Checkers went public in 2001. I looked up the SEC filings—now I was in familiar territory—and guess who sold all their shares for one lowly nickel on the dollar? The Hopewell children.

I went back to *Battleship*.

What Hoppy thought was ten million dollars was actually one-twentieth of that. That's half a million bucks. Not bad, but not what he thought he had to play with.

Another hunch. Down went *Battleship*, up came the names of the sugar companies Checkers had forced to shut down.

Score.

Dryfoos Brands, based in Nashville. Purchase price: fifty grand. And with that, the title to all the recipes. Including, I was willing to bet, the cow patties.

"He didn't mention that in *Dessert Professional*," I said.

There was a footnote that cited a confidentiality agreement signed by all parties, probably crafted so that Dryfoos could never spill the cocoa beans.

Up came *Battleship*. I blew up, and put on my forensic accountancy hat while I rebooted.

"So let's say the shop is a break-even proposition, solid volume but high overhead," I thought aloud. "The man was low on cash, needs to start another revenue stream. Maybe he went to his sister, maybe he didn't. Maybe she came to Nashville to tell him no to his face. Maybe she knew he was a lying sack and didn't trust him. So he puts the touch on Hildy to start another business, it flops—"

On purpose? I wondered suddenly. *Tell me, Mr. Bialystock. Did you build in failure so you could keep most of the money? Did you tip McDonald's off yourself so you could tell Hildy you spent all the money fighting their lawyers?*

It was possible. But was it enough to make her want to kill him?

I still didn't know. Worse, among the other things I didn't know was whether she was an isolated case or whether, as Jennifer had suggested, collecting checks and wooing available women were all part of the same scheme.

There was only one way to find out.

I saved my game, went to the online White Pages, grabbed the unfinished bagel from that morning, and went out.

Chapter 8

My next person of interest—and I use that term loosely because I wasn't the least bit interested in her as a person—saved me the trouble of figuring out a reason to talk to her. She found me.

I had intended to go to the Confederate Hill home of Gary Gold, whose role in the entire matter had not yet been examined much less thought about by me. He was the local mystery author whom Lolo had commissioned to write the scenario for the party. I would get there—but not just yet.

Rhonda Shays was driving her BMW along Korean Veterans Boulevard when she spotted me. It was more like an eagle catching sight of a field mouse, her head rotating as though her sternomastoids were made of putty. We were in the middle of the Cumberland River when it happened. Her reflective sunglasses fixed on me, followed me as I headed away from downtown, and a moment later my cell phone rang.

"Wait for me on the other side," she growled and hung up.

Ordinarily, I don't respond well to commands, unless they involve mustard or mayo or some other condiment. But, as I said, I did want to talk to Rhonda. I also had a real good idea why she was so angry, and saw this as a good opportunity to put that behind us. If it was possible to put anything behind an insane person.

There are a series of parking lots on the other side of the river. They service LP Field, home of the football Titans. I know that because Thom's a big, big fan. Me? I know nothing about sports. I pulled into one of them, got out of the car, and waited.

I don't know where and how Rhonda turned, but she arrived about a minute after I did. She parked diagonally across two spots—a habit born, no doubt, from years of selfishly protecting BMWs. There was most definitely a Cruella De Vil vibe happening. She was wearing a poufy white blouse, a dark black skirt, stiletto heels, and the smoke from a cigarette curled about her straight black hair. It had the definite aspect of a mushroom cap. But when she yanked off her sunglasses as though she were Clark Kent about to change, those eyes blazed through it as she stalked over.

"Are you in love with my ex-husband?"

If I'm ever asked that question again, I'll have a better answer. Something like "Why, are his friends asking for me?" or "Yes, and they're going to be twins!" All I said was, "What?"

She stopped inches from my face. She's only five-three, but the heels brought her eye level. "Are you. In love with. My ex. Husband?"

"No," I said. I wonder if she could see me shudder.

"Liar!" she charged. It sounded more like a Katharine Hepburn "Li-ah!" I wondered if the rest of her sounded that way. This was the first time in our lives we'd ever spoken, though I'd heard about her from Royce and at the deli.

"I really did just have sex with him," I assured her. "But if I did love him, why would it matter? You were already on the way to being divorced, weren't you, when he tried to buy my property."

"*Your* property!"

She did it again: "Your" became "Yoh-ah" and "property"—well, each syllable was accented, the middle one pronounced "puh."

"You sassy city thing," she said, no longer an eagle but a hissing snake. "You didn't earn that place. You *inherited* it!"

I don't think there's any need for me to continue parsing her enunciation. You get the idea. Anyway, I admitted she was right about that, then added, "Isn't that how you got your money?"

"Good God, no! I *divorced* for it!"

"But your former husband was old money. So in a sense you inherited too." I couldn't believe I was trying to reason with this lunatic. "Anyway, what's that got to do with the price of potatoes in Idaho?"

"Oh, listen to you! Listen to you, you witty urban slut."

I closed the gap between us by an inch or two. The "urban"' part of me, the "Asshole, the line is over *here*!" part of me, was beginning to boil. "Now look. I didn't pull off the road to be called names by someone like you—"

"Someone like *me*?"

"A poseur, a society mountebank, a *zoyne*."

She looked at me blankly. She suspected she'd been insulted, but she didn't know how. I used the break to regroup.

"Now, was there something else? Because if not, I've got a couple of questions for you."

She folded her arms daringly. "Do you now?"

"I do."

"Go ahead, *Gossip Girl*. Shoot to kill!"

My insults were vocabulary. Hers were the CW. It figured.

"Actually, it's funny how this discussion started out, because I wanted to know if you were in love with Hoppy Hopewell."

Her eyes became shiny plums. "Love?"

"Yeah. Rumor has it you two were tight."

I swear, it was like I suddenly dropped into *Gone With the Wind* and Scarlett was about to play one of her parts. Or else it was the *Three Faces of Eve* and the woman was truly suffering from Multiple Personality Disorder. She half-turned, her cigarette hand dropped, and up came her other hand *with a handkerchief*! Either she always carried one up her sleeve for effect, or she had mastered sleight of hand, in which case the movie would be *Houdini*.

"Who—who says such things?" she sobbed, touching her eyes in turn.

"All of Nashville, including the surrounding suburbs. Maybe some folks in Charleston."

She appeared not to hear. "It is true. I loved him, even though he was a decade older than I." Her eyes and manner became imploring. "Who wouldn't?"

Me? Thom? I thought. *And if you're thirty-eight, I'm a Vernicious Knid.*

Rhonda suddenly had a rhapsodic air about her. "Hoppy was funny. He was vivacious in a manly sort of way, he was romantic, he was an amusing lover—"

"Great," I cut her off. "The question is, were *you* a *jealous* lover?"

The tears stopped. I swear I heard the squeak of a faucet. "What are you implying?"

"I hear he was also close to Hildy Endicott."

A beat, and then she laughed like Blanche DuBois. "Hildy Endicott! That's almost comical!"

"They were in business together."

"Were they now?" That seemed to throw her a little, but she recovered. "People cannot be in business without being lovers? Weren't you and my husband lovers and yet *not* in business together?"

I wasn't sure that made sense, but the laws of physics didn't really apply to this woman. "Let me put it another way," I said. "Did Hoppy ever lead you to believe you were exclusive?"

"Ms. Katz, may I ask *you* another question?"

"Go ahead." She would have asked it anyway.

"What in the name of the father is this any business of yours? I asked you about Royce because he was my husband. What was Hoppy to you?" The evil Rhonda was back, the handkerchief gone, the cigarette—though now a stub—back between her red lips. "Were you lovers? Did you fancy a man of mine *again*?"

"Rhonda, even if I were a nymphomaniac with a sweet tooth, I would have found some other solution."

She recoiled as though I'd slapped her. "You rude Northern hussy."

"Yeah. Well, that still doesn't tell me whether you were possessive enough to want to terminate your little slice of Heaven."

"I didn't kill Royce," she replied.

"That's not really a defense. You never loaned Royce money. Did Hoppy borrow? Did he default?"

"That is none of your business," she said. "Anyway, I wish you would stop being so tawdry. What is all of this to you?"

"I was there."

"Where?"

"At Lolo's party."

Judging from her expression, that may have been the most shocking news yet. "*You* were invited?"

"No, I was catering."

"Oh." She seemed relieved. She *was* relieved. Nashville society was intact. "Still, I don't understand why you're so interested—"

"It was our first party. Unless I become the

caterer who solved the murder, I'll always be the caterer who buried Hoppy Hopewell."

"Yes, I see," she said. "It's always business with you people."

I'm sure she intended that to exonerate me of salacious involvement with Hoppy. With friends like that. . . .

"Getting back to the other business for just a sec, answer me this."

"Why?"

"Because you have nothing to hide and you want to prove it to me," I said. That confused her just long enough for me to ask, "How do you feel about imported vegetables?"

"I never eat them," she huffed. "I don't feel like living in the water closet!"

That derailed my line of questioning. I thought I had her.

Rhonda moved closer. Our eyelashes could have weaved each other. "What has that got to do with the price of tea in Nepal?"

Aha, thought I. "What about *exotic* tea?"

Rhonda's plum eyes had long since shrunk to black olives. Now they became evil, beady things. "What. Do you know. About exotic. Tea?"

"I only know from Lipton," I said, recovering. "But I'm guessing you know a lot more."

The fixed-nose wrinkled. This close, she looked like a bat. "Why should I know anything about Ceylon Green, Darjeeling Glenburn White Peony or Bolivian Black that any well-bred woman would not?"

"Because they didn't give Hoppy Hopewell money to bring them into the United States?" I suggested. "What did he call the company? No, let me guess. *Mr. Tea? Tea for the Seesaw?* Something designed to get sued?"

"Model Tea," Rhonda said. "He said the Ford Motor Company shut him down and it cost him everything fighting them. How did you know? Were you balling him too—?"

"God, no." I shivered. Twice. "Because Hildy Endicott gave Hoppy a whopping bunch of money to develop a healthy eating option called *Hoppy Meals.* A certain fast food chain didn't like that either."

The woman looked like she'd walked into a glass door. Her red lips parted, the filter of her cigarette stuck stupidly to the upper lip. I'd never seen that before.

"So he got you too," I said. "And I'm willing to bet there were other ladies in his development fund."

"Others?"

"A whole Cozy Foxload, and maybe beyond. I wonder if there are any spinsters in the state legislature? Or handmade *Kit Kat*-loving spinsterly aides to the senators?"

"So what?" Rhonda said, recovering somewhat. "Hoppy was a businessman."

"Apparently not a very scrupulous one—"

"Businessmen put together deals." She ran right over my remark. "Not every investor has to know every other investor in different projects."

"True, but not every investor is sold a one-hundred-percent investment in a fatally flawed corporation," I pointed out. "You did stake him to the entire claim, didn't you?"

"It . . . it was a healthier alternative to coffee," she muttered.

"Not for you. And apparently not for Hoppy."

Rhonda stepped back. If she had a fan up her sleeve, she'd be batting away the vapors. She leaned heavily against the hood of her car. The impact knocked the cigarette from her lip. She crushed it instinctively as though she'd simply dropped it.

"Are you saying one of those women killed him?" she asked. Her manner had shifted subtly. She was now in personal survival mode.

"I'm saying it's possible that 'a' woman killed him." I looked at her like a field mouse who had decided "Never Again."

"I'm sure there's some other explanation for what happened," she said, still grinding the butt with her pointed toe.

"I may have to agree with that," I told her. "Hoppy was a scumbag who was having money problems."

"That's silly."

"Is it?"

"The shop is doing well."

"How do you know? Did he leave it to you?"

"To me? Heavens, no."

"Any idea to whom?"

"Not the vaguest."

"So how do you know it was doing well?" I pressed.

"It was always busy," she said.

"People browsing, not buying?" I said.

"He *told* me it was doing well," she insisted.

"Right. Hoppy Hopewell never lied to anyone."

"No!" she shot back. "There has to be *another* explanation for this . . . this. . . ."

"Subterfuge?" I said. "What, like there was a Hoppy from another dimension? A twin brother who was going around scamming people while kind-hearted, hardworking Hoppy ran a business he really knew very little about?"

"Don't be ridiculous," she said. "He was the candy king!"

"He was full of fudge," I said. "You're still being a sap, Rhonda. The guy was a con man. He had no regard for anyone, for the truth, or even for chocolate."

"But he studied the art of German chocolate cake in Weimar!"

"If he was in Weimar, that's not the batter he was whipping up," I said. "Rhonda, Hoppy stank like week-old lox. The question is whether one of his investors was off-the-wall angry enough to kill him or whether there's some other reason."

"Hoppy," she said wistfully. The woman was suddenly Greta Garbo. Her head went back and she said to the football stadium, "I want to be by myself, please."

"Believe me, so do I. Just tell me where—"

"I will tell you nothing more," Rhonda said. "If you wish to see me again, contact my attorney."

She was becoming defensive. Her mourning period had definitely ended; it was time to cover her ass.

"Is that where you were going?" That was what I'd wanted to ask before she cut me off. She gave me another way in.

"Where?"

"To see Solly?"

"Who?"

"Solomon Granger, Esquire."

The nose wrinkled again as if she'd smelled that spoiled lox. "The New England attorney? Lord, no. Of all the ideas. I have no interest in *him*!"

I was being uncharacteristically slow here. I forgot that in her world, every business associate was a potential lover.

"My attorney is Jefferson Davis Forrest," she said. "As for myself, I'm going to have my hair done. For the memorial," she added, as though that justified vanity at a time of mourning.

"Oh. Do you know when it is?"

"I do not," she admitted. "I wish to be prepared."

Rhonda got in the car with *"pre-pay-uhh-ddd"* trailing behind her. She drove off without another word.

I stood there in the waning sunlight wondering at what point I'd fallen down the rabbit hole. Because everyone I'd talked to about this was definitely "out there." I got in the car and continued to my original destination. Maybe, I thought, outside this ridiculous world of the Southern aristocracy, Gary Gold would prove to be surprisingly, refreshingly normal.

I don't have to tell you how wrong I was.

Chapter 9

I checked in with Thom as my GPS squired me along Shelby Avenue.

"How's everything?" I asked.

"Slowish," she said.

"Coincidence?" I asked.

"I don't think people're avoiding us," she said. "I don't imagine most of 'em know."

"It was pretty dead at Hoppy's place."

"That's different," Thom said. "That's the house of the dead."

"Seriously?"

"Oh, yeah. They take that stuff seriously down here."

"Wow. Up North, a mob guy gets bumped off at a steak house, it's booked solid till the next hit somewhere else."

Thom tsked me. "You got some funny ways up there. No respect for the dead."

"Not for those who deserve it."

"Or privacy."

She had me there. "We've got ten million people living and working in side-by-side stacks. We hear strangers' cell phone conversations, read their iPad newspapers, walk through their cigarette smoke. What the hell is privacy?"

Thom sighed. "No wonder you have the mouth you have, always gettin' elbowed and havin' your foot stepped on." I didn't tell her that my "mouth" was mild by comparison to most: The shock might kill her sweet, Baptist soul. "I'm guessin' our afternoon customers were just hangin' by their TVs or computers, waitin' for the next shoe to drop on the Belle Meade crowd. Stuff like that is blood sport down here."

"Literally."

"Yeah, and I'll tell you somethin' else. No ordinary person would do Hoppy in like he was done."

"By 'ordinary' you mean—"

"That was a rich person's freak-out," she said.

"I don't understand."

"They can't kill people as themselves. That would be a mark on their status. They have to become someone else, like a blue-collar worker—"

"An electrician?"

"Exactly. They'd have to playact to do something that gruesome."

"You truly believe that."

"I do," she said.

After my encounter with Rhonda, I wasn't about to dismiss momentary schizophrenia as a component of this crime.

"You find anything out while you been nosing

around in something that I still don't see is any of your business?"

"Just what you knew from the start," I told Thom. "That Hoppy was no damn—I mean, no darn good."

"Hah. You see? There's no grapevine like the service industry for reliable information. You bettin' on any horses yet?"

"Too early," I told her. "I'm off to Confederate Hill to see the writer now. Your grapevine tell you anything about him?"

She chuckled. "He came in here once about a year ago as a guest of the Cozy Foxes. At least, I think it was him."

"What do you mean?"

"I gotta go," she said.

"What do you *mean*?" I pressed.

She replied, "He was the right man for this job."

I wasn't able to extrapolate anything from Thom's parting comment, so I filed it away as I drove to his home. It was on the also unhappily named Fatherland Street. Just seeing the street sign gave me shuddering racial memories. The address was a small, newish little bungalow—I'd put it about 1960, which was about a century younger than some of the other places in the neighborhood. I got out when the GPS told me I'd arrived and walked up the short, narrow concrete path. There was a simulated gold bar hanging from the black lamppost in place of a number sign. The mailbox beside the front door was painted gold. I guessed this was indeed the place, and rang the bell.

An intercom crackled. I hadn't seen it, cobweb-covered under the mailbox. "Leave it by the screen door."

"I'm not a delivery person, Mr. Gold."

"Who are you?"

"Gwen Katz. We haven't actually met—"

"What do you want, Gwendolyn?"

"Actually, it's Gwenette."

"Is that French or something?"

"I think it's Welsh. My mother was fond of Dylan Thomas."

"Then she should have named you Myfanwy or Christmas, should she not have?"

"I can't say and sadly I can't ask her, since she is deceased. Mr. Gold, I'd like to—"

"Katz is Hebraic, though," he said.

"It is."

"Gold is not," he mentioned. "It's short for Goldholdt. That's German."

"I'm not surprised," I said. "Mr. Gold, these pleasantries aside, I was wondering if I could talk to you."

"We're talking. What are we talking *about*?"

"The Baker party," I said patiently. "I believe you wrote the murder scenario—"

"You believe? It's true! But are you true? How do I know you're not a process server?"

"I told you, I'm Gwen Katz, owner of the Nashville Katz deli. You've eaten there."

"Not good enough."

"Are you *expecting* a summons for any reason?"

"One never knows, does one?" he asked.

It would take another minute of this before I kicked in the door and beat him with the gold bar from the walk. So, once again, I lied.

"Mr. Gold, I'm thinking of hosting a murder party and I would like to read what you wrote for Mrs. Baker. She recommended you highly."

"I am emailing her as we speak to make sure that she did, in fact, send you to me."

"Great, fine. In the meantime, do you have a copy of the scenario? Something I could read?"

"Hard copy or PDF?"

"A printout, if you have one," I told him. I didn't want to leave without it. I didn't ever want to talk to the man again.

"I am making one as I type to Lolo Baker *and* as we speak."

I could hear the printer chugging. When it stopped I heard a door open and close.

"It is around back, on the patio, in the milk box," he informed me.

I went back there and saw a single sheet of paper sticking from under the metal lid. I took it, made sure it was what I wanted, and left. I left jogging toward the car. I guess some people are writers for a reason—creative drive and an anti-social nature were the two I would have guessed before coming here. Add to that lunacy. When I had Googled Gary Gold back at the house, it had listed him as the author of several children's books published by a small local press in the 1990s,

Policy Press with only a P.O. Box. They were ghost stories like *Wagner and the Spook* and *Carl Is Afraid of the Closet*. Lolo had hosted publishing parties for both at the estate. One newspaper archive had a photo of the author, from the back, signing copies for guests. I was morbidly curious to find those now. Just as I was to read the mystery scenario he'd written. But not as much as I was to get back across the River, to which I sped like Ichabod Crane racing for the covered bridge.

Chapter 10

My two cats are night creatures. They emerge from their big, plastic cat homes when the sun goes down. They can't see it from in there; they sense it. They had done the same thing in New York; I wasn't sure they had ever actually seen the sun.

Their names are Southpaw and Mr. Wiggles, and they're both about five years old. They were left behind by a neighbor when she moved, and I couldn't turn them over to be euthanized. They were spayed, declawed, and generally pretty lethargic. But they were something to care for, and care about. When you live alone, don't have a lot of close girl friends because most of your college roommates are married, and are usually more sick of male friends than not, cats are acceptable companions.

They emerged like furry little vampires, their big cat-guts swaying to and fro, their eyes bright with hunger. I spooned out their canned cat food, then took a pair of Hebrew National hot dogs from the fridge, slit them lengthwise, and slapped them in a frying pan for me. While I held them flat with a big metal spatula, I spread Mr. Gold's paper on the counter and read:

The Baker Murder Mystery by Gary Gold
Created for Lolo Baker by Gary Gold.
(c) 2011 by Gary Gold

Marley was dead. For just a couple of moments.

At first it looks like he's just sleeping in the patio swing but he's not. He's dead! Harley Marley, the infamous night time biker (played by Gary Gold) had been intending to crash the party . . . but someone crashed his. This will be announced, during dessert, by the loud breaking of a beer bottle over his head. (I will, myself, strike a bottle against the metal studs of the leather wristband I will be wearing. All of the guests will come to investigate.)

Lolo (poking the corpse): "Who could have done this to Harley Marley with his own beer?"

Lolo will look around quickly (so Gary doesn't have to hold his breath for very long). She will find an unsigned note on the ground (which Gary will leave there). She will read it.

Lolo: "I don't love you. I don't want to see you again. Do not follow me."

Everyone will go back inside. Lolo will detect a faint stain on the note. Under examination from her magnifying glass she will discover tomato sauce.

Lolo: "Whoever did this wrote it while she was eating pasta!"

The guests will smell each others' breath. Only one will smell of garlic, but she will explain it is the result of having eaten a canapé before dinner. Then she will die: she is the actual murder victim! Harley Marley is gone. (The dead woman should be Lolo, so that the other guests will have to figure things out on their own.)

Lolo: (near death): "I knew this would happen! Search me!"

The dead woman is searched. *There are hate letters written in the same hand as hers!* That means Harley Marley faked his own death . . . and he's not really dead. He poisoned the snack in the truck because he knew his lover loved eggplant!

Now Harley Marley is among them, but in disguise and hiding. Is he the butler? Is he one of the caterers? Is he the electrician who has been working quietly upstairs? Is he the florist who has arrived with a wreath from Harley Marley?

That is for Gary Gold to know and the guests to discover.

I was cold with horror. It was the stupidest "mystery" I had ever read, with more holes than the Bunny Ranch. The only good thing was that now I saw where the eggplant canapés fit. I slid my franks onto a plate, grabbed a jar of Gulden's, and considered that mess as I ate. The only real information it provided is that Gary Gold was there.

I finished eating, made decaf, and called Grant Daniels. He was in the middle of his happy hour, I'm-off-duty-now vodka martini. Probably with a date, because I could hear the background clatter and he didn't say my name when he answered.

"Hey, you," he said.

"Sorry to interrupt, but I just read the scenario for the murder mystery Lolo's guests were supposed to solve at the party. Did any of Deputy Chief Whitman's people interview Gary Gold, the author?"

"Not that I know of," he said. "You sure he was there?"

"Gold was supposed to be a victim and then not—it's complicated, but yeah, he was there."

"We'll check it out. I'm assuming you talked to him?"

"Kind of. Through a door. Strange duck."

"Thanks for the tip. I was actually going to call you later."

"Oh?"

"The memorial is tomorrow at 10 a.m. I thought you might like to go."

How unbearably romantic. Okay, we hadn't exchanged vows, just . . . well . . . but still.

"I'll see you there," I said.

"Great. Thanks for the tip about Gold."

"Sure."

I hung up and immediately slammed my forehead with the heel of my hand. Not lightly, but enough to cause the cats to jump from their bowls.

Dumb, dumb, dumb! Not that I was the poster child for fidelity. I came to Nashville a free woman for the first time in a decade, no longer tied to an inattentive, self-absorbed *putz*. I had some catching up to do and I did—with a pair of sweet-talking Southern gentlemen to boot. If a third and fourth hunk had walked in the deli door and stayed, they'd have gotten the special of the day as well. I had no right to be anything stronger than disappointed.

But I was.

I forced myself not to think about it anymore. Neither the inside nor the outside of my head could take it. I got myself a pint of Mountain Jim's hand-packed strawberry-with-strawberry chunks from the freezer, put on the CW—if someone was going to *Gossip Girl* me, I figured I should at least know what it's about—and chuckled when I thought about Gary Gold's scenario. At some point during the ten o'clock news, I dozed off.

There was a ringing sound.

It was still dark, I fumbled with the phone, knocked over the melted ice cream, and mumbled out a hello. The ringing recurred. It wasn't the phone. It was the door. The cats had already gone to hide—maybe they were still expecting the grim cat reaper—so I was on my own. I got up, stumbled to the door, switched on the outside light. I looked through the frosted glass. A man was waving.

"Hey, Gwen. It's Grant."

I was now very awake. I leaned back to look at the stove clock. Nearly eleven. I stole a quick look in the small teakwood mirror hanging beside the jamb—my own addition, Uncle Murray didn't care how he looked—and after fluffing my hair, threw back the bolt and opened the door.

The man looked tired. His fawn-colored blazer looked tired. The five o'clock shadow was now six hours older than that. I waved him in; after the briefest hesitation, he crossed the threshold, propelled by an upward jerk of his head, like a man who was convincing himself he'd made the right decision.

"I didn't like how that call went," he said with that endearing smirk.

"Whatcha mean?" My tone was so carefree I made myself sick.

He shrugged carelessly. "It just seemed kind of cold and abrupt."

I shrugged carelessly. "You were busy."

"Not really," he confided. "I guess I thought I was. Old colleague from Kingston, here to collect a prisoner."

"Now *that's* hot."

"It is?"

"If you're into handcuffs," I said. *Stop joking, idiot,* I warned myself. *He's being serious.* "Listen, you don't have to explain—in fact, you don't have to do anything."

"I had to tell you that," he said.

The door was still awkwardly open. I'd forgotten to shut it. If I did now it would seem like he had to stay. If I didn't, it would seem like I wanted him to go.

I reached my hand outside and fussed with the empty mailbox. A good detective would notice what I was doing. A good man would pretend not to.

"Not very popular," I said, and shut the door.

I noticed the melted ice cream and picked up the container. I snatched some tissues from the end table and mopped up what little had been left to spill out.

"You want to sit down? I've got some decaf brewed—"

"Actually, I only came by to tell you that face-to-face."

So much for my mailbox improv. "Oh. You could've called."

It was his move. He hesitated to make it, whatever it was. The smirk returned then blossomed. "Think I will have that decaf if it's no trouble."

"It is not," I said.

I walked briskly into the kitchen so he couldn't see me grinning. There are few things in life so satisfying as being miserable about something that turns out to have been imaginary, like a bad grade or a misread pregnancy test. This was one of those things.

I tossed the ice cream container, heard Grant follow me into the kitchen. I set sugar and cream

on the butcher block table and got him a mug—
my vintage *Phantom of the Opera* mug, one where
the mask became visible on the side as you filled
it with hot beverage. I handed it to him and refilled my own *I Love NY* mug.

"This is cute," he said, admiring the mug.

"It was the last show I saw with my mom," I told
him. "She loved it."

"Isn't it a musical about a monster?"

I nodded. "All the best ones are." They weren't.
But it made me sound smart and just came out of my
mouth. Now that I'd said it I tried to think—*Beauty
and the Beast, Sweeny Todd, Assassins . . .* that was it.
"Beauty and the Beast, Sweeny Todd, Assassins. . . ."

"What did she love about it then?"

"He was a monster with a good soul."

"Like a hooker with a heart of gold?" Grant said.

"I guess so. He helped a singer realize her potential and died for that. Actually, he died for
killing people, but he did it for her."

"Grease is my speed."

"I like that one too," I said, putting down my
mug and doing a bit of the Hand Jive.

Grant smiled. I think he was a little embarrassed by my hyperactivity. I know I was. I suggested we go back to the living room. We sat on
the sofa.

"So, this murder," I said, looking for anything
else to discuss.

"It's a strange one," he said. "I gave your writer's
name to Whitman—I have to do this through

channels—and he said he knew about him. They haven't talked to him yet."

"Reason?"

"He didn't show up on the initial tag run."

"Tag run?"

"One of the officers got the tag numbers of all the cars in the driveway. Cell phone photos. We've got an app that IDs them instantly. His didn't come up."

"Hmmm. It was too far to walk. Maybe he thumbed a ride?"

"They're checking on it."

"I assume someone asked Lolo about it," I said.

He nodded as he sipped. "She said he dropped off the scenario the day before, then told her she wouldn't see him again until she found him—and these are her words, not mine—'pretending to be pretending to be dead.'"

"It makes sense," I assured him. I went and got the scenario from the kitchen.

Grant took a moment to read it; while he did, I read him.

He was more relaxed now that he was in the police work groove. Truth be told, so was I. More truth be told, I wish we weren't there. I wanted to—well, I wanted to not be doing police work.

"Wow," he said.

"I know."

"I wonder what she paid for this," Grant said.

"Whatever it was, it was too much. Any idea how they met?"

"Local author, wrote some thrillers—"

"The Cozies, right," Grant said. "Like gas on a match."

"What was?"

"Their attention, his vanity."

"Probably," I said. "Though it was pretty strange he wouldn't see me."

"What, a writer? Strange?" Grant said.

I chuckled.

"Maybe he's got a mother fixation, only talks to women over forty or fifty," Grant went on. He turned and looked at me with those soft but spicy eyes. "You're too young and hot. You scared him."

Talk about gas on a match. I put my mug on the little coffee table where Uncle Murray's keyboard still sat, a reminder of the nuttier yet dream-driven side of the clan. I took Grant's mug and set it next to that.

I kissed him, everything on one role of the dice.

He grew a tongue and arms, and I had no further thoughts that night of Gary Gold, Lolo Baker, or Hoppy Hopewell.

Chapter 11

Remember what I said about the happiest thing in the world being when you were proven wrong about something bad that had its claws in your soul? I'd like to amend that. It's happy only so long as the bad thing stays away. If it comes back, metamorphosed into something even uglier, the happiness turns to ash.

Grant didn't stay the night. He left sometime after—well, just after. I didn't know he had; I was sleeping. A deep sleep. A grateful sleep. I woke about seven and the bed was empty, the covers crudely straightened on "his" side. I listened for the sounds of water running in the bathroom. Nada. The *plip-plub* of Mr. Coffee hard at work turning McNulty beans into morning glory. Also no-go. I stretched myself from a fetus position, looked on the floor where I knew we had left his pants. They were gone.

It felt like my heart had become stone and my brain numb. The first thoughts were a rerun:

Dumb, dumb, dumb! What did I expect? A little velvet box with a ring? Crap, I didn't even want that. Life returned swiftly to my two stupidly impressionable organs.

Brain: One-night stands crash. Even second one-night stands.

Heart: That's usually because the participants are usually too drunk to go. I thought this was more.

Brain: No, *I* think. *You* feel. You felt this was more. I knew what it was.

Heart: Really, hotshot? What was it? Just a skinny dip? I'll show you mine if—

Brain: Something like that.

Heart: I don't believe it. You saw how he was acting.

Brain: He was uncertain—

Heart: Not during.

Brain: Of course 'not during'! Before.

Heart: He didn't know how to approach me, how to broach how he felt.

Brain: Uh-uh. He wasn't *sure* how he felt. Probably still isn't, which is as good as a loss.

Heart: What are you talking about?

Brain: He likes you enough to have wanted a return visit, but not enough to want you to think it's anything more than a visit.

Heart: You don't know that. He may have had to get to work.

Brain: You're an idiot and you're blind.

Eyes: Hey, I saw!

Brain: What did you see?

Eyes: How he was behaving. And you're both wrong.

Heart and Brain: Oh?

Eyes: He came here to stop thinking of the chick he was with. Eyes know eyes, and I could see he was looking backward, not ahead.

Gwen: Shut up, all of you.

I beat Thom to the restaurant by forty-five minutes. The place smelled of the floor-washing Luke had given it and I left the door open. I turned on the grill, made the coffee, and pulled the chairs from the tables. It felt good to be active, distracted from Grant and Hoppy. I was just about to open the cash register to make sure we had enough change when my manager clunked in the door. It wasn't that she had a heavy tread; it was that she was always burdened with bags. One for her stuff—mail-order catalogues, water bottle, Bible, breath mints, keys, wallet, pepper spray, brush, and hair clips, which she was always breaking— and one for her clothes, which she changed when she got here. Thom did not like to go home in her work outfit, "Smelling like a sa-lami," as she put it.

"You think this is gonna get you extra points with the boss for missin' mosta yesterday?" she asked.

"The boss is a jerk. I don't care what she thinks."

"Oooooh. That sounds like—"

"It is. I don't want to discuss it."

Thom thunked her bags on the counter. "You

can't just drop that egg and not expect me to call you butterfingers. What up? And you might as well tell me because I ain't leavin' it alone till you do."

I caved. I hadn't wanted to whine, but I had to talk to someone. Now, Thom had her puritan side, but she wasn't naive or judgmental. She had that side for a reason.

"Men," she said and collected her bags. She shook her head. "Oh, man." She went into the back to change.

That was it. That was the extent of her advice, her strong shoulder, her compassion. But the effort wasn't wasted: all the thinking I had done had brought me to the same conclusion. Maybe that was as far as the equation could be reduced. They were what they were and you couldn't expect them to be more. If they were, then they ceased becoming pronouns. They became Clark or Bruce or Peter. They became a boyfriend or husband. Until then, they were just guys.

I had thought Grant Daniels was more than that. My brain interrupted to tell me that she had nothing to do with it: the heart had been doing the thinking, which was the problem. I couldn't argue with that.

I was curious about something, though, and I grabbed Thom when she returned to set out the napkins.

"Was my uncle happy?" I asked.

She stopped and gave me a hand-on-the-hip

look. "You got some kinda MapQuest I don't know about?"

My look told her I didn't follow.

"How the heck you get to that, girl?"

I saw her point. Two minutes before, we were talking about my broken-hearted fling with Grant Daniels.

"Two things," I said. "First, I see his keyboard a couple of times a day. He ended up being a dilettante—"

"A who?"

"A dabbler," I explained. "He never really made music work as a career. Second, as far as I know, he was alone all his life except for my dad. I was wondering how that worked out for him."

Thom paused and smiled. It was different from her usual big smile for the customers, or her sassy smile for the staff, or her wouldn't-it-be-wonderful-if-you-did-some-more-work-around-here smile for me. This one was honest.

"Your uncle may have been a dabbler, and he may only have been Luke-level good on his keyboard, but he loved making his melodies. He carried that keyboard everywhere. And I mean everywhere, sometimes to the john. Went through six Double-A batteries every two days. I know 'cause I ordered them by the case."

"Did you like what he composed?"

"Not a note of it. But I liked that he liked writing it. He came alive." She looked at me. "Sort of like you did when you got yourself another little mystery to pick at."

"Yeah, I guess that's sort of what I was asking," I said. "Somebody asked me why I cared who killed Hoppy Hopewell and I made up some shi—some sugar about it being bad for business that we catered the death gig."

"But that's got nothing to do with it. In fact, we got calls yesterday to cater two other parties."

"Did we?"

Thom nodded. "A confirmation and a bachelor party. I asked them how they heard of us. The confirmation was from your online menu. The other was from the news reports of Lolo's party."

"How about that."

The world suddenly seemed a little brighter. I wasn't incompetent. Some part of me had made a right decision, however ill-advised my romp with Grant may have been. Or maybe wasn't. I had no idea. Heart sulked about that, but Brain was right-pleased with its business decisions.

"Your uncle made us his family," Thom went on. "Music was his girlfriend. He dated now and then, but if the gal wasn't into music, he lost interest. If she was, she lost interest."

"His stuff was that bad?"

"Not so much bad as completely awful."

I thought about that for a moment, and it still didn't make sense. "You're going to have to explain that."

"His tunes weren't bad but he thought he would sell songs, if they were—" She looked for the proper word, gave up. "Check out these titles. *White Christmas Shoes. When Doves Fly. Great Vibrations.*"

"Seriously? He wrote those songs?"

"He wrote them, shopped them around, played them here when I let him—when there weren't enough customers to scare away—but was so, so sincere about them. He never saw that there were . . . problems."

My heart was happy to be distracted. It hurt for Uncle Murray.

"How did my dad put up with that?" I wondered.

"I'm guessin' he just loved his brother and was happy to see him happy. I never met your father, but from what I hear, that was something that eluded him."

Now my heart hurt for my father. It was more like an emotional bungee jump: it pained me to think that he was chronically unsatisfied. What a sad fate for both my parents. Unhappy together, unhappy apart.

I hadn't realized my head had dipped. Thom bent and looked up into my eyes. "You okay?"

"Sure," I lied. There were tears on the way, so I turned to flick on the heat lamps. Thom probably knew better, but she let it go.

"You can't let yourself dwell on what was or wasn't," she said, "on opportunities people missed or were afraid to take. I spent a lot of time doin' that, regrettin' how I threw myself at men or family members or employers who didn't respect me."

"Then you found Jesus," I said. I wasn't being sarcastic; she had.

"Yes, but He was only part of what saved me. The other part was your Uncle Murray. He had this joy about him, this love of each day and each hour in that day. He was a *positive* man. Whatever delusions he had about his music, he had those same delusions about the folks around him. He thought I looked pretty and smelled nice and treated customers better than they deserved. He saw me fuss about how lettuce or a pickle looked on a plate if it had just been tossed there during a rush. He noticed things and made you feel good about yourself, whether you worked for him or were a customer or just passed him on the street. I think that must've been one of the things that sustained your father. I dunno—maybe your mom was jealous of that, the fact that from what I hear she wasn't able to do that for him. It isn't enough to love somebody, hon. You gotta enjoy being around them and they you."

Thom had rounded the bases and my heart and brain were waiting in the dugout with open arms.

"Thanks," I managed to choke out.

"You're welcome," she said.

"I *did* have a good night last night."

"Of course. Sometimes it's okay to just want to be held or feel attractive." She was still smiling sincerely . . . until she wasn't. "You turn on the grease?"

"Oops."

And she was gone into the kitchen to flick it on, and get out the eggs and butter and fill the salt and pepper shakers and sugar. I finished at the cash register and went into the office, and shut the door and let it all out. Years of it. I had spent a lot of time crying about my failed marriage, but not about my parents' failed marriage, or my uncle's failed career, or looking at the shores of middle age with a slightly scary new home and career and warm but provincial new associates I didn't know well. And men like Grant and Royce, who were like New York men but without the courtesy to be honest about interest that was only marginal.

I cried into my open hand until I heard customers. I washed my eyes with warm water, let hair fall over them to hide the red, and went out to help Newt on the grill. Luke was peeling potatoes for early morning latkes—done shredded, hash-brown-style, instead of pureed so we could sell them *as* hash-browns—and I worked the toaster.

There was no idle talk during rushes, and that suited me perfectly. I needed the distraction. The regulars kept coming through 9:30, after which it slowed enough for me to duck out and change. My head was back in the game, "my" White Christmas Shoes, the desire to figure out who killed Hoppy Hopewell. I found myself even more motivated than before. Rational or sane, fueling my darker emotions or not, I really, really wanted to figure this sucker out before Grant Daniels or his fellow officers did.

* * *

The memorial was like a wake.

I was expecting people to be talking to one another or popping over to the open coffin to say good-bye to the Chocolate King. They were doing anything but. There were thirty-odd people in the funeral home chapel, and that included the three black-suited ushers. Neither Pinky nor Jennifer was present, I didn't recognize anyone from the state legislature—though they may have been there; I just didn't know those people—and Solly was sitting with his junior partner, a young lady with pearls, blond hair, and a headband holding it in place. A couple of local merchants were present, probably to network.

Rhonda was there with her newly done hair, which looked frighteningly like the oddly wind-blown hair I saw the day before. So were Grant Daniels and Deputy Chief Whitman, who were standing together beside the door. I nodded to them both. Grant seemed to pay me a hair more attention than he would have before last night. Then he was back checking out the crowd and talking to Whitman.

The only Cozy Fox in attendance was Lolo. Besides myself, she was also the only one there who had also been at the dinner party.

Royce was also there. He was in the back, as far from his former wife as the space would allow. He waved as I entered. I waved back. That was it. He could drop dead.

I walked over and said a quick farewell to Hoppy Hopewell. He looked okay, better than he had the last time I'd seen him. I noticed there were no trinkets, no parting gifts in the coffin. This was not going to be an emotional send-off.

I sat in the middle, on the aisle, my heart trying to convince my brain that Grant shouldn't be joining Royce on that fiery ferry ride to hell. That was when he surprised me by coming over. My brain agreed to move him off the dock.

"Sorry I had to go," he said.

"No need to be sorry," I said. "I was asleep." My heart was screaming murderously at my brain-controlled mouth.

"I know, but I should have left a note or something."

"What, like thanks for the Joe?" *Take that,* said my heart, wresting command.

"No, seriously," he said in a strong whisper. He was trying not to lean close and create the wrong impression, which left him talking almost like a ventriloquist. "The case woke me up around two and I couldn't get back to sleep. I didn't want to wake you."

Oh. That worked. I felt good again. "Thanks, I said." My brain had the reins again. "What did you wake up thinking about?"

"What I was just discussing with Deputy Chief Whitman, the secrecy surrounding Hopewell's estate."

"No duh. I couldn't even find out who got the chocolate shop." No duh? What was I, twelve years old? Maybe that was my problem. Grant made me feel like a teen again.

"And you probably won't find that out," Grant said. "Solly Granger filed a series of motions, along with the will, pertaining to Section 29-25-104 of the state code regarding probate. It has to do with forestalling the intervention by any third-person claimant."

"In non-legalese?"

"Basically, Granger moved to bar Hoppy's sister from making any claims against the estate."

"Really? So she's not—"

"She's not."

That was a little bit of a surprise. I was willing to guess that if anyone had inherited whatever he had, it was Sis. As we were talking, Solly walked in with Father Virgil Breen of St. Joseph's. That was obviously to protect Solly from any further questioning, which Father Breen could dismiss as inappropriate.

Grant now had an excuse to lean closer: decorum. "Granger also told me this will be the only public event involving Hoppy Hopewell."

"Not surprising," I said. "Funerals tend to be private."

"This is more than private," Grant said. "I was led to believe that his sister wouldn't even be there."

We both sat back as organ music began and Father Breen took center stage and kind words were uttered about the deceased. But, like Grant, my mind was elsewhere, sorting through what little we knew.

I was still sorting when the clergyman finished after about ten minutes, Solly rose and left, and the memorial was, evidently, quite done.

Chapter 12

Rhonda slipped through a side door so I didn't have to talk to her again. But I did excuse myself from Grant—who gave me a handshake instead of a peck, which sucked the tiniest bit of joy from me—and chased Lolo down in the line filing out.

We emerged into the sunlight together. She looked lovely in a clingy black blouse and knee-length skirt with elbow-length black gloves and a black pillbox hat and veil.

"That was almost lovely," Lolo said.

Well-said, I thought. She seemed as nonplussed as I was by the whole thing. I asked how she was doing.

"I feel a little like Lady Macbeth," she replied.

"Having trouble with spots?"

"No, not that," she said. "'What? In our house?'"

High school English came back to me. After conspiring to murder the king with hubbins, Lady Macbeth caused a stir when she was apparently more upset that he died there than that he was dead at all.

"But I don't apologize," she said as we walked toward the parking lot. "I enjoyed Mr. Hopewell's company but I was not a great admirer."

"Some history there?" I asked.

"Some indeed," she replied.

When she didn't elaborate, I said, "Did you invest with him too?"

She turned toward me so fast I could swear her hat shifted. "*You* gave him money?"

"Exotic aphrodisiacs," I said, trying to think of something he might not have asked her to invest in. "Egyptian pomegranate, century-old ginseng, oysters from Pitcairn Island." I stopped there because those were the only aphrodisiacs I knew about.

Lolo's eyes lowered, dragging her face with them. "Then the rumors are true."

"What rumors?"

"I knew that he was running several businesses on the side, poor man—"

"Why poor man?" I made a mental note not to lose track of my subsets here.

"Because he was always so tired when I wanted to talk about ours," Lolo said, her eyes on some sad memory. "I thought it was just two or three of the Cozies, maybe a few other wealthy matrons. I didn't know he had gone to the gentry."

She didn't mean to be insulting, so I didn't take it personally. That was just the way a lot of these old Southern moneyed widows were. "Apparently, he had his fingers in a lot of peach pies. At least I wasn't romantically involved with him."

Again, the look. "Who was?"

"I couldn't say," I told her. "Those were rumors too."

She sighed. Her harsh looks were like lightning flashes, scary and then gone. I couldn't tell whether she was protective, jealous, or both. I was betting on just the first.

"*That* is even more exhausting than business," she said. "I told Hoppy from the start that I would never become involved with him. For myself, I would never indulge in that sort of thing out of wedlock."

"I'm sure he appreciated that on many levels," I said.

"As a matter of fact, he did. He told me so."

"What was 'your' business?" I asked, eagerly changing the subject.

"Hmm?" She glanced back toward the funeral home. Maybe she really did just like the guy.

"Your business with Mr. Hopewell."

"Oh. Exotic mystery memorabilia."

I was expecting plants or pets or something a little more ordinary. Perhaps, given Lolo's nature, I should not have been surprised.

"What kind of memorabilia are we talking about here? Jack the Ripper's moustache wax?"

"That would be something, wouldn't it?" she said, brightening. "No, he found handwritten notes by Mr. Conan Doyle for an unwritten children's tale called 'Who Cooked Jemima Puddleduck,' the flask of Mr. Raymond Chandler—whence he sought comfort while writing of *The Big Sleep*—a fake leg belonging to Cornell Woolrich on which he carved the names of critics who disliked *I Married a Dead Man*—wonderful things like that."

I was both speechless and dumbstruck. First by the awesome, almost inspirational *chutzpah* it required to tell someone, even someone as gullible as Lolo, that those artifacts were genuine; and second by the fact that she believed him.

"Do you actually possess these items?" I inquired.

"Alas, I do not," she said. "Do you remember the tragic plane crash in Smolensk, Russia, in April of 2010?"

"The one that killed the Polish president?" I asked.

"Yes, that very one!" she replied enthusiastically. "It so happens that Maria Kaczyńska, the president's wife, ran the equivalent of the Cozy Foxes in Warsaw. Those and several other items were part of her personal collection. They were onboard that plane with her—all tragically destroyed."

"And you had already paid for them," I guessed.

"I had. Hoppy was working with the insurance company to recover the funds but—well, you worked in the financial world. You know how complicated those international dealings can be."

"I do indeed," I said. "Weren't they going to some kind of memorial service in the middle of nowhere?"

"The Katyn Massacre of 1940," Lolo said. "Hoppy

and I discussed the event. The Russians killed Polish soldiers there, you see. It was terrible."

"Massacres usually are," I said. "What did Hoppy say those items were doing on the plane with the first lady?"

"She was bringing them to give to him."

"Couldn't he have just flown to Warsaw?"

"Hoppy was going to the memorial anyway," she said. "He told me he lost a distant relative in the massacre."

"Let me guess. He canceled his trip when he learned of the crash."

"Not entirely," Lolo said. "He got as far as Europe. Then he came back. No sense going to Smolensk if you're not going to pick up someone's collection of mystery memorabilia."

"I guess not. Did he tell you about Maria Kaczyńska before he left or after he got back?"

"After he got back," she said. "He didn't want to trouble me with details of the negotiation until they were finalized."

"Did you pay for his airfare?"

"Of course, though he offered," Lolo said. "This was a business venture, my venture. He was going to amass these pieces, let me select a few I wanted to keep, and sell the rest for a profit. I suppose he knew I could never have parted with any of them, but how many business opportunities promise to be so much fun? Think of how exciting the Cozy Foxes gatherings would have been if we'd had Alfred Hitchcock's eyeglasses on the table."

I told her I'd try to imagine. Now, at least, it

made sense. Hoppy had this scam working and waited for a European air disaster to pin its failure on the demise of Maria Kaczyńska. He would have let the insurance angle play out for a year or two and finally given up, by which time Lolo would have forgotten all about it.

It spoke again to money problems, though it didn't seem as if this one had a romantic component. It didn't need one, and there was only so much of Hoppy Hopewell to go around.

We reached Lolo's car, a classic Jaguar XKE coupe. People were moving around us, in wide, arcing trajectories like we were magnetically repulsive. Either they were giving Lolo privacy, or they saw her as toxic at worst, a murderess at worse-still.

She gave the car a loving stroke. "It was my husband's baby," she said. "I only take it out for special occasions."

"It's a pip."

"Tell me, Ms. Katz. You meet ordinary people every day."

"I do. I'm one of them."

She didn't appear to have heard. "Do you think that what happened will taint me in their eyes?"

The old gal must have noticed the motion of the mourners. It got to her.

"You mean, give rise to the Curse of Baker Plantation or something like that?"

"Exactly like that," she said.

"I don't think so. People are easily distracted by things like unemployment, inflation, terrorism, war, their kids."

"I'm glad to hear you say that," she said. "I do so fret about my station in the community. The Bakers have a reputation, you know. I should be horrified if I failed to uphold it."

"Before you go," I said, "I was thinking of asking Gary Gold to write a family history for the back of our menu. Is he a good person for that?"

"Gary is a very inventive fellow," she said. "He is a mystery novelist, you know."

"I know."

She had said that almost reverently, as though he had seen the face of God and drew her a picture.

"I own *all* his original manuscripts," she added. "Two copies of each, in fact. He printed them out for me. It's very thrilling. That was what got me interested in the idea of possessing other memorabilia."

"Poe, Hammett, Gary—I can see how it all fits."

"As for non-fiction, I do not frankly know if facts could contain his imagination."

"Do you think he would meet with me to discuss it?"

"Oh, I doubt that, at least initially," she said.

"Why is that?"

"He is a very private man."

"Really? Because Thom, my manager, said she saw him with you at the deli a while back—"

"I coaxed him to come out, but he wore a mask."

"What, like the Lone Ranger?"

"*Exactly* like the Lone Ranger! How splendid

you said that—I knew he reminded me of someone. Without the hat or silver bullets, of course."

"Or the faithful Indian companion," I guessed.

"He has trust issues, I believe. It took me a long, long while to get him to come and see me."

"How did he get there. On Silver?"

I had to explain my comment. She smiled.

"No, he borrowed one of my cars. He doesn't own one, you see. Mystery writers, unless they are extremely fortunate, are not extremely wealthy."

That would explain why the police didn't notice an extra one in the drive.

"What did you do, pick him up earlier?" I asked.

"I had Lizzie collect him," Lolo said. "Then she went home in her car."

"I see." At least, I saw another piece. I still had no idea how they all fit.

"I hope to come by the deli soon with the Cozies," she said. "I simply must have life return to normalcy as soon as possible. Fictional murders are so much less oppressive."

Particularly for the victims, I thought as she honest to God "toodle-ooed" me and drove off.

I checked my watch. It was just after eleven. I had time to eat a quick brunch and prepare for lunch rush. Plus, I had some equilibrium where Grant Daniels was concerned.

All in all, a good morning.

Chapter 13

As I helped Newt in the kitchen, I ran through the evidence and leads. It was the same way I'd operated when I was still a practicing accountant. I would do something unchallenging—like walking around the city or hitting a Starbucks and playing *Angry Birds* when it was still the hot new thing-to-do—and think.

I had a lot of pieces; they just didn't make much of a picture . . . unless you care for Jackson Pollock, in which case I had a masterpiece on my hands.

One thing was clear. Most of the people in Lolo's circle were uncommonly self-absorbed. That complicated things a bit. At some point during our initial time together, Grant had mentioned to me—and subsequent reading bore this out—that most killers tend to be like that. They think they're the center of the cosmos, so taking a life is not so troublesome as it is for the rest of us.

I say "us" because there were times in my life when I asked myself that question, whether I *could*

kill someone. I don't mean the spontaneous stab-
an-intruder-with-a-fork sort of thing, which I think
we're all capable of, but something premeditated.
On numerous occasions, especially during the unhappy parts of my marriage and the onerous parts
of my divorce, when I pondered the age-old "If
you knew you could get away with it. . . ."

I always came away thinking I wouldn't, couldn't,
shouldn't. At least, not where Phil was concerned.
And I never hated anyone more than I hated
him—except maybe my high school boyfriend
Esteban, a foreign exchange student. I fell for the
accent, the swarthy good looks, and let him take
me across the finish line. After which he disappeared from my life except in hateful thoughts.
Part of me had really believed the scumbag would
continue to be interested in me, if for no other
reason than a potential green card.

So there have been two people I've hated, and
I never got to the point where I felt I could put a
knife in either of their dark, Satanic, bloodless,
pig-hearts. That told me either someone had to
hate Hoppy a whole lot—which was possible, of
course, for reasons I had not yet uncovered—or
else the killer was a crazy narcissist, of which I had
plenty. And was about to acquire one more.

Mollie Baldwin came to lunch with her teenage
daughter Poodle. That's right: like a dog. Not a
nickname, not a nom-de-guerre, that was her real
handle. Mollie was a big woman, not very tall, but
very wide. She was big in breeding and showing
circles as well. Naturally, Mollie's favorite mysteries

involved canines. I know that because she once came in all a-quiver, having just acquired a mint condition first edition of the classic Philo Vance novel *The Kennel Murder Case.* I asked why it was so special.

"Dogs are the only creatures unscathed and un-touched since the first falling of man," she said during the course of our little chat. The other Cozies had nodded, not necessarily because they agreed, but because they agreed that Mollie believed that.

The good news was that she never brought any of her babies with her: they only ate filet, and my meats weren't good enough for them. They were good enough for Mollie and Poodle, though, and they usually came by before their weekly manicure and pedicures.

Poodle was height-weight proportionate, a pretty early twentysomething except for balls of her curly hair affixed to the sides of her head. She didn't seem self-conscious about it, however; Poodle was every bit as into dogs as her mother. She was also openly, famously into young men; aggressively, like a dog in heat.

Mollie was a little more reserved today than usual. Not that she barked and panted, but she usually had a kind of wide-eyed eagerness about her that was absent today. Either she was still a little shellshocked from the other night, or else one of her dogs had a worm.

I took their order myself. It was a pair of chicken salad platters, not hot dogs. I passed it to Luke, who was bussing, to take to the kitchen. Poodle excused herself and went to chat with a pair of Nashville Electric Service hardhats.

Mollie smiled thinly. "Youth," she sighed. There was a disapproving tone in her voice, one that suggested that there were probably fights at home like the ones my mother and I used to have. Except when I dated older doctors or lawyers.

"What were you like as a kid?" I asked.

"Not like that." She leveled a red fingernail at Poodle. "I waited until I was older, then—just between us hens, yes, I made up for lost time."

Mollie was only in her early fifties, but she had put two husbands in the grave. I was guessing she made up for her time off the market with a vengeance.

"But this—this offering herself," Mollie sighed. "And then to keep a diary of her experiences."

"What girl doesn't?"

"And what mother doesn't peek?" she asked rhetorically.

Plenty, I was willing to bet.

"She isn't bad, you know," Mollie said.

"Of course not, Mrs. Baldwin. Your daughter is just experimenting."

Mollie frowned. "I meant as a writer."

"Oh."

"Yes, she meets that local fellow once a week for tutoring."

"Gary Gold?"

Mollie nodded.

My only response was a silent *Oy*. It was time to change the subject.

"How are you holding up?" I asked.

"I am in mourning, of course," Mollie said. She pointed to the black Victorian flower pin tacked to the lapel of her beige jacket. Poodle had nothing for show-and-tell. She was apparently less grieved.

"You weren't at the memorial—"

"It would have been too, too upsetting."

"Were you very close to the deceased?"

"*Very* close, at one time," Mollie said. "We were lovers after my first and second husbands passed."

"That worked out," I said.

"Hoppy was a great consolation."

I didn't know Mollie well, but I decided to push. "Why didn't you two hook up? Permanently, I mean."

"I asked, several times," Mollie said. "But he had another love."

"Who?"

"He never shared that with me," she said.

"That seems a little . . . selective, given everything else you shared."

"Oh, that was just torrid fornication," she said with a dismissive wave of her thick hand. "There was a lot about Hoppy he kept to himself."

"Such as?"

Mollie's brow dipped. "I don't know. He kept it to himself."

"I meant personally, professionally, about his past—"

She drank some water, seemed reluctant to say more.

"I don't mean to pry," I fibbed. "It's just that— I remember that when my Uncle Murray died it was good to just talk about him."

She smiled wistfully. "Ah, Murray."

Uh-oh, I thought. I wasn't going to ask.

"He was a sweetheart," Mollie said.

Don't say it—

"I miss him."

Don't tell me how much or in what way—

"He used to write folksy songs about my loves," she said. "*God Bless the Puppy. What a Difference a Dog Makes. You Go to My Tail.* He would sing them to me right where you are standing."

I relaxed as though cables had been cut. I literally *phewed.* It wasn't that I begrudged my uncle a sex life. It was just the thought that any part of my gene pool could be amused for very long by someone with a two-track mind.

"Hoppy was different," she said. "He wasn't creative. He wasn't that entertaining, though he imagined he was. He wasn't even that smart, though he thought he was."

"In what way?"

"He asked me to invest in some speculative new business about seven or eight months ago, something I knew was bogus."

"Exotica?"

"You could call it that," she said. "He told me he had met an artist in Europe who created Pet Chias."

"Which were?"

"Floral growths that one affixed to the tail of a dog," Mollie said. "They grew, nurtured by the dog's own water. He said it was very green."

That was not the color I would have guessed.

"Did you give him money?"

"Of course," she said. "There was an earnestness about him one simply could not deny."

"Let me guess," I said. "He decided to abandon the business because the Chia Pet people sent him a legal letter."

"Yes!" Mollie said with a look of surprise. "How did you know?"

"Just a hunch," I said. I grabbed the water pitcher from Luke, refilled Mollie's glass, and handed the pitcher back to him. The coquettish smile she gave him made me wonder if I had appeared so obvious and needy to Grant the night before. I resolved to practice my man-looks in a mirror before I went to bed. "Did you know that Hoppy had a number of start-ups that met similar fates?" I asked when Luke had gone.

"I didn't know for a fact but I suspected," Mollie said. "He had a lot of ideas. He was an extremely driven man."

"Is it possible that others didn't see it that way?"

"How so?"

"Hoppy was taking money and failing to deliver on his promises," I said. "Do you think that what happened the other night might have been the work of one of his less understanding partners?"

"There are dogs that walk and others that speak and one that plays computer games using bark recognition software," she said. "I suppose anything is possible."

"True," I agreed.

"What I told the police officer was that while I couldn't imagine who would want Hoppy dead, I could imagine a woman, any woman of a certain age and situation, pining in his absence. Unless, of course, she had distractions."

I followed her eyes to the blue-collar hunks. As much as the idea of Poodle bird-dogging for them both had its skeevy side—and it did, enough to dry my mouth and chill the skin—I had to admire her pluck. While Mollie was distracted by visions of doggy-style shenanigans, I decided to ask—

"I wonder if Hoppy used the chocolate shop as collateral in any of these dealings."

"He didn't with me," she said, her eyes sizing up the human chew toys. "He wasn't a particularly courageous businessman. I'm not sure he would have risked something certain for something speculative."

Poodle returned with an email address written on her wrist. Their food arrived as she was transferring it to her iPhone. I wished them a good day and went to the back to the kitchen, intrigued by three things Mollie had told me. This was the first I had heard of a love in Hoppy's life—not just a paramour—and the first intimation that someone had realized the chocolate shop, not a family fortune, was the dead man's financial lifeline.

Scoundrel Hoppy Hopewell may have been, but there was something sad in the story she told.

Chapter 14

If you had told me that Pinky and Jennifer hadn't moved in twenty-four hours, I wouldn't have argued. They were wearing the same clothes, doing the same off-loading of pretzels as the day before.

"I guess you sell a lot of those," I said as I walked in.

"A ton, but all to one guy," Pinky said.

"An S&M freak," I suggested.

Both girls froze and fired me a look.

"Sugar and monosodium glutamate," I said.

They relaxed, snorted, then air-high-fived me. I dual-handed them back.

"Did I miss you at the memorial?" I asked.

"We didn't go," Pinky said. "We're both hourly. I wasn't giving up seven-and-a-quarter to see someone dead who I saw for free alive."

"Me too," Jennifer agreed.

Pinky looked at me suspiciously. "Hey, you're not asking us for a reason, are you?"

"What do you mean?"

"*You're* not the new owner, are you? Scoping us out, like, undercover?"

Both girls were suddenly alert, like flamingos who think—if flamingos think—a floating log might be an alligator.

"I'm definitely not the new owner," I said.

"Yeah, because, like, honestly—when we were talking about it later, we didn't think you really came in here to place an order yesterday," Pinky said.

"You've got a good sense of things," I said appreciatively. "If things do go south here, you can come work for me."

I meant it too. I was thinking about how few hard hats came to the deli and how these two could make a difference.

"Hey, thanks," Pinky said. "Sorry if we were, like, weird about that."

"Not a problem," I said. Solly could probably go after me for allegedly raiding the ranks, but I decided not to worry about it. My offer was contingent.

"So did you really want to place an order?" Pinky asked.

"No," I admitted.

The girls high-fived.

"I was the caterer at the party where Hoppy died. I saw your boss crash-land about as close as you are to me."

"Too bad you didn't shoot that," Jennifer said.

"Probably would've been top video on YouTube for, like, a week."

"Probably," I said. It also might have helped us solve the crime, but I didn't want to confuse the matter. "Anyway, that's why I've been asking about Hoppy."

"Like, to finish the story," Pinky said. "You saw part two, you want to see part one."

"*New Moon* without *Twilight*," Jennifer said. "Could frustrate."

"Exactly." *Christ, was anything real to these girls, to that generation?*

"So what do you want to know now?" Pinky asked.

"Hoppy took a trip," I said, incongruously reminding myself of a movie my dad once made me watch—what was it? Hopalong Cassidy served something. "I was wondering if you remembered when that was and where he went."

Pinky held up a finger. She came around the counter and went to a door in the back, one that was painted, jamb and all, to look like a gingerbread house.

"Let me check the calendar," the young girl said. "He used to write important stuff for us there."

"Write" I thought, then suddenly remembered "writ." *Hoppy Serves a Writ.*

"Mr. H was gone in October," she shouted from the back.

"What does it say exactly?"

"It says, 'H in Europe,' and it has a line from

October 17 to October 24. He wanted to be back for Halloween, which is our busiest time."

That didn't work out. "What about before that?" I asked.

"He was gone in the spring," she said. "Let's see—that was April 11 through the 23rd."

Those dates coincided with the crash in Smolensk; or rather, they followed it closely. My guess was that he heard about it and got out of sight *tout de suite,* so he could tell Lolo he was going to meet the Polish First Lady.

"Do you happen to know where he went that first time?" I asked.

Pinky emerged from the back. "No, but I remember thinking that it wasn't, like, a beach or anything."

"Why?"

"Because he came back as pale as when he left."

That wasn't much help. He could have gone to Memphis.

"Do you know if he arranged the trip through a travel agent?" I asked.

"Yeah, yeah, yeah!" the girls said in unison.

"Okay, what am I missing here?"

"Paul McCartney," Pinky said. "McCartney Travel Agency."

"He's always playing Beatles songs on his car boom box."

Obviously, I needed to go to a few Lions Club meetings, or whatever kind of business networking went on down here. I would have remembered a name like that. "Let me guess," I said. "He drives a Jetta."

The girls looked at me like I was Kreskin. "How did you know?"

"A bug," I said. When they didn't get it, I added, "A beetle?"

"Ohhhhh," they said as one, nodding with wonderment as though I'd worked out a proof for trisecting an angle.

I was surprised they knew the Beatles. I asked if they knew Mr. McCartney.

"Do not," Pinky said.

"He's kinda creepy," Jennifer added. "Looks at us like we're peppermint patties."

They gave me the location of his storefront, which was just two blocks away, and I thanked them for their time and trust.

"You want a chocolate chip before you go?" Pinky asked, pointing to the tray they'd just filled.

"Thanks, but I'll pass," I said. "I'm more of a yogurt raisin kinda gal."

"Health food, huh?" Jennifer said.

"I don't know about that," I told her. "I guess I just don't like comfort foods that crunch."

"Diggin' that," Pinky said. "Your heart's breaking, you, like, don't want to be reminded of that with every bite."

"I guess," I said.

I left trailing that hollow tinkle again, thinking Mountain Jim's ice cream . . . cheesecake . . .

yogurt raisins. Soft and smooshy. Maybe the girl had hit on something.

A valuable reminder, I thought, not to equate youth with a lack of savvy.

Or the reverse, I thought with visions of Rhonda and Lolo and her Cozy Foxes in my head.

Chapter 15

I felt the small of my back tingle with a kind of disbelieving embarrassment as I reached the office of the McCartney Travel Agency. His motto, printed boldly on the window, was honestly and for real "Wings Over the World."

As it turned out, no one was likely to mistake this Paul McCartney for the other. The travel agent was an African-American man in his early thirties. He was sitting behind a glass tabletop and was on the phone when I arrived, so I had a chance to look at the photos on the desk. They showed him with a white man and a black woman—clearly Mom and Dad in front of a variety of landmarks. He kissed the mouthpiece and hung up with an "I love you too." I didn't notice a wedding band. I was guessing—

"My mother," he said with a deep Southern accent and an air of apology as he quickly yet unhurriedly finished the conversation. "She'll only call me on a landline. *Hates* drop-outs."

"Who doesn't?" I laughed.

"Exactly," he said, and offered his hand. "Paul McCartney."

"Gwen Katz."

"Of the Nashville Katzes?"

"Niece of the last owner, daughter of the co-founder," I said.

"I knew your Uncle Murray," he said. He was still holding my hand, and now clapped the other upon it warmly. "He was a card!"

"Which one?" I asked, wondering why I suddenly found myself so Borscht Belt. It must have been the silliness of the whole McCartney vibe.

"I'd say the Joker," he replied after a moment of mock thought. "He was one funny dude."

"Intentionally?"

"I honestly don't know," he admitted. "He did a *terrible* B.B. King whenever I saw him, which wasn't often—I'm more of a Cajun man myself—and I always wondered if he was being serious or jivin' me. Anyhow, welcome to Nashville. How you likin' our town?"

"Nice."

"You're from New York, right?"

"Born and raised."

He whistled. The guy was all practiced style, but it had a certain charm. "Culture shock much?" he asked.

"I've got to watch my mouth a little and be nice to people. Oh, and I had to remember how to drive a car. Other than that, it's been fine."

He laughed warmly, also practiced. "You look

like the kind of gal that nothing fazes. I'm sure you picked it all up just fine."

He was good.

"Mr. McCartney, I'm sure you've heard about what happened to our mutual friend Mr. Hopewell—"

"Poor Hoppy," he said, giving my hand a final squeeze before setting it free. "A genuine tragedy. A terrible loss for our community."

"All of that," I agreed. "Did you know him well?"

"Very," he said. "We often played pool at Swifty Felson's down the street."

"Was he any good?"

"Terrible!" McCartney laughed. "I took him for a C-note every time."

"He was a gambler?" I asked, perhaps a bit too eagerly.

A tiny, tiny shield went up. I could see it in the momentarily frozen smile, the slight, almost imperceptible droop of the eyelids. "Not really," McCartney replied. "How did you know him?"

"We're merchants in the same town," I said.

McCartney looked at me. "I'm a merchant in this town and I never met you."

"That's true," I said. "But you don't sell food."

"I see," he said. "Of course." There might have been a lingering trace of caution in his voice; I couldn't be sure. It was time to get away from the chit-chat minefield and head for the heart of the matter.

"Anyway, a couple of months ago he was talking about some trips he had taken," I said. "I've been putting in long hours at the deli and I thought it might be time to take one of them myself."

"A trip is never a bad idea for any reason," he said, raising a finger as he slipped into what was obviously one of his many handy mantras. "Where did you want to go?"

"Honestly, I just don't know."

"Well, which of the places sounded especially interesting?" The hands opened, welcoming, inviting, encouraging.

"All of them," I said. "Maybe if you run down his itinerary it will refresh my memory."

The hands did not move to the computer keyboard, but alighted flat on the desk. "Ms. Katz," he said, "I have spent enough time at Swifty's to know when I'm being hustled. I don't like it. It gets the Irish up in me."

That sounded absolutely surreal.

"Did you really come here to book a trip?" he asked.

"I did not," I confessed, seeing as I had no other option.

"Then what exactly do you want to know and why? First, tell me—are you really Gwen Katz or are you a PI?"

"I am not a private investigator. I'm definitely Gwen Katz. Gwen Katz is not someone that someone would claim to be unless they were her," I said convolutedly. "My life's not that super-cool."

"Then what interest does Gwen Katz, deli owner, have with the travels of Hoppy Hopewell, whom you've probably only known, at best, about what—six months?"

"Not even," I admitted. "Our contacts were . . . limited."

"The cops think you killed him or something?"

Now *that* was a taste of home, the first street-wise question I'd heard in half a year. "No, no, nothing like that," I assured him.

"Then—?"

I hunched forward as though I was about to share a confidence. Paul McCartney sat where he was as if he was Judge Roy Bean. "Mr. McCartney—Paul, if I may—I have a confession."

I waited for him to soften. All I got was, "I'm listening."

"I did something stupid. I gave him money."

The face cracked a smile. "Another one of you."

"Of me?"

"Gullible women," he said. "Hoppy was always putting the touch on the ladies. Invest in this, stake me to seed money in that."

"That's me," I said. "Uncle Norman always called me Gwen the Gullible." He didn't, but this was the first bite I'd had from Paul McCartney. "How did you know about that?"

"Hoppy always got a little loose-lipped after a few beers. What did you buy into?"

"European coins," I said. It was all I could think of that Europe had for sure, besides postage stamps; at least I know something about money.

"You mean, currency or—"

"No, vintage specie. Prussian pfennigs, Swiss

francs from Liechtenstein, prewar Polish zlotys. He was buying—he said—mint condition collections for resale to collectors in the United States. He was going to cut me in for half of the three-hundred-percent markup." I added, "No pun intended."

"Mark," he said. "I got it."

"I figured you would," indicating the travel posters on the wall.

The hands steepled. "What were you planning to do?" he asked. "Visit every country where he supposedly bought a collection? If I were going to scam someone, Ms. Katz, I would say I was going to Brussels and then head for Antigua. It would cost less and be much, much sunnier."

"I thought about that," I told him. "But when he went away in October, he didn't come back with a tan."

McCartney nodded. "Good get."

I felt bad appropriating Pinky's observation, but I didn't think she'd mind.

"Ms. Katz, if any of these investments ever ends up in court, I do not want to have been responsible for sharing information that the law might consider confidential."

"I appreciate that, but it's not like you're a psychiatrist—"

"Please!" A halting hand went up. "Allow me to finish."

I shut up.

"I am not, however, an unsympathetic man," he said. "I have a mother I love dearly and it would pain me deeply ever to see her feminine trust taken advantage of. So I will tell you this. If you are looking to collect any of those monies you mentioned, you would not be likely to encounter any European who has met Mr. Hopewell."

I stared at him, stupefied. Not only did he stereotype my gender, he told me that out of 27 member nations of the European Union Hoppy could have visited, one of them wasn't Liechtenstein.

I sat there looking at the Berlin Wall of travel agents, wanting to hit him with a mallet. Not that I could blame him. I'd been deposed in many, many litigations involving clients; even being peripherally involved was stressful and distracting. It was an area where you wanted to stay as clean as possible.

I rose. "Maybe I should've played pool with him instead," I said. "Thanks for your time."

"You're welcome," he said. "Let me know when you do want to book a trip. I have excellent relations with the Von Harbou Hotel Chain in Germany."

I looked at him and he looked at me. There was nothing in his expression to indicate that he was helping me, if in fact he was. Maybe my Hail Mary "pool" line had touched a soft spot.

"I appreciate that," I said. "Very much."

"You're welcome," he said, a little of the smile returning.

Chapter 16

Germany.

What could Hoppy have done in Germany, apart from that bizarre claim that he had studied chocolate cake making there.

Maybe nothing, I thought. Maybe Hoppy just went there for a vacation, like normal people do. For all I knew, maybe he was there on business, either for the chocolate shop or actually trying to make one of the investments work. Not one of the obviously ridiculous ones, but a business deal I hadn't yet found out about. The information Paul McCartney had so kindly imparted was something, but where or whether it fit was still a mystery.

I went back to the deli to work the lunch shift and do my mindless-work-while-thinking drill. That got slightly sidetracked when Grant Daniels came to lunch with Deputy Chief Whitman. I fantasized that while they had a wide selection of places they could have gone, Grant chose the deli so he could lay eyes on me.

If that were the case, he was really subtle about it. So subtle, in fact, that it never came up. Then again, it was a working lunch and when I showed them to a table—I was playing hostess for Thom who was taking phone orders—I was happy to be invited to join them if I had a minute.

I made a minute. Several of them, in fact. After taking their order, I slid into the booth beside the Belle Meade detective. I didn't want to go thigh-to-thigh with Grant.

"You two have met," Grant said by way of breaking the ice.

"Hi again." I shook Whitman's hand as he grumped out a hello.

"I want to say up front that Deputy Chief Whitman isn't entirely onboard with this, but he's agreed to let me talk to you about the investigation so far."

"Okay," I said. What else was there to say?

Grant leaned back and Whitman leaned forward. It reminded me of those tag team wrestling matches my grandfather used to watch. Maybe it was a politer version of good cop, bad cop—reluctant cop and outside-the-box cop.

"I'll be frank, Ms. Katz," Whitman said. "We aren't exactly drawing aces here. People seem reluctant to talk about Mr. Hopewell and we can't compel them."

"Why reluctant?" I asked.

"People seem conflicted," he said. "Most of them seem to want to remember the deceased as they knew him in life. Jovial, a welcome guest, always bringing chocolates—"

"Santa Claus," I said. "For widows and spinsters."

"That's a good way to put it," Whitman conceded. "They would welcome finding out who killed him, but they don't seem to want to know why."

"It's a strange world you inhabit," I told him.

"The Old South and its adherents do have a different way of looking at things. Not a bad way, in many respects. There's privilege but there's also honor."

"Do you think the women are closing ranks to protect one of their own?"

"I don't have an answer for you," Whitman said.

"The other part of this is Solomon Granger," Grant said.

"I'm not a fan," I said.

"You may actually know him better than we do," Whitman said. "I understand you had dealings—?"

I explained how he tried to help Royce steal my restaurant to build their entertainment complex. I said that while he never did anything illegal, as far as I knew, he was not above withholding information.

"He's the kind of guy who won't turn on the light so he can tell you that white is black," I concluded.

Whitman actually broke a little smile at that. "Nicely put."

"And just in case, if you're suggesting that I use my exhaustive feminine charms to woo information from that human tombstone—"

"God, no," Grant said. He said it very quickly. Possessively? I probably read that into it, but he definitely didn't like the idea.

"We would never suggest that," Whitman said, which was only halfway there; he didn't say I shouldn't think of it on my own. "We mention him because he's stonewalling the investigation."

"How?"

"We went to Judge Footwise."

I interrupted. "What is he, a Hobbit?"

"She's a Cherokee," Whitman said. "Askini Footwise."

"Oh. Oops."

"Tennessee does not presently have any tribes in residence," Grant said.

"Her family has been here since before Davy Crockett, but that's beside the point. Before she was appointed to the bench, Mr. Granger did pro bono work for a Choctaw family that was living on public lands in the western part of the state. He managed to get old squatter laws declared unconstitutional, had the area redefined according to a map from 1819, and the family was allowed to stay."

"So he's not all bad?"

Grant's mouth twisted. "The family sold the land to a developer and Granger got his thirty-percent contingency fee from that five-million-dollar deal."

"Nothing illegal," Whitman said. "Just—well, like you described it. He didn't reveal the end game."

"So how does the judge fit in, besides feeling

like Granger got some of her kin a good deal from a once-corrupt system?"

"That's it entirely," Whitman said. "She won't break the law for Granger, of course. But she does let all the breaks fall pretty much on his side."

That concept was not only foreign to me, it was orbiting somewhere beyond Pluto. The great oral tradition of my family has it that all fifty-odd souls in my great-grandparents' *shtetl* in Russia went out of their way to wheel-and-deal fellow citizens out of land, money, goods, betrothed, natural resources, and even secure hiding places when the Cossacks were near.

"We went before Judge Footwise to get a search warrant that was limited to Mr. Hopewell's home and telephone records," Whitman said. "Mr. Granger petitioned the court to disallow the warrant on the grounds that Mr. Hopewell committed no crime and therefore his privacy was inviolable."

"What?"

Grant shook his head. "I know. The problem is, under a narrow view of state civil liberties law, he's right."

"You're saying that unless Hoppy was somehow complicit in his own murder, his estate can't be investigated?"

"Only through interview and public scrutiny," Whitman said.

"That's ridiculous."

"It gets better," Grant said. "The things that were private when he was alive, like whatever he may have told a shrink or a priest—those things we're allowed to look into."

"Unfortunately for us, he never went to church and we don't know if he ever saw a psychiatrist," Whitman said. "That's one reason we need his records."

Grant added, "The catch-22 for us is that the records are now owned by the estate, and in order for us to petition Judge Footwise to force the state to cooperate, we need to implicate them in some way."

Their food arrived and while they stared at their turkey clubs, I was busy digesting what they'd told me.

"You've managed to talk to a number of the individuals who are persons of interest to us," Whitman said, touching the napkin to a spot of Russian dressing in the corner of his mouth. "Detective Daniels tells me you've got scraps of information that might help us."

"Scraps is right," I said unhappily and I ran down what I knew.

Hoppy needed money.

Hoppy's sister did not.

Hoppy had an active libido, which he may or may not have used to charm said funds from well-to-do older women.

Hoppy was a fraud chocolatier.

That said, Hoppy taught the Cozy Foxes how to melt chocolate, possibly to expedite access described above. (It occurred to me then that if this were a James Bond novel, that would be a cover for a gold smuggling operation. Except that it wasn't, so it probably *was* just chocolate.)

Hoppy liked having access to the corridors of power.

Hoppy was a bad pool player.

Hoppy went to Germany within the last few months.

Gary Gold is a weirdo.

Lizzie Renoir, the housekeeper, is another weirdo.

Rhonda is a bitch, though I knew that.

Pinky and Jennifer didn't much care for Mr. H.

There's a back entrance to the second floor of Lolo's mansion.

When I finished, both men just stared at me.

"Pretty much a lovely mess, right?" I said.

Grant finished chewing a mouthful. "Did not know about Germany," he said.

"Found that out this morning," I said proudly.

"Or the poor quality of his pool game," Whitman said. "Did he bet?"

Ha. I was ahead of him there. "Only in the hundreds," I said. "Gambling was not the source of his debt."

"Nice," Whitman remarked. It was the first time he had said anything that had a hint of open admiration.

"Here's the thing," Grant told me. "We've reinterviewed all the members of the Cozy Foxes except one. Helen Russell."

"She's the one I'm missing too."

We compared notes on the others. I had a few things the detectives didn't, and they had a few things I was missing, like the fact that Poodle was adopted and Lolo owned the property where the chocolate shop was located. That didn't appear to add much to the investigation, though one could never tell.

"Ms. Russell does not want to talk to us," Whitman said. "She says she's too upset to revisit—and these are her words—'the life he lived.'"

"Who was he, Saint Francis of Assisi?" I asked.

Whitman looked at me with surprise. "You know about St. Francis?"

I called his surprise and raised him. "I did go to school, Detective. I have an education."

"Sorry, I just thought that—separation of church and state."

"Religious studies, NYU," I said.

Grant cut in. "Does Ms. Russell come here often?" he asked.

"Only with the Cozy Foxes, as far as I know."

"Is there any reason you can think of to go to her?" Whitman asked, recovering from his embarrassment.

"That depends. Where can she be found?"

"She's got an old mansion on Acklen Avenue," Whitman said.

That was just a short hop down I-65. "What do you want me to do, break in?"

"Ideally," Grant said.

Whitman and I both looked at him.

"Kidding," he said. "She bikes, Gwen. Every afternoon following her in-house tai chi class."

"We were thinking you might run into her?" Whitman said.

I hadn't ridden a bike since I was ten. I didn't even own one.

"I took the liberty of bringing my own," Grant said.

"You ride it here?"

"It's in the trunk," he replied.

"Boy's or girl's?"

"Boy's," he said. "Is that a problem?"

"Not at all. I like riding boys."

Grant buried his mouth in rye. Whitman looked like he wasn't sure he heard right, but didn't want to go there in any case. He pressed on.

"I know you've got an establishment to run, but we need—we'd *like*—to know if there's some other reason she doesn't want to be interviewed."

"Like, 'Did you punch a hole in Hoppy Hopewell's melon?'"

"We don't expect she'll own up to that, but she may tell you *something*," Whitman said earnestly.

I wasn't being serious, but poor Deputy Chief W. W. Whitman, Jr. didn't realize that. He was probably a good egg, just not cracked enough to get me.

"You'll owe me a thigh massage," I said to Grant.

He stiffened and Whitman turned red.

"At the Chin Spa," I added with genius timing. Both men relaxed.

"There's a Chin Spa here?" Whitman asked as

he returned to his sandwich. "And I thought Belle Meade was chi-chi."

"Mary Chin," I said. "From Taiwan."

Grant grinned and Whitman shut up. I left them my car keys and excused myself to help with what was left of the lunch rush. Fifteen minutes later, Grant gave me my keys, gave me his thanks, and told me the bike was in my trunk.

"I'll talk to you later," he said.

I didn't tell him the door would be unlocked and I'd be soaking in a tub of epsom salt with a glass of red wine. Therein lay the road to disappointment. I said simply, "Yeah."

And once again I lost myself—distracted myself?—thinking about the strange world of Hoppy Hopewell and company. . . .

Chapter 17

The antebellum South.

The period before the Civil War, a time of gentility and breeding, of gentlemen and ladies, of plantations and—

Slavery. That's the big ugly shadow. Like thinking of famous Austrians or Germans and sticking to just Mozart, Goethe, and Gutenberg. The shadow of human bondage hangs over the South the way Hitler hangs over parts of Europe.

It's indelible.

But locals have learned to live with the stain. They balance it with a pride in the lives they otherwise lived, with all those qualities that glow brighter in their absence. As much as my grandfather loved wrestling and watched old videotapes until they broke, my dad loved John Wayne. And his favorite John Wayne movie was *Stagecoach*. There's a scene in that film when Hatfield, the gambler-gentleman played by John Carradine, is about to put a bullet in the head of Lucy Mallory, played by Louise Platt, because they're going to be overtaken by savage Indians. I remember being horrified by that as a child.

"Daddy, is he going to *shoot* her?" I remember crying.

"Be quiet," he said.

After the movie, he explained that Hatfield wanted to spare her being captured by the savages, that murdering her was actually a kindness.

I didn't see that. I saw murdering her as killing her. Years later, I still felt that way, though I saw how it could be interpreted as an act of charity and perverse goodness.

The South is like that. There's no getting around the awfulness at the center of that prewar society. But the crepe that was hung from it was thick and gay and, if not transformative, at least an effective camouflage. When pressed, Tennesseans will point out, with pride that sounds more like an apology, that their state *was* the last to secede from the Union and join the Confederacy.

All of that aside, they did build beautiful homes. Short of a Caribbean beach house or a Central Park triplex, you might agree to marry a so-so guy just to live in one of those plantations. Helen Russell's estate was no exception.

I had stopped at home to put on sweats, then scooted down the highway and parked around the corner on Elliot. I hoisted the bike out with an appropriately aggrieved "Oy." It was a compact mountain bike, mud-splattered where my manly friend had no doubt tested that manhood against hill and stream. He had thoughtfully provided me with a helmet and full water bottle. As I adjusted the flimsy-feeling headwear, I hoped that the old saw was true, that riding a two-wheeler was something you didn't forget. I thanked God that at least the roads were flat here.

Helen was supposed to emerge in about ten minutes so I'd have to circle or fuss with the chain or do something until she appeared. I pedaled to the corner—without falling, though I wobbled a little at the start—and was delighted to find that stalling would not be necessary; a woman in spandex was just emerging from the driveway. I was less delighted with the prospect of having to catch up with her; she was a good tenth of a mile ahead of me, I guessed, calculating her distance by the only measure I knew: New York block lengths. Twenty of them made a mile and this was about two blocks.

I chugged after her, trying to think of what I'd say when I caught up. *"Fancy meeting you here"* wasn't going to cut it.

I was out of breath before I'd gone one block. I don't work out; it's not that I'm lazy, but walking in New York and being on my feet at the deli have always been all the exercise I needed to retain my svelte figure. Calf muscles I've got; "wind" is not my strong suit. I was *shvitzing* like a marathoner by the time I caught up to Helen. At which point I had to stop to take a drink. I wasn't sure she'd seen me until she swung the bicycle in a tight, skillful circle and came back. She continued to pedal around me as we spoke.

"Are you all right?" she asked.

I nodded while I drank, then managed to gasp out, "Fine, thanks." I looked at her. "Hey, fancy meeting you here!"

"Who is it?" she asked, still circling like an eagle—but without the same kind of menace Rhonda had displayed.

"Gwen Katz, of Murray's Deli."

"I see now, yes," she said. "You're a little far from home."

"Tell me about it," I said, hoping she meant the deli and not New York. Jews are paranoid that way. "This is how I'm trying to learn about Nashville," I said, "by biking through its communities."

"If you'd care to join me, I'd be happy to show you around," she said—not breathing hard, the little hummingbird.

I accepted eagerly and got my legs working again. She kindly let me dictate the pace.

I caught glimpses of her as she talked about the neighborhood and its history and the homes. I listened as well as I could with blood slamming in my ears, the helmet partly covering them, and the wind scooping up the rest. When we were all finished with our multiple circumnavigations of the block—and when I was about all-in—she invited me to the house for a lemonade.

Success was never harder won.

A groundskeeper took the bicycles, a butler

opened what used to be the servants' entrance, and we made our way to a sunroom the size of my house.

"It's got lovely light, don't you think?" she asked.

"I think you could fit the sun *in* here," I said.

She laughed coquettishly, she did. A practiced Southern laugh, charming and designed to put a guest at ease. We sat in cobra-backed wicker chairs just a few feet apart. Only hers was facing the afternoon sun.

"That's why I take my ride in the afternoon," she said as a servant brought our drinks. "So the rays of the sun can help me recuperate."

We had just been *out* in the sun, which wrung us dry as toast. She seemed to read my mind.

"It's a question of sweating out the bad humors and then replenishing them with healthful vitamins."

She pronounced the word with a short "i" like the British. I was still on the fence as to whether the woman was genuinely cultured or totally affected. She certainly looked like I had always imagined a Southern Belle to look—except for the form-fitting cycling outfit, which revealed zero body fat. She was petite and fluttery, the delicate bones of her fingers always in motion, her eyes lively and alert, her mouth always upturned and painted very red.

"I certainly did the former today," I said, forcing myself not to chuck the unsweetened lemonade.

"Then you have not been taking these tours for very long?"

"I just started," I said. "Went around Confederate

Hill yesterday, Belle Meade the day before, two other communities before that."

I was watching those big eyes carefully. At the mention of Belle Meade they twitched just a little, like a gnat had buzzed them.

"We've been behaving like criminals," she said unexpectedly. There was a trance-like quality to her voice. She seemed to be looking at something distant, or past.

"Who has?" I asked innocently.

"All of us who were there," she said. "The guests. We've been keeping away from one another, afraid that our eyes would betray us."

"Betray what?"

"Our secret," she said in a rough whisper.

I set the drink on the glass-topped rattan table that stood between us. I edged the chair around it, closer to her.

"What's going on, Ms. Russell?"

"We planned this murder," she said.

"We?"

"The Cozy Foxes," she said. "We—"

And then she erupted in laughter. I nearly fell back. The laugh was big and real, not like her previous titters.

"You haven't ridden a bicycle in years!" she said. "And I haven't acted in years—oh, at least twenty of them. But I was very good, don't you think?"

I was flabbergasted. If I looked half as stupid as I felt, that was too much. What was worse, I couldn't tell if she were truly amused or if she was Disney villainess amused, laughing at me before she turned me into some kind of creature or locked me in the castle dungeon.

"Don't try to put one over on a mystery aficionado," she said, still sputtering out chuckles. "Never mind the mud, when it hasn't rained here in weeks. Your sweat clothes smell of nothing, not even fabric softener from a recent washing, and your *waitress* shoes have white soles that show nothing of the black rubber from the pedals. Also, poor dear, poor silly dear, I told you nothing but lies about the community and you didn't challenge a single one. Did you really think that Margaret Mitchell lived on this street?"

I dimly recalled her saying something about *Gone With the Wind,* but I honestly couldn't remember what.

"Child, she was from Atlanta!"

"I couldn't hear very well," I said lamely.

"No, I'm sure not," she said. "You were too busy trying to figure out how to work that mountain bike—which you borrowed from whom?"

"A friend," I said timidly.

She took a long draught of lemonade. I waited for the ax to fall. I was too ashamed to move.

"What is your interest in Hoppy Hopewell?" she asked. "Were you a lover? Did he promise you money?"

"No, nothing like that—"

"Then you *are* interested in him!" she charged.

Ow. I fell for that old gambit.

"Yes. I *am* interested in him," I said.

"Then I repeat: why?"

I wrestled with that one a moment before replying. "Because I'm trying to impress the man I'm dating."

That took her by surprise. "And that is?"

"Detective Grant Daniels."

"Indeed! Son of the Civil War historian who named one son each after the competing generals."

I didn't pretend to know that. For all I knew, she was lying again. "That's the man," I answered.

"Did he tell you about me?"

"No."

"Let me rephrase that. *What* did he tell you about me?"

Christ, she was good. "That you declined to talk to the police again."

"Is that all?"

"That's all."

She finished the glass and poured more from the pitcher—refilling mine as well, which gave me some hope.

"I used to live in this estate with my brother, the eminent philanthropist John Warden Russell," she said. "Have you heard of him?"

I said I had not.

"He endowed hospitals throughout the state, including our own beloved institutions here in Nashville. When Mr. Hopewell came to town, he befriended my brother—who had a fondness for chocolate and young ladies, both of which were to be found at that shop—and persuaded him to put said Mr. Hopewell on the board of his philanthropy. That was five years ago. He then proceeded to use his position there to try and insinuate himself in the good graces of every highborn family in this town.

"Mind you, John had nothing against a man trying to get ahead—but it became personally embarrassing, as you can, I hope, understand. After several months, John asked him to resign. It created a local scandal, since Mr. Hopewell did not go quietly into that good night. It was insidious—he spread rumors about John and his liaisons. Before very long, my brother became the brunt of jokes at the club, at parties. The matter was not just tawdry, Ms. Katz. It was vicious. There is, as you may know, a rivalry between many of the families in this great state. It was easy and convenient for them to use this to tear him down.

"John took his life within a year," she said, the life gone from her eyes, the mouth curving down, the voice dropping. She suddenly seemed much older than her fifty-odd years. "I have always blamed Mr. Hopewell for that." She regarded me with a hint of fire. "I was not sorry to see him gone."

It took me a moment to collect my thoughts. I did not for a moment think that this one had been a performance.

"Do you think Mr. Hopewell intended for things to go that far?" I asked.

"What he hoped is of no interest to me," she said

"Of course. May I ask, Ms. Russell—if you hated him so much, why did you go to the party?"

"To change my activities to suit his comings and goings would have given him power over me," she said. "That I would never allow. No, it was better to remind him of his low place merely by being where he was. True to form, he was a coward until the end. I did not acknowledge him, but I did not ignore him. He hid from me, first in the kitchen and then upstairs."

I perked. "Did you see him go upstairs?"

"I last saw him slinking in the direction of the staircase," she said. "Until he crashed loudly and deservedly through the ceiling, I had no idea nor interest where he had gone."

"I'm sorry," I said after a long silence. I had sat in silence, watching her; I'd wanted to make sure she had nothing left to say.

"For which part?" she asked.

"All of it," I said.

She looked at me, remembered her lemonade, and took a sip. "Don't apologize for your entrapment. Despite its rather amateur conception and execution, I respect ingenuity. And I imagine you did not have long to plan it."

"I did not," I said.

"No, you did not take time to rinse the odor of grease from your hair. I infer from all this that Detective Daniels came to you during lunch?"

I nodded.

"If I weren't so fiercely grateful to whoever did this, I would offer to solve this case for him. As it is, I hope they get away. Though I trust you will have the good manners not to tell him that," she added. "He might think the killer was me."

She took my silence as assent.

I felt all kinds of inept, not to mention embarrassed, as I walked the bicycle back to the car. I would have to tell Grant the story, of course, at least the bulk of it to make sure it was true. It probably was. There were too many elements that could be easily checked.

The one uncertainty that lingered, though, was whether she might have done it. One of the hallmarks of any good lie—and this is true in business as it is in crime—is to keep as much of the story as real and airtight as possible. The lie is best disguised by hiding it in the truth.

Once again I was leaving an interview with a little more information and no clear idea where it belonged.

Chapter 18

.

If you've never had one of those epiphanies that makes you question everything about your present life and tries to convince you to chuck it out the window, all I can say is you're not missing anything.

I wouldn't say the experience with Helen Russell had been transformative in the way that a bad relationship or mugging can be. But it wasn't good. It reminded me how alien I was here. This woman of the Old South had not only made me feel out of place, she'd made me feel like an idiot. The smart, master's degree New Yorker led by the nose into a brick wall by a one-time belle who—I checked in the online social register as soon as I got back to the deli—had graduated with a bachelor's in art history from the Christian-identified Belmont University. Quite possibly a great school, but it wasn't NYU.

I changed into my work clothes, wanting to get out of the sweats. I shoved them hard in the small locker I kept there. I didn't want to see them again, maybe ever. I'd got my ass kicked, and I fought the urge to get on the next jet back to my home, back to the great melting pot where the Trumps and the homeless live side by side—at least as viewed two dimensionally on Google Earth.

What stopped me, ironically, was something Helen had said: how she wasn't going to let Hoppy dictate her moves. She was right. I couldn't let her dictate mine, as much as I absolutely wanted to for the rest of that long, long afternoon.

Thom noticed something was wrong, but didn't say anything until after we locked the door.

"You want to talk about it?" she asked as we counted out the day's receipts.

"I do, but I shouldn't."

"Why? Is it those cops you were talking to?"

I was surprised she had made them; then I remembered Deputy Chief Whitman had been at the party we catered. Duh. "It isn't the cops, though it should be, right? Talking to cops about a murder, wondering if you might be a suspect. . . ."

"Are you?"

"Huh? No!" I said. "That's another thing that's wrong!"

"That they don't think you killed Hoppy? Girl, you lost me."

I took a breath, stopped trying to count singles. "What I'm saying is that all the normal reflexes were not working, until now. After all these months I'm finally having the right reaction to being here."

"And that is?"

"Flight, as in 'fight or flight,'" I told her. "I've got panic going on, big-time."

"New boss lady, that's just your mental house settling, telling you you're here."

"It's more than that," I said.

"Hon, you have to relax—"

"I can't."

"You got to."

"No, don't you see? It's like everything has caught up to me at once and is piling on: moving from New York, the divorce, changing my career, playing detective instead of playing *Bubble Ball* on my cell in the subway. What the hell am I doing? What the hell was I *thinking*?" I looked at her looking at me. I couldn't tell if she was concerned, confused, or hurt; probably all three. "It isn't you," I added. "I like you. A lot."

"And I like you," she said. "Which is why I'm holdin' back hittin' you in the ear with this roll of nickels."

I looked at her left hand. It was a fist and it was pumping lightly at her side. "What would that accomplish?" I asked.

"If it didn't clear *your* head, it would make me feel better," she said. "I hate when the Devil gets the upper hand."

"The Devil? Thom, I just described why I'm suddenly scared out of my head and you introduce a unified theory that has nothing to do with it."

"I don't know what you just said, but the Devil is at the root of every bad thing that happens, every bad decision we make. He plays us like that app you described. He helps move us through events with a hand that's familiar but ain't no friend. He takes us to a place where we are weakest and therefore he is his strongest."

I didn't want to insult her faith or her intelligence. "I didn't need anyone's help getting here," I said. "I did it all by myself."

"You only think so," she insisted. "Do you mind if I ask you something? Something personal?"

"Go ahead."

"When did you first know your marriage was over? I don't mean when you first suspected and not when your divorce papers finally got signed. When did you know there was no turning back?"

I thought about that for a moment. The bottom of my throat began to constrict. "When I was looking in the mirror and saw a girl that wasn't in her twenties any longer and realized that that face, with its couple of wrinkles from age and lots of lines from stress, was going back on the market."

"In other words, you were alone."

"Oh, yeah. Very."

"That, honey, is when the Devil gets you."

I took a moment to let that Medieval notion seep through all the filters of my Jewish upbringing. We have no devil, at least not like that. Our demons are guilt, mostly self—

"Crap."

"What?" Thom's fist was no longer moving. She was all big, inquiring eyes.

"You aren't wrong."

"Talk to me."

"It isn't the upheaval that's killing me. It isn't what other people do to me. It's what I do to myself, what we all do to ourselves. Guilt. Remorse. Fear. Insecurity."

"You got it. God tests us," Thom said. "He sends famine and floods and even crabby customers. It's the Devil who tries to make sure our worst instincts come up to deal with those challenges. I heard something in church about a year ago, something I truly believe: that the door to hell is locked from the inside. I see you doing that right now. Turning the key, backing away, wanting to run."

"Maybe," I said, my doubts rising again. "On the other hand, who says that going forward is the right thing? Sometimes it makes sense to fold and get out of the game."

"Uh-huh. So why not just hang yourself and get out of all the games?"

"That's a little extreme," I said. "I just listed a buttload of things that have piled on. I'm feeling the weight. It's natural to want to get out from under it and go back to where the world makes some sense. How do you know I wasn't running when I came here? Some people would say that was weakness, leaving New York."

"Do you think it was?"

"No. I think of it as a fresh start."

"So would leaving here now be a fresh start?"

"No." I had to think about that.

"No is right. It would be running. You know the difference."

She was right again. Tragically, that made me

want to run from her. I saw her and suddenly didn't know her. Who was this woman? What was this *place*? There was nothing comforting or safe. From me, the zones of unfamiliarity radiated outward: the street without a single Chasid, the block without a street vendor selling Rolex knockoffs from a battered briefcase, the city district without a porn shop, the metropolitan region without anyone I knew a year before. Each one of those was an impenetrable circle—

Like the circles of hell.

I shuddered and exhaled loudly. It must have been loud enough that Thom thought I was going to pass out or something, because she slapped the nickels in the till and grabbed my arms with both hands.

"What is it?" she asked.

"I'm not sure," I said.

"He left you," she guessed.

"What?"

"The Devil. You chased him away."

I hadn't; I was guessing that what just happened was a mini-anxiety-attack. Tension had been building since I got down here, like pressure under a crystal plate, piling on until I'd just vented it out.

It came again. I breathed in, then out—more than I'd taken in—and the deli got a little tipsy. My legs trembled and refused to hold me upright; Thom was on it and hugged me to her, supporting me, keeping me from falling.

"Holy crap!" I said.

"It's okay," she cooed.

"Holy *crap*!" I repeated, and I started to cry.

"Let it all out. Thomasina's got you."

This time, I took her advice. With effort, I raised my arms and laid them on her shoulders and heaved out tears I had been holding back for months. I felt her cheek against my tears, her heart against my breast, her hands patting me.

I felt like I hadn't for about thirty years: like a kid frightened by a big, strange world with only two people I could rely on. In a way, though, it was just what I needed—to go all the way back and start over again on a different path.

"You're gonna get through all this," Thom said.

I was too busy crying and sniffling to answer.

"I know 'cause I been there," she went on. "It gets a bad rap from all you Northern type folk, but it really does work."

"Wh-what does?" I choked.

"What just started for you," she said. "Being reborn."

There was no way Thom and I had the same view of that word or what had transpired. But I couldn't dispute the fact that I felt better after my cry. I didn't want to be my usual argumentative self, so as we resumed closing I admitted that I felt—"renewed" was the word I used. She didn't want to badger me then either, so she accepted that. In her mind, I'm sure, God was responsible for it all anyway.

I don't know. Maybe He was. My accountant's brain had always had problem with the logistics, like Santa Claus; it isn't possible to take care of everyone on the planet. But I wasn't a rabbi and I didn't pretend to have the answers. Only questions.

After locking up, we had an impromptu girls' night out. I wasn't a big drinker and Thom didn't believe in the stuff so we started our little adventure at Starbucks. I had always hated the fact that they were all over Manhattan, like a fungus, but I had ended up going there out of convenience, for a fix, when my Chocolate Cherry wore off; now I was glad to be in one. It was a touchstone. For a flashing instant, I could have been in the West Village or on Fifth Avenue or on the Upper East Side. That helped to settle me further, like an architectural Tums.

I used snatches of the familiar there to nail my feet to the ground. The smell. The heads bent over cell phones or underlit by laptops. The texture and design of the napkins. I felt like crying again, grateful for the reconnection, but that was pushed aside by embarrassment. I was angry at myself for having a positive response to a chain store. Then I was re-angry at myself for complicating something that didn't need to be complicated.

Get thee from me Satan.

We followed the not-bad Joe with a trip to the Mall at Green Hills, where we shopped for utensils we needed at the deli and clothes we didn't need in our lives, after which we bought a box of doughnuts and went to the nearby Limpscomb University campus. We planted ourselves on the grass. The night was warm and a couple of stars were visible and there were students moving here and there. If I squinted my puffy eyes we could have been sitting in Central Park after a free concert by the New York Philharmonic, waiting for the crowd to leave before venturing out.

"Okay," I said as I licked creme filling from my fingers. "I guess I'll stay."

"You guess?"

"I'll stay," I told her. I lightly pounded the ground like a ladylike gorilla. "I'll definitely stay."

"To prove something or because you want to?"

"Probably both," I said.

"Glad to hear it," she told me. "You gotta look at beat-downs as learning experiences, not defeats."

"I guess." That went against my heritage. My mother and both of my grandmothers and, now that I thought of it, all my aunts were in-your-face arguers. It didn't matter whether they were right or wrong; to them, every loss had to be a Pyrrhic victory for the other side.

"What say we head back?" she suggested. "The sugar rush should carry me home, after which I do need to collapse."

"Me too," I said. I was physically and emotionally tapped-out.

I packed up what was left of our baker's dozen of doughnuts and we left arm-in-arm, drawing frowns from some of the students we passed. Maybe to them we were devils. Lesbian devils. It's funny the things you can get wrong about people when you rely on first impressions.

Which, as it has a way of happening in my life,

brought me back to the matter of the murder of Hoppy Hopewell. And Helen Russell's performance this afternoon before her grander—truer?—performance. How much of that, how much of what the others said and revealed, was a lie? Or, at the very least, a withholding.

I would stay in Nashville and I would hit this thing hard and I would find out who killed that son-of-a-bitch.

I was back.

Chapter 19

The day was not yet through with me.

I got home around just before midnight to find the cats hidden. They were tucked in their kitty rooms, unwilling to come out even for eats. I brought their bowls of tuna to them so they wouldn't starve. Then I went back to the kitchen, tossed the cans in the metal recycling bin, and flashed the nine-inch kitchen knife I had casually picked up during my first trip. I picked up my cell from the counter, ready to speed-dial 911. I was two-fisted danger and ready to rock-and-roll.

There was only one reason the cats would refuse to come out for their nightly stroll: an intruder. Didn't necessarily have to be someone inside the house; the cats were known to hide when my neighbor in New York came for the mail I'd picked up or because she'd left her keys in the apartment.

I first gave the house a quick once-over before turning to the backyard. As I went to the door to check, the front bell rang. I went over, flipped on the outside light, and cracked the door slightly. The chain was latched; for New Yorkers, that was as natural an act as flipping a red-light runner the finger.

"Hi," said a man on the other side.

I had seen him once before and there was no mistaking him for anyone else. He was in his mid-to-late twenties, five-foot-five, and shaped roughly like a pear. His hair was black and long and hung from a green wool cap. He wore a shabby tweed jacket over a white T-shirt. A Nashville Predators hockey necktie was knotted loosely around his neck. His jeans were bulging; he appeared to have put on about twenty pounds since buying them. At least he didn't need a belt.

"Gary," I said.

"I hope I didn't scare you," he said; it was a statement, not an apology. "I was sitting on the back porch, waiting for you to come home—I think I scared your cats."

"How did you know I have cats to scare?"

"I heard them *rowrr* and then patter away when I got here," he said.

Possibly, I thought. Except that I had carpet all through the house. I'd been meaning to tear it up, but hadn't gotten around to it. Maybe that was part of my one-foot-out-the-door subconscious at work. More than likely, this odd little fellow had gone around peeping into all the windows.

"What can I do for you?" I asked.

"May I come in?"

I'm a sucker for good grammar, even when it comes from a bad writer. I shut the door, undid the latch, turned the knob, and sort of concealed the knife along my forearm. I stepped aside and pointed toward an armchair. It was Uncle Murray's favorite seat, I gathered, given the deep depression in the cushion and its proximity to the TV and coffee table both. Gary wiped his feet on the welcome mat and waddled over. If he was trying to look pathetic, he was succeeding. If this was really him, I felt bad. I reminded myself that he fancied himself a performer of sorts, having been prepared to play a part in his own murder mystery.

I checked him out as he walked, didn't see the bulge of a gun or knife. I relaxed a little and lay the knife on top of the DVD player. I didn't do my usual hostess thing and offer him a beverage. I wasn't sure I wanted him to stay.

He sat carefully, like a balloon settling, lowering himself with his thick hands on both armrests.

"I was wondering if you had time to consider that work you wanted me to do," he said.

"I don't know about you, but for most people, the time to inquire about such things isn't midnight."

"Yes, well, it wasn't when I first got here," he said. "I took a taxi to the deli, but it was closed, so I thumbed a ride here. I've been waiting for four hours."

I felt a twinge of bad about that, though I was more amazed that someone actually picked this man up. Then again, people were friendlier and less suspicious down here than they were up north. A lot of them were also as strange as this guy.

"Sorry," I said. "I've been busy—I haven't been able to think about it any more."

"I understand," he said. "Whatcha been doing?"

The casualness of his question made it sound threatening. It wasn't curious, it was demanding, softened only slightly by the gentle Southern accent. Maybe that was just his way. I sat on the sofa. *Okay,* I thought. *Gary wants to talk. He was there the night of the murder. Let's see how this plays out.*

"I was the caterer at Lolo Baker's party the other night," I said. "Mr. Hopewell's death traumatized me. I've been working through it, I guess, by talking to people."

"I see."

There was a big, fat period at the end of that sentence.

"You were there, weren't you? Didn't *you* find it disturbing?"

"Disturbing," he said as though weighing the word. "I don't think things really *disturb* writers."

"Oh? What do things do?"

"They nourish us."

"Do they?"

"Like the offerings at a salad bar," he said. "Surely that doesn't come as a surprise."

The idea that this portly fellow had ever laid eyes on a salad bar was a surprise. The rest was a natural fit with his pompous, inflated self-regard. "I guess that makes sense," I said charitably.

"What did you think of my scenario?" he asked.

I wasn't sure what he'd do if I told him the truth. "Fascinating," I said. "Very layered. Surprising." I wasn't trying to make with the double entendres, secretly insulting him. I tried to say things that he'd buy, that would open him up.

"Surprising in what way?" he asked with the trace of a self-satisfied smile. Once again, he wasn't really curious. He was encouraging me to stroke his ego.

"The twist at the end," I said. "Harley Marley faking his death."

"That was fun, wasn't it?" he said proudly.

"Very. I'm sorry I didn't get to see it acted out."

"Could I have a glass of water?" he asked. "Sitting outside dehydrated me."

I smiled as sweetly as I could and went to the bathroom. I had a glass there. I was afraid that if I went to the kitchen he would follow me and settle in at the table, where I had put the remnants of our doughnut dinner. I filled the glass and turned, then started: he was standing in the hallway, right outside the door. So much for hearing cat paws on the carpet.

"Why did you come here?" he asked.

"You mean to Nashville or the bathroom? Because I've been wondering one of those—"

"The latter." Again, the demanding tone of voice. I didn't like it. I wondered if it would be possible to defend myself with a hairbrush.

"I had something in my teeth," I told him.

His eyes dropped to the wastebasket. "There's a

piece of dental floss . . . but it's under a tissue. I didn't hear you blow your nose."

"I used the rubber end of my toothbrush," I said. If he touched it to see if it was wet, I was going to knee him in the groin and run.

"Ah-ha," he said without any sense of discovery. He was just taking the information in.

His gaze shifted. "My water?"

"Your water." I handed him the glass. He left with it.

We returned to the living room. He stood in the center of the room as though he was on stage, feet planted squarely, shoulders back as far as his belly and waistband would permit. He drank half the glass.

I stood close to the TV . . . and the DVD player where I'd placed the knife.

"I am naturally interrogative," he said unapologetically, "probably bordering on the inquisitional. I don't know. I can't see myself. I can only be what I am."

That was some of the most convoluted hash he'd yet put forth. As a writer, he was a terrific meat grinder.

"It's a constant fueling process," I said.

"Yes!" There was a glimmer of appreciation in his voice. "That is why I lock myself away for stretches. I'm like a boa constrictor. I need time to process things without additional overstimulation."

"Perfectly understandable." It was my turn, now. "So, Gary—applying those qualities to what happened the other night, I have a question. What do *you* think? I assume you've given the aborted mystery night a fair amount of thought."

"I have," he said. "I think it was someone who wasn't there."

"Come again?"

"By that I mean figuratively—someone who wasn't invited to the party."

"Why do you think that—and who would that be?"

"Those are two questions," he said as he drained the glass. I don't think he was being snarky. He was simply anal. He was correcting my misstatement that I had "a" question. "To answer the first one second, I think it would be a woman."

"Why?"

"Because the party was mostly women," he said. "That would help to effectively disguise one. If someone happened to see her they would say, 'Oh, was she invited?'"

He acted that last part out with a little mince. I said, "I would have guessed that too—"

"Not a *guess,*" he said. "Reasoning."

"Right. I would have reasoned it to be a woman but for an entirely different reason."

He gave me a look that asked, *"And that reason is?"*

"It would have been easier for a woman to get close enough to a man to push a drill bit up his nostril."

"By pretense of affection?"

"Something like that," I said.

"That is a stereotype," he replied.

"Of what? Human interaction?"

"No, of one of those horridly trashy romance novels that I refuse *ever* to write. 'Oh darling, I must have you now! Take me here, on this floor that appears to have been cut away, so that if we fall through it we will be together for eternity.'" He shook his head. "Ridiculous!"

That was snarky. "Has anyone ever asked you to write one of those?"

Gary waved his pudgy hand dismissively. "They know better. I never would."

I didn't ask what publishers he was in contact with. Fish in a barrel.

Gary was still standing there in the center of the room, but as we spoke he had become more agitated. Either the juices were flowing, or he was just becoming more relaxed around me, or else there was a full moon and I hadn't noticed.

"To answer the first question second," he went on, "I think it was someone who wasn't invited because then the police would not know to talk to her."

"But then if it were proven they were there, by evidence—say, a fingerprint or an eyewitness—wouldn't it make them *more* of a suspect?"

"A calculated risk," he said. "There is a perception that criminals are a cowardly and superstitious lot—"

"Where did you hear that?"

"*Detective Comics* number twenty-seven," he said. "The first Batman story."

"Not canonical," I suggested.

"Of course not! The author was only seventeen years of age, so how could he know better? Yet that flawed notion has pervaded criminological circles."

Of comic book fans, I thought.

"My point is, some are clever and most are risk-takers," he said. "I believe, based on the fact that there are apparently no viable suspects, that our felon was both."

"How do you know there are no suspects?" I asked.

"There's an invention you may have heard of. The Internet?"

"Sounds familiar. Just not getting from here to there—"

"The blogosphere," he said as though it should have been self-evident. "People post things on sites such as *Nashville Nuggets* and *The Confederate Hill Yell.* No one knows anyone who has been arrested."

I didn't mention that the news also would have been on the news. Moreover, none of that meant there weren't any *suspects,* just that no one had been formally charged. I didn't explain any of that because there was no winning with this guy. And as it happened, he was accidentally right. Grant and Deputy Chief Whitman were as stymied as I was.

Gary came over. He handed me the glass like I was his mother. He clasped his hands behind his back and regarded my right cheek. He had trouble making eye contact, I'd noticed.

"What about you?" he asked.

"Regarding—?"

"The case. What do you think?"

That nearly knocked me on my doughnut-enlarged backside. The sensei, apparently, of all things wanted to know what Grasshopper thought. For a moment, I thought I saw the boy in the man.

"I think you're right, that whoever killed Hoppy Hopewell brought to bear a little bit of ingenuity and more than a little bit of planning," I said. "Who and why is something that will probably take some time to uncover."

"Why do you say that?"

"Well, apart from the lack of witnesses and evidence, there's a lawyer who does not want the police prying into the private life of the deceased. Did you ever have any dealings with Solomon Granger?"

He shook his head once, vehemently, and said, "I do not believe in attorneys."

Neither of those facts surprised me. "Until the detectives can get into Hoppy's apartment, assuming it hasn't already been cleaned out, and access to his phone records, things are probably going to proceed very slowly."

He pushed out his lower lip as he took that in. "Perhaps I shall write a play about this," he said.

"A lovely idea," I said.

"I believe I will call it *Death of a Chocolate Salesman*."

I had to stop myself from asking if he knew my Uncle Murray. They had the same creative bent, and I meant that as being something unsound. I didn't want to talk to Gary any more about anything. I was tired and I just wanted this visit to end.

"Thank you for your hospitality," Gary said as though he'd read my mind. "I will show myself out." He strode to the door, his hands still clasped behind him like Captain Bligh.

He opened the door, shut it behind him, and was gone. I shuddered. Gary Gold might not have been the hands-down oddest of the people I'd met, but he was definitely the creepiest. He was preposterous enough, unseen in his own element; in mine, he was like one of those science fiction androids with a software tic.

While the meeting was not especially enlightening, it *was* exhausting. The entire day had been a real challenge. But with Thom's help and some of my own boot-strapping, I'd survived it. Maybe my manager was correct about one thing. Maybe this was some kind of overdue settling, turning a corner of some kind.

The kitchen clock told me the new day was a half-hour old. I was too tired to think and, as they always are, the problem would still be here tomorrow . . . and would probably seem less onerous in the daylight.

I pulled off my work clothes, fell into bed, and was asleep before Gary's heavy tread had disappeared down the street.

Chapter 20

I woke up feeling proactive.

Now that there was a go-get-'em vibe in my body, I appreciated just how absent it had been. Not just since the murder, but since I got here. I had gone through motions, did what I had to do, but without a real fire-in-the-belly desire.

I had that now. It wasn't because I'd had a long sleep—it was six a.m. when the alarm dragged me from a dreamless, narcotic-like super-slumber. And it wasn't a late-blooming sugar high from the doughnuts. Rather, it was because that old New York steam had crept back in the engine. I didn't have to be like them, do the old, Jewish fit-in thing. I could be me.

On the way to the deli, I left a message for Dag Stoltenberg, the semi-retired attorney who had handled my family's affairs down here. An expert in international copyright, the Norwegian expatriate liked—or took pity on, or both—my Uncle

Murray and had tried to help him place his songs overseas.

We hadn't spoken in about two months. Dag had gone to Tromsø for a visit and had only just returned. He was an early riser—he ran an hour every morning on his treadmill while listening to Grieg—and, in any case, was still on Norwegian time.

"God morgen!" he said in Norwegian. The heavy accent thinned when he switched to English. "How is my favorite and most beautiful client?"

"Not so bad," I said truthfully.

We exchanged a few pleasantries about his trip, after which I asked if he had heard about Hoppy Hopewell.

"Ja, I just caught up with dat news," he said.

"I was there," I said. "Catering."

"Herregud!" he said, which, from experience, I knew meant "My God!" The only other Norwegian I knew was *ja* and *ikke*—yes and no—and *forbanne,* which meant damn.

I told him that I was thinking of putting in an offer on Hoppy's shop, but that Solomon Granger was throwing up all kinds of roadblocks.

"Vell, you understand he can do dat," Dag told me.

"You mean, solicit offers without providing access to any kind of financials?"

"Sure," he said. "I would not recommend someone to buy under those conditions, but it is not a publicly traded company. If Mr. Granger is the executor, he can set whatever terms he wishes."

"Why would he, though? Why wouldn't he even say who owns the place?"

"Maybe de individual vas a girlfriend *or* boyfriend. Maybe dey do not want to be asked about Mr. Hopewell. Maybe dey do not vant to reveal *vere* dey are."

Oy. I hated the idea that Solly had any rights at all.

"Dere *is* one ting ve can do," he said. "If he has been named executor, dere must be a power-of-attorney document filed vit de county. Dat can only be sealed if de assignee is not actually an attorney."

"I don't follow. Are you saying that if I gave power of attorney to Thom, that could be sealed—"

"*Ja*. Because it does not run a reasonable risk of having been coerced."

Light bulb *on*. "Gotcha. An attorney could theoretically fake someone's signature, or have them sign a bunch of documents which they wouldn't read, and thus conduct business for them without anyone else being able to check."

"Without *anyone* being able to check, not even de person who signed!" Dag said. "So de state enacted dis law to protect people like you from people like me."

That not only made sense, but it explained why Grant or Whitman had not thought to check on it. They stopped at the will being sealed, at the probate being sealed, at the corporate papers being sealed, but didn't bother to look into the single document that gave Solly the authority to seal them.

"I vill make a call over dere as soon as dey open at ten," he said. "I vill get dat information for you."

I thanked him. I wasn't sure what that might tell us, but it was like chicken soup: it couldn't hurt.

The morning rush came and went. Thom was a little more solicitous than usual, keeping an eye on me as I did the hostessing, helped in back, worked the counter, and even bussed. I wanted to keep busy.

It was a quarter past eleven when Dag called back. I went to the office, sat with coffee from my private office stash and a fresh-baked bialy, which I ate plain. I found I was eating healthier, or at least less greasy, since keyboards and keypads became so important. They didn't work as well with a coating of shmear or butter.

"Find anything?" I asked the attorney.

"*Ja, ja,*" he said. "Power-of-attorney was granted by a woman."

That got my attention. I almost tipped over my coffee. "Who?"

"Anne Miller," he said. "I took de liberty of looking for her—but dere's a problem."

"Let me guess," I said. "You get a million hits for the movie star."

"*Ja,*" he said.

"I don't think it was her."

"She was dead when dis paper was signed," Dag said. "If it is important, ve can hire someone to go through de listings—"

"Thanks, no," I said. "It will be easier just to ask people if they ever heard of her."

"You going to tell me vhy dis is so important?"

"Because I'm not accounting, I'm not using that forensic part of my brain. It's what I was trained for, what I've been doing almost my entire professional life."

"Dat's a good reason," he said. "Dat's a very good reason!"

"I'm glad to hear you say that, Dag, because I appear to have absolutely no control over myself."

He laughed. "Just be grateful you have got a manager."

"The best," I agreed and hung up. I ate the bialy and stared at the wallpaper on my computer monitor, a photo of my parents and me at my high school graduation. It was the last picture I had of the trifecta: the three of us smiling, really smiling. It was one of the last times I could remember the universe seeming to have some kind of order. *Maybe that's why I do what I do, why I do this,* I thought. To try and restore some of that discipline to my world.

"What about fun too?" I asked, taking a last look at the smile.

I picked up the phone and called Solly Granger.

"Mr. Granger is busy at the moment," the receptionist told me. "Would you care to leave a message?"

"Yes," I said. "Tell him I want to talk about Anne Miller."

"Hold, please."

That got her attention. Probably his too.

"Ms. Katz, Mr. Granger will be right with you."

Sweet, I thought. I might finally be onto something.

Solly picked up and said without a hello or preamble, "You found the loophole. Congratulations."

"I wasn't looking for a 'loophole,' only more information about—"

"Don't tell me you were looking into the chocolate shop," he said. "That was old the day you ran it up the flagpole. You've been looking into the death of my client Mr. Hopewell."

"All right. What if I am?"

"Leave Ms. Miller out of it."

"Why?"

"Because she's suffered enough," he said. And hung up.

Okay. That wasn't the fun I expected it to be. It was actually a little scary: I had never heard Solly so angry.

I was about to call Grant when there was a knock at the door. It was followed by Thom poking her head in.

"You've got a visitor," she said.

"Who?"

"Poodle Baldwin."

"Send her in," I said, thinking that if she was here by herself it was to discuss something in private.

The young woman entered and Thom shut the door behind her. "Sit," I said, indicating Thom's chair. As soon as I said it, I realized she could have

taken that as a dig. She didn't. I guessed she had
built up a tough skin in school to all the dog jokes.

The photo on the computer caught her eye.
She leaned over, not quite allowing enough clear-
ance for those hair balls. One of them brushed my
face and I had to do a cobra-head move to escape.

"Your parents?"

"Yup. High school graduation."

"That's so nice," she said.

Poodle didn't sit. She stood fussing with the
end of the orange pashmina scarf thrown casually
around her neck.

"Something wrong?" I asked.

"I heard my mom talking to Helen Russell on
the phone this morning," she said. "I guess you
went to see her yesterday. Helen, I mean."

"I did," I told her.

"You talked about Mr. Russell—John."

"A little," I admitted. I had an awful sense about
where this was going.

"I . . . I . . ."

"What is it, Poodle? You want something to
drink? You sure you don't want to sit?"

She nodded and went to the chair. She worked
it out from behind the other desk, and sat beside
me. "I don't know you very well, but you come
from New York and you probably have a different
view of things than people down here."

"You could say that."

"Did Helen tell you about John and Mr. Hopewell and the kind of things they did together?"

"A little," I said cautiously. I didn't think she was

setting me up the way Helen Russell had. She really seemed to be struggling with something. But I didn't push. I wanted to make sure that she got to where she was going of her own accord. The words, the truth, had to come because she wanted them to.

She sobbed once—it was more like a hacking cough—then caught herself and regained her composure.

"I didn't know," she said.

"Know what?"

"That they both liked . . . *other* girls." She said the last two words quickly, suddenly, as though she'd sucked venom from a wound and was spitting it out.

"Talk to me," she said. "It's okay."

She sucked down a breath and let it out. "Hoppy . . . was my first."

"How old were you?"

"Sixteen," she said. "And two days."

I didn't know what the age of consent was in Tennessee, but that still seemed pretty young. Not cut-your-junk-off young, just pathetic.

"Poodle, do you mind sharing something? Can you try?"

She nodded again.

"How did they do it?"

It took a second before she blurted out, "Gift cards."

"You mean, to stores?"

"Yes. It started as a birthday gift, they said. Mom

had put a sweet sixteen notice in the paper. They gave me hundreds of dollars worth of cards."

What a pair of pricks. But that couldn't account for Hoppy's money problems. Besides, Russell was well heeled.

"Go on," I said. "Where did they meet you?"

"The first time it was at the pool parlor. I went there to celebrate with my friends. After that we'd meet at the mall late in the afternoon. They'd give me my choice of stores and off I'd go."

"They had a selection of cards?"

"Big-time," Poodle said. "Hoppy would fan it out like he was a magician or something. They'd wait for me in the food court and when I was done they'd drive me back."

"Where?"

"To Hoppy's home," she said. "He'd pull into the garage, close the door, and we'd go to the den. They'd ask to see whatever clothes or shoes or jewelry I'd bought."

"You modeled for them."

"In a way. It was kind of a joke. He had this long carpet that was like a runway and I'd walk it like they do on those VH1 shows. Then they'd toast me, we'd all drink a toast. That was how it started."

"Wine?"

Another nod. Underage drinking; even that didn't help us. With both men dead, even if Poodle gave a statement to Grant, there wouldn't be a reason to search Hoppy's home.

"How often did this happen?"

"Five times," she said. "About once a week for a month."

"And then?"

Her miserable expression was my answer.

"You never knew that there were other girls?" I asked.

She shook her head once.

"Did you love Hoppy?" I asked. "Did you think you did?"

"Yeah, I thought I did," she said with the hint of a smile. "He was fun to be with. John not so much, but Hoppy was funny and attentive."

"Were you with John too?"

"I was with him *mostly*," she said. "Hoppy said he liked to see me enjoying myself." The little smile turned crooked. "I pretended to. For Hoppy."

I felt sick now, not because I was a prude, not because the whole May-December thing held any kind of special freak status in my world, and not even because the girls had effectively been turned into hookers. That was scummy, but sort of par for the course where men of means were concerned. I saw a lot of that in cooked books back in New York, though the price of seduction was a little higher—private jets and Mediterranean yachts. What sickened me was that these two bastards had come up with a plan to make this happen again and again. It wasn't like a CEO with a crush on his secretary or a film producer seducing a day player with the promise of a line or two. It was a program to take advantage of Poodle and other young girls and then not care whether they messed them up.

I took her hand. "Y'know, I've done some pretty nutty things in my life," I said. "We learn from our mistakes."

I sounded like a mother, from the platitude to the compassionate tone of voice. I have no nephews or nieces or young employees; that was a first for me. And then I thought something no mother should ever think.

"Poodle, I need to ask you something."

"Sure."

"Were you—*angry* at Hoppy?"

She didn't answer at first. Her hand suddenly felt clammy. She looked at me with tears in her eyes. "I was when he said he couldn't see me any more, when he said it was time for me to date young men my own age."

I didn't for an instant think he was looking out for her. He was a man and he probably got bored once the novelty of Poodle had worn thin. I didn't ask if she was angry at Hoppy now. The way she'd said it through her teeth answered that.

"What about your mother?" I asked. "Did she know about—"

"No!" Poodle cried. "At least, I don't think so! I was so careful. I told her the gifts were from a med student at Vanderbilt who I was supposedly dating. It wasn't that I was ashamed of what I was doing, not at first, but I knew she wouldn't approve. That's why I'm here. I've been thinking about that since the night Hoppy was . . . since the night he died. Mother doesn't like the way I cat around with men. We've had some terrible fights about it. I know she was there, at the party, but I wanted to tell you that I don't think she knew. And even if she did, I don't think . . . I can't believe . . . she wouldn't *do* something like this!"

Poodle was full-out hysterical now. I pulled her to me and held her tight. Thom opened the door a crack, making sure I was okay, then quietly withdrew.

The emotional storm passed in two or three minutes. I gave Poodle some paper towels—I didn't have tissues but I was always spilling coffee on my desk—and she patted her cheeks and eyes.

"I was so stupid," she said.

"You were trusting, not stupid. We've all been there." I know I was. The big love of my life, or so I thought, was a lug of a jock of an asshole—stop me if you've heard *this* one before—who was three years ahead of me in high school and who happened to have the same dentist, Dr. Murray Stone. And while this gentleman-who-shall-remain-nameless wouldn't be seen dead with a wallflowery type like me around his football buddies, he was only too happy to chat me up while waiting for his time in the chair to get that megawatt smile buffed. We went on a date, I fell for his shoulders and stubble, and when I left his apartment the next morning I never heard from him again—except for one time about a year later when he was horny and drunk. I left the message on my answering machine as a reminder not to *not* bang guys like him, but not to be surprised when they disappeared.

Poodle and I sat in silence while she collected herself.

"In a way, I have to thank Hoppy for introducing me to sex," she said. "Otherwise, I would have missed out on a lot."

She was obviously feeling very comfortable, very quickly, with Ms. With-It New York. I tried to act as cool as she thought I was. Inside, I was hoping that she'd stop there.

"I just wish I had known about the others," she said, the teeth clenching again. "That's what really bites."

Poodle left after securing another promise from me never to tell her mother about Hoppy or John. I promised, though I didn't tell her that it wouldn't surprise me if Mollie already knew. One thing I'd discovered down here is that the society rich talk, especially about each other. A lot. And not kindly.

I was back on duty in time for the lunch rush. Breakfast seemed like it belonged to another day.

In about an hour, lunch would seem that way too.

Chapter 21

I had been intending to call Grant all day, but work and then Poodle and then more work got in the way. So I was glad when he showed up shortly after two.

I was wiping a table. The cloth smelled of everything on the menu. He didn't seem to notice, and my gladness evaporated when, approaching me, his expression stayed fixed in cop-neutral.

"Can you get away?" he asked.

"Sure," I said. He was clearly not inviting me for an arm-in-arm stroll through Centennial Park. "What's going on?"

"Lizzie Renoir didn't show up for work today," he said. "C'mon. I'll tell you as we go."

I held the rag toward Luke, who was about to start his afternoon strum-from-a-stool concert. He set his guitar aside and hurried over as I rushed out, waving to a puzzled Thom. We got in Grant's unmarked Dodge Charger and he screeched from the curb.

"Lolo called Deputy Chief Whitman when Lizzie didn't show up," Grant said. "She lives in that old mansion near the cul-de-sac on South 6th, which is way out of his jurisdiction. He called us and we sent a cruiser over. We found her on the kitchen floor with her head bashed in, one of those blocky, steel hammers beside her—"

"A tenderizer," I said.

"Right. She was unconscious but still alive. Best guess is that she'd been there for two, three hours. They've got her at VU Medical Center. Lolo's got a research wing named after her."

That was a lot to take in. I backed up. "If Lizzie lives in a mansion, why—"

"Sorry. You're so comfortable I forget you're new here."

Comfortable? Jeez. That's one not designed to make you smile when you roll it over in your memory. I backed up over that speed bump and replayed the words he said after:

"It's not a mansion now, it's apartments," he said. "The fourteen bedrooms were converted about three years ago, when Lizzie moved here."

"From?"

"Montreal."

"I've been meaning to ask why she doesn't live with Lolo."

"I didn't have time to read her interview. The cop who talked to her said she wanted to have her independence. I can't blame her. Would you want to live with Lolo?"

Probably not. In fact, I wasn't sure I wanted to live with anyone ever again. Especially not someone who called me "comfortable."

"Clues?" I asked.

"So far, nada. I've been trying to think of a motive. That's why I hijacked you."

Would the compliments never cease? *What the hell,* thought the proactive me. We had a matter-at-hand and I was going to focus on that.

I said I'd have to ponder that one. Then I told him about Gary Gold's visit and what Dag had discovered.

"Anne Miller?" Grant said. "Wasn't she a movie star?"

"A dancer," I said. "But it's not her."

"Any ideas?"

"None," I said.

Then, after getting him to swear to keep it confidential, I told him about Poodle.

"I had heard that John Russell had exclusive tastes," Grant said.

I tensed a little when he said that. Some things just don't deserve to be euphemized. Taking advantage of defenseless teenage girls was one of those. "Happily," I said, "that piece of shit is gone and Hoppy won't be pimping for any more like him."

My tone drew a surprised look from Grant. He was savvy enough not to say anything else on the matter. We drove the rest of the way in silence. Not that I was taking in the scenery. I was thinking about Lizzie and the fact that she wasn't at the party. What reason would anyone have to take her out, unless she had found something in the house afterwards.

And then did what with it? Tried to blackmail someone? That didn't seem to fit. Even if it did, if the killer came after her, she or he probably took the thing with them.

I paid absolutely no attention to the rest of the fifteen-minute drive. I missed the house because I was still inside my head—alternately thinking about the attack and how I'd like to never see Grant again—and I didn't emerge until we were inside the kitchen.

I wasn't prepared for the crime scene. Yet the sight of blood smeared across the white tile wasn't the most disturbing thing. It looked like a broken bottle of ketchup. It really did. The watery kind we don't use at Murray's. What upset me was the way everything in the place had been overturned.

The apartment consisted of a kitchen—a kitchenette really—a bedroom, a bathroom, and a very small den. Officers and plainclothes personnel, fourteen of them altogether, were moving with silent purpose through the residence. Grant's arrival was acknowledged, when it was at all, with nods.

Police tape had been strung from cabinets to appliances to mark off the spot where Lizzie's body had been found. We stepped gingerly around it and went to the den. Grant walked over to a sergeant who was waiting for a photographer to finish taking pictures.

"Sergeant O'Rourke," Grant said.

"Detective," the other replied. The burly sergeant gave me a who-the-hell-are-you look but didn't say anything.

Grant asked, "Who was first on-scene?"

"Officer Bolton," he said.

Grant looked around, saw the man in the bedroom. "I heard there was a hammer? A tenderizer," he added.

"Bagged and on its way to the lab," he said. "But first pass was clean."

"Thanks," Grant said, and we went over.

The young officer was moving clothes aside with a pen. They had been spilled from a drawer which lay on a rug.

"Officer," Grant said.

The young man stood. "Sir."

"Anything?"

I have to admit, I wasn't used to this shorthand. It didn't strike me as familiar necessarily, but respectful. They were guests in someone's home and were behaving as such.

"Whoever did this was thorough and quiet," he said. "The drawers are intact, they weren't thrown aside."

"Neighbors might have heard," Grant said. "Any of them see or hear *anything*?"

"Melody is taking statements in the rental office," he said. I gathered that was his partner. "It's just inside the front door."

"Yeah, saw it when we came in."

"I helped get everyone down there," Bolton went on. "Mix of college kids and the elderly.

Everyone seemed shocked as heck—most of them were probably asleep and, like I said, whoever did this was pretty quiet."

"The door was jimmied," Grant said.

"That was me," he said. "It was intact when I got here. Locked but not bolted. The windows were also locked."

"She let them in," Grant said.

"That'd be my guess."

"Video anywhere?"

"We're running plates that were picked up by the cameras at the stadium," he said. "That's the closest."

That would be Shelby Avenue, where Rhonda and I had our confab. It was a main drag, not likely to tell them anything.

Grant took me back to the den, where we found a quiet corner. "I don't think she was trying to extort anyone, do you?"

"Not likely," I agreed. "Where does Rhonda live?"

"Why?"

I told him about our encounter up the road.

"Lockeland Springs," he told me. "Big place on the golf course east of here. Even if she turns up on surveillance, it won't mean squat."

"Fine. That aside, I think it's fair to say that Lizzie stumbled on a piece of evidence that some-one was afraid would implicate them. This wasn't planned."

"No," Grant agreed. "The tenderizer was an impulse."

It annoyed me how he used that word now, like it had always been part of his vocabulary, like he had known what the hell to call it before I told him. "Comfortable" made bigger waves than I expected.

"She may not have known the item was important and was just being nice," Grant said. "Maybe they came to pick it up. Maybe that's when Lizzie realized it wasn't as innocent as she thought."

"Or else the attacker was afraid she knew more than she let on," I suggested. "I only met her a few times, but Lizzie had a kind of reserve that someone might have interpreted as secretive."

"And that could've cost her," Grant said.

More than he knew. As we stood there looking at the place, waiting for a eureka moment, he got a call from the hospital.

Lizzie had died.

Chapter 22

People talk about emotional roller coasters, but that doesn't really describe anything. A roller coaster is made of a little anxiety and anticipation, a bunch of nervous laughter, and the rest of it's pretty level.

What we should really be talking about are emotional boxing matches. You mostly take a lot of blows and maybe land a few yourself, and unless you're really lucky, the entire experience is mostly painful, occasionally exhilarating, but primarily just draining.

That's how I felt when Grant dropped me back at the deli. We hadn't spoken for most of the ride. I was pretty much over his stupid man-vision view of our relationship. Despite what I'd told Poodle about being worldly-wise and guarded, I had let *his* shoulders in, among other things, without the proper safeguards being in place. That was my fault, and now I was paying the price of feeling emotionally abandoned. Let the buyer beware.

I was not, however, over the death of Lizzie Renoir. I felt it would be appropriate to pay Lolo a courtesy call. Grant was going to go straight to the hospital to talk to her—she had arrived shortly after Lizzie did; I would wait until after we closed. I wanted to work. I also wanted to avoid the press that were beginning to arrive as we were driving off. They were sure to be at the hospital and at Lolo's for at least an hour or two. I didn't want any further identification with the fallout from Lolo's party. About the only thing Grant had said on the way back was that at least he and Deputy Chief Whitman would be able to play "This Cop, That Cop," which he explained as an advantage of having a case spread across two jurisdictions. Each lead detective could tell the press that the other was in charge of releasing information, with the result of being able to bat them back and forth and say nothing for hours. There was nothing worse for an investigation, Grant said, than being pressured from above when they were taking heat from the press.

One of my projects since arriving had been to add some healthier choices to the menu. People didn't come to Murray's to lower their cholesterol or chow down on roughage, but some of the people who came with those other people might want dishes that had greens and soy instead of egg or meat or dairy. I charted the sales of those menu specials and, when there was something that seemed to spike, I made it a permanent fixture. I was reviewing those figures now, standing behind the counter. I didn't feel like closing myself in the office—not after spending an hour in Lizzie's place, which had been claustrophobic with cops and tape and just plain bad karma.

As part of my newly confident self, I made the first move and, toward the end of the day, told my manager that everything was fine with me. I didn't open up with anyone, but she had been there for me the day before and I wanted to keep that door ajar. There were things I wanted to know about her life, and one day soon I hoped she'd share them. Whatever badness had visited me the previous afternoon, good came out of it.

It was six-thirty when I pulled up to Lolo's house. There were other cars in the driveway, one of them an inexpensive model; probably a temporary housekeeper, I guessed. Lolo didn't look like the kind of woman who ran her own dishwasher.

I'd brought a quart of potato salad from the deli. I didn't know if gentiles brought food the way Jews did making a shiva call. If not, it didn't matter. It was one of the sides we'd made for her.

The door was ajar; I later learned this was the way Society acknowledged the loss of a domestic— sort of like riding boots reversed in the stirrups to symbolize the loss of a warrior. It had a certain patronizing charm. The first thing I noticed upon entering was that the roof had been seamlessly repaired and the hall floor waxed and polished.

Hoppy had been plastered over and scrubbed away. *Good riddance,* thought I.

I could see seven other people besides Lolo. I didn't know any of them, but a few seemed to know me from the deli. I pretended to recognize them.

Lolo seemed genuinely upset, which was hardly surprising. Two murders in one week, a party guest and an employee; tragic and, from a purely functional perspective, it could have a real chilling effect on her social life. And that's what Lolo was mostly about, directing the A-list of Nashville society from its peak . . . not from a base camp. Right now, she had to feel like she was in Everest's Death Zone.

She was seated in a big armchair in her huge living room, which was lit by a chandelier the size and brilliance of the *Close Encounters* mothership. She was dressed in black and drinking red wine. This was also a salute to Lizzie, who—she explained while her new helper got me a glass, which I had initially declined, then accepted when the reason was forthcoming—kept the wine cellar stocked with the best of the Canadian vineyards.

"I was told by dear Lizzie that the Canadians are the top vinifiers of imported grapes," she said.

I wasn't sure that was a great distinction, but maybe it was.

"I'm going to miss her," Lolo went on as a gentleman scootched along the adjoining sofa so I could sit beside Lolo. "She was a steadfast companion."

Like Tonto, I thought, but for a Lone Ranger who couldn't ride, shoot, rope or do anything much except display his silver bullets.

I let my eyes take a turn around the room, then asked with sudden cagey inspiration, "Has Anne Miller been here?"

Lolo's blank expression wasn't an act. "Who, dear?"

"A-a friend," I stuttered. No one else seemed to react to the name, except for the man to my left who asked if it was the movie star.

"No Ms. Miller has been here," Lolo said. Unless—"

Lolo tinkled her dinner bell, which sat on the chair table to her right. A black woman came in from the kitchen. "Ma'am?"

"Are you Anne Miller?"

"I'm Sabrina Brown, ma'am," she said.

"Thank you," Lolo said. She looked at the container in my lap. "Would you like her to take that?"

"No," I said. "I was taking it home."

Lolo dismissed the servant and returned the bell to its place. I don't know what disgusted me more, her making the point that my friend must be a servant or that she didn't know the servant's name. I was about to get up to go when Lolo raised a finger as if to forestall any thought of departure or extraneous conversation.

"I heard from Officer Clampett that you were at Lizzie's apartment," Lolo said.

All the whispered, respectful conversation

going on around us winked out, like the passing of demure little clouds. Every eye shifted in my direction.

"I *was* there," I said. "I didn't see him there."

"He heard it from Deputy Chief Whitman. Why were you there, dear?"

This time, "dear" sounded accusatory, like "You little busybody" or "Yankee." Maybe it was just my imagination. Or maybe Lolo was genuinely ticked off. She had been nice enough when we were planning the menu for her party, she was pleasant when she and her Cozy Foxes slummed it at the deli, but now I was in her club and bound by her rules.

"Detective Daniels had some questions for me," I said as I was trying to formulate a reason.

"How thrilling for you," Lolo said. "May I inquire, were those questions about my party?"

There was definitely some ice in her voice now. Society stuck together, even when one of their own banged young girls or took his own life. Could she also count on the discretion of the gentry?

"Noooo," I said, dropping my voice about an octave as if that would dispel any such notion. "The officers—well, this is rather tawdry."

"My ears have heard much."

I edged closer. "You know how she was killed."

"Certainly."

"Detective Daniels wanted to know if I could tell them anything about the tenderizer before they moved it. The pulverizing capacity per square inch—you know, could it have done the damage or was it a plant."

The leader of the Cozy Foxes considered my testimony. "Very clever," she said.

I didn't know whether she meant me or Grant. "Wasn't it?" I said generally.

The conversation resumed around us as people drifted away. Obviously, nosiness had a shelf life in high society. But thinking of the Cozy Foxes again gave me a sudden inspiration. "There is one thing that occurred to me while I was there, in poor Lizzie's kitchen."

"What was that?"

I leaned forward to make sure the others would not hear. "Detective Daniels seemed a little stymied at the crime scene. Wouldn't it be interesting, thought I, if the Cozy Foxes had a go at it?"

"At what, the bloody scene of the crime?"

"No, no. Not in person, but—at the deli, say. What if I could convince the detective to let me have the file and we all review it. Would that fall under the charter of what your literary club can do?"

It was as though I'd attached alligator clips to her big toes and turned on the juice. She literally trembled with excitation.

"Could you manage such a thing?"

"I believe I could."

"We would meet . . . after hours?"

"No one else there."

She sipped the wine, her mind no longer on

who had purchased it—if it ever was. "I love that idea, Gwen Katz. I love it to the marrow."

"Then why don't we plan it for tomorrow?"

"I will phone the others at once and tell them to be there," she said.

I didn't doubt that they would be.

Her manner was considerably more respectful now that I'd shown some kind of fealty, and she was still giddy with delight as I rose to go. She extended her hand knuckles-up for me to clasp rather than shake.

"Tell me something, though," I said. "I hear that a lot of the women at your party didn't especially like Hoppy Hopewell."

"That is true," she admitted.

"Then why did you invite him?"

She smiled sweetly. "Simply to see whether my party was more important than their hate."

Chapter 23

Grant happened to call while I was driving home. He wanted to warn me that the grapevine had heard I was at Lizzie's house and we should have a story prepared.

"Too late," I said.

I told him where I'd been and what I'd said. He was impressed.

"So now they know I a playa," I said, trying to sound ghetto. It was lost on him. "Hey, it's good that you called. I need a favor."

"Of course."

"I want to borrow your Lizzie Renoir file."

"Sure. You want security code to the arms locker too?"

"I'm serious."

"No, you're crazy. I can't do that."

"Then give me an unofficial version in an official-looking folder," I said. "A redacted copy of the report, some of the less upsetting crime-scene

photographs, floor plans, and all the key facts.
Also the financials, everything you've got."

"Why those?"

"Bank statements speak to me, like tombs to an
Egyptologist."

"I assume you're going to tell me why you want
all of that?"

"I want to see what the Cozy Foxes have to say
about this."

"You want culpability findings from Lolo's
coffee klatch?"

"This killing is probably related to the first, do
you agree?"

"It seems to be."

"Fine. The Cozies have been involved with this
party from the start and they have all been to
Lolo's place countless times," I said. "They know
each other. I want to see how they relate when
they're forced to review this morning's crime.
And who knows what else might come out of their
chatter?"

"If one of them *is* involved, what makes you
think she'll show?"

"Because no one declines a Lolo Baker invita-
tion. To do so would damn near be an admission
of guilt."

I heard him sigh.

"We've got nothing to lose," I said. "Even if none
of them was involved and they decide that Lizzie
was killed by space aliens, we've at least eliminated
them from the list of possible suspects. Except,
maybe, for Helen Russell."

"Why Helen Russell?"

"Because she's a hell of an actress."

Grant agreed to put something together. He asked if I wanted to pick it up or if he should drop it off.

"However you're *comfortable*," I said, certain he had no idea why I hit that word with a snap like a fly swatter.

"I should have it in about two hours," he said. "I'll bring it by?"

I told him that would be fine. Then girded my mental loins to accept it at the door and send him on his way.

My father once told a joke that lasted a full fifty minutes.

It was Yom Kippur and there wasn't much else to do, beside talk. We couldn't watch TV. We couldn't eat. I was fourteen or fifteen and it was my mother, father, my mother's parents, and a stray aunt and uncle—a minyan at least, if women had been allowed to participate. (An aside: one reason I became a non-practicing Jew is when I discovered that a slave could be one of the ten people but not a woman. Nice, right?)

After about twenty minutes, everyone knew that there was no way even the greatest punchline ever written could satisfy the build-up. Still, there was something about it. . . .

The joke went like this:

It was during the Depression and the circus was

coming to a small Midwestern town. *(He spent about ten minutes describing the town, the weather, the population.)* Buster and his son Cuffy were excited as could be about the circus, since there wasn't a lot of excitement in their impoverished region. *(Sort of like that high holy day, but I digress.)* Buster scraped together the admission price and he took his son on opening night. *(At this point, the tent and sideshows were described for another ten minutes.)* Finally, it was time to enter the big top. Buster had secured them seats in the front row so they would have the best view of all three rings. *(At this point, seven or eight minutes must be invested describing the aerialists, the elephants, the trick riders, and of course the ringmaster.)* After a while, it was time for the clowns. The last one to emerge from the clown car was the headliner Peskio. He ran along the front row squirting water from a flower at the pretty women and throwing confetti on the children. Buster and Cuffy were literally jumping with anticipation as he reached their seats. Peskio looked squarely at Buster.

"Are you a giraffe?" he asked.

"No-ho-ho!" Buster laughed uncontrollably.

"Are you an ostrich?"

Buster was laughing so hard he couldn't answer, only shook his head.

"Then you must be *an ass!*" Peskio yelled.

Buster stared at him, stunned, as the clown guffawed and moved on. Cuffy stared up at his father in tears. The man's world collapsed. He had been insulted in front of his boy. The rest of the night was a blur to Buster, who stared blankly at Flingo the Human Cannonball, Steppy the Stilt Walker, and other amazing sights. Before leaving, Buster took a flyer from one of the hawkers. The circus was headed to California and then it was coming back. They would be here again in exactly one year. Buster resolved to be ready for them. (*Dad invested another ten minutes on what Buster did: he took a correspondence course in public speaking, read books of philosophy, trained with a heavy bag so he would be fit and intimidating, and went to free courses at the local high school to learn rudimentary Latin so he would have a better understanding of language and its meaning.*) Sure enough, twelve months later, the circus was back. Buster made sure that he and Cuffy had the same seats. They psyched themselves up with games along the midway, and gorged on cotton candy for energy. They took their seats and barely heeded the trapeze or animal acts as they waited. Finally, the odious red car appeared and from it the clowns emerged. At last, the moment arrived. Peskio unfolded himself and made the rounds of the front row. He reached Buster and Cuffy and without even a glimmer of recognition on his big painted face, he stared at Buster.

"Are you a giraffe?" he asked.

"No!" Buster said proudly.

"Are you an ostrich?"

"I am not!" Buster replied.

"Then you must be *an ass*!" Peskio yelled.

At which point Buster squared his shoulders and said to the clown, *"Screw you!"*

That was the joke.

I tell it because, as I said, while it isn't funny, it's got something. What it has is a life lesson, one that applied to me so perfectly that it causes me to wonder what else my dad knew about life that I don't, and makes me sad I won't ever get to ask him.

After a day of plotting, and then of refining my plotting about how I was going to put Grant Daniels in his place, he came to the door, I invited him in, we had some wine, and he stayed the night. All of it, until just after dawn.

It isn't that I'm weak. I've gone toe-to-toe with some of the toughest CFOs since the advent of Christianity. I tossed my husband when, after avoiding our marital bed with this excuse or that—from work to late night TV—he told me, *"I'm not having an affair, I'm just not interested in you anymore."*

What's happened, as you've seen, is that down here I'm disgraced Army lieutenant Philip Nolan, the Man Without A Country. I've been set adrift with nothing familiar but myself—and so much of me was tied up in the work I did and where I lived and who I lived with.

All gone now, except for Starbucks. I mean—Starbucks? My only lifeline? How desperate and lonely am I?

Grant, flawed and clueless as he can sometimes be, is one of the few new buds that looks like it could flower. Him, and now Thom. That's why my brain overruled my heart on this one and I'm glad it did. We had a good, good night.

There was a little awkwardness as we dressed the next day. For one thing, I hadn't even cracked the folder he brought. I'm not sure he was convinced how bad I really wanted it. I didn't tell him it really was all about that. For another, I wasn't even a little convinced that he had a relationship in mind. That was something a sleepover seemed to hint at, at least to him. I decided to take that bull by the oysters.

"This wasn't a commitment," I assured him as we checked ourselves side-by-side in the bedroom mirror before heading out. "I'm talking about what we did, staying over, the whole *megillah*."

He didn't answer at once.

"Is that what you were thinking?" I asked, ramping up the awkward factor.

"No," he said. "I was thinking, 'What's a *migeel-luh?*'"

We laughed for different reasons. I told him that, technically, it was a big story . . . but in this case, I meant it as everything that had transpired from the time he walked in the door until now.

"Nice," he said. "It sounds like one of those Japanese monsters. Like Mogera or Mothra."

I had to admit that now he had me at a disadvantage. We chuckled our way out of that fix and out the door. I imagined the neighbors to be watching, though it was probably too early for any of them. I didn't care—New Yorkers are used to that—and I hoped it didn't bother him. It didn't seem to.

He saw me to my car and gave me a peck on the lips. "I liked it," he said. "A lot. I'm glad I stayed."

"So am I."

"Would it be insensitive to bring up work?"

"Not at all. That's why you came."

"It wasn't, but it was a good excuse. Are you really serious about doing what you said?"

"Serious as death."

"I'll let you know what the morning brings," he said. "I've got someone checking on your Anne Miller lead. Could be helpful."

Another peck and he was gone.

The sun was just rising across the street. It seemed unusually bright this morning, but I knew that was delusional. And that was okay. Sometimes it's good to be a little sunstruck.

Chapter 24

"Somebody's walkin' on sunshine," Thom observed as I set up the slicer.

"That would be me," I said.

"Do I wanna know why? You medicated?"

"Hell—*heck* no," I said. "This all natural."

"Your man," she said.

"Not the pronoun I'd use but, yeah. We had a good night."

"Stop there!" Thom said, disappearing into the walk-in to stock the tins of shredded lettuce, dressing, and other tools of Newt's trade.

The morning blew by, the rush was a breeze, and I was planning to give Lolo a shout when Grant called. I took the call in my office.

"We found Anne Miller," he said. I had gone into the back room expecting a somewhat different, possibly more romantic, opening line, like *"I've been missing you."* I got mad at myself, not him. *You had a great night. Don't let big, dumb expectations taint it.*

"And?" I asked.

"Thirty-two years old and a fugitive from German justice. She's a member of the Red Army Faction."

My disappointment was gone with the wind. The day had taken a sharp right into terra incognita.

"How do you know?"

"We have lawyers too," he said, sounding a little wounded. "We got the power-of-attorney agreement and put the document up on IPABB—the International Police Assistance Bulletin Board. Police computers around the world check it constantly, searching for a match to new, hot 'red notice' postings."

That was fun to know.

"Anne Miller's signature came up on file with both the *Bundespolizei*—the German Feds—and Interpol. It was an old sample, from high school, but it's definitely hers."

"Germany, eh? That would explain Hoppy's trip. Question is, what was she to him."

"An old friend, that's for sure."

"Oh?"

"BPOL surveillance caught them together in Berlin seventeen years ago," he said.

Seventeen years, I thought. *She would have been fifteen. The goddamn pig. I wondered if John Russell was with him, just so I could hate him more too.*

"Hold on," I said with sudden alarm. "Are you saying that Hoppy was a terrorist or that he was killed by one?"

"No," Grant said. "I don't think he knew about

her affiliation and the RAF had no reason to go after him."

"How do you know?"

"She wasn't in the group in 1993. She was just a kid who was interested in becoming a florist, according to her high school records. Her older brother Karl was a member. He hated his grandfather, who was a Nazi, and went the other way. Karl is the one who recruited her."

"Charming."

"But Hoppy obviously cared about Anne. I don't know how many times they were together, but she obviously made a big impression for him to leave her the shop," Grant said.

"Meanwhile, good luck getting a passport."

"Which is another reason Hoppy may not have had any idea about her affiliation," Grant said.

"Solly did," I said.

"Yeah, now." Grant said. "He probably didn't find out until he had to execute the will. Probably had contact information from Hoppy."

"Fast turnaround," I said. "Hoppy dies, he has the power-of-attorney next day?"

"Germany's eight hours ahead," Grant pointed out. "She gets a PDF, signs it, sends it back, it's filed electronically. The whole thing could take under an hour."

"Well, at least her terrorist past could explain why Solly warned me off," I said. "Christ, do you think he was actually looking out for me?"

"Probably not," Grant said. "He's just a dick

covering his own ass. Not that you aren't worth looking out for."

Oooh, that was nice. My good mood came galloping back.

"I'm thinking our attorney friend took Hoppy at his word whenever the will was drawn up, that she was an old friend. Now that he was going to be her de facto counsel, he did a quick due diligence."

"How did he get through all the movie star Anne Miller clutter? Special lawyer filter?"

"In a way," Grant said. "All he had to do was type in her name and 'criminal record.' That's what we did."

"Tricks of the trade," I said, annoyed that I hadn't thought of that. "So he was afraid of being linked to violent, left-wing urban guerrillas," I said. "Then why did Solly contact her at all?"

"He had no choice. The probate process ensures that all the terms of the will are carried out to the letter. If Solly screws up, he can be disbarred and jailed."

I reveled in that prospect for just a few seconds. "So where are we now? Where do the German police stand on all this?"

"Right—I've only told you part of that story. The BPOL lost her in 2002."

"How'd they manage that?"

"She went to ground. Got a fake ID, a new name—not legal, mind you, because that would have shown up on official records. They picked up her brother in 2001 and would have loved to find Anne. But she buried herself well. I'm guessing—

and this is just my gut talking—that she had lost interest even before Kurt was pinched. She chose to go inactive because she never really believed in the cause. A lot of radicals do that, especially when the heat is on. And with Hoppy as a potential sugar daddy she might have renewed her dream of being a florist or becoming the perfect *hausfrau*."

"Question: why, then, did she use her real name on the power-of-attorney?"

"Solly's activities would have had no legal authority otherwise," Grant said. "Hoppy probably told her what he did, whenever he wrote that will, and she would have known what she'd need to do. She just never expected a document from Nashville to end up in the hands of the BPOL. And even if it did, there's no address other than Solly's—"

"Of course!" I gasped. I had been chewing on something he'd said a minute before.

"What?"

"A new identity. New papers. A new passport."

"What are you talking about?"

"The money!" I said. "Hoppy needing it, cheating people to get it. That time period—it's about when he started rolling the older women."

"Shit. Good one. I think I love you."

"Don't joke," I warned.

"I wasn't. You know I have a sucky sense of humor."

That was true, but I didn't want to lose my groove by sprouting wings and flying off into relationship fairy land.

"If he knew she went underground, he would have had to know about her past," Grant said. "That would have left him open to arrest and extradition. Did Hoppy have that kind of courage, even for love?"

"I don't know," I said. "Maybe he didn't know about *that* past."

"You lost me."

"She was underage when they met. They had an affair, a relationship, something that was more than a fling. You know what I would have told my lover under those circumstances?"

"Do I want to know?" Grant said.

Whoa! Grant was hittin' that stuff hard today. I told myself it didn't mean anything. He was just turned on by the Nick-and-Nora-ing. "I would have said, 'Herr Hoppy, mein papa found out about us and wants to kill you and put me in a convent. I have to get away from him.'"

"But she was in her mid-twenties when she changed her name. Why would she have waited nine or ten years to run away?"

"I don't know," I admitted. That *was* a problem with my whole scenario. Regroup, brain: what do you know for sure? Hoppy met and fell in love with an underage girl when he was in Germany, at a time when he thought he still had a fortune. He came home to start the chocolate shop to stabilize his own finances. At some point, he reconnected with Anne Miller. Maybe that wasn't until 2002. She expressed a desire to come to the U.S. but had a problem. Her thinking: if I can get to the U.S., it'll be easier to stay lost from the BPOL. Maybe she loved Hoppy, maybe she didn't. He tries to help her with money—

"And connections," I said.

"What did you say?"

"There's something else that fits," I told Grant. "Hoppy sucking up to local politicians. Maybe he was trying to convince them to get their counterparts in Congress to pull strings for him. Or set up face time for him."

"Possible," he said thoughtfully. "Damned possible. Constituent meetings are a matter of public record. I'll check."

The data flood was a lot more to process than anything we'd come across so far, as was the idea that Hoppy might actually have cared about one of his little chicks. It softened my regard for him just a little, and I couldn't help but wonder why. Then it dawned on me: maybe Anne was his first. You've got a poor little rich kid, a stunted adolescent from all I could tell, falling in love with a girl who was his own mental age. He fell for Anne just like Poodle did for him. It didn't take a shrink to see that Hoppy cutting a swath through the young ladies of Nashville was his attempt to recapture that lost feeling of love and acceptance.

Unlike John Russell, who was simply a goddamn perv.

But then I realized something else:

"You know," I told Grant, "all of this might have nothing whatsoever to do with Hoppy's death."

"I was just thinking that," Grant replied. "Well,

I'm going to turn Solly over to the Feds and let them worry about him and Anne and the estate."

"Can't you just go over and bust down the door?"

"Afraid not. The FBI is the only law enforcement entity with the legal authority to execute claims against individuals by foreign police services on American soil."

"That's a mouthful of disclaimers," I said. "Do we at least have gloating privileges?"

"We'll see how that pans out. As far as we know, our obstructionist friend hasn't done anything illegal."

"No, he's just representing the interests of a member of the Baader-Meinhof Group."

"Former member."

"Not in the minds of Nashvillians."

"You've an evil bent," Grant said playfully.

"Only when it comes to rat-bastards who tried to steal my property," I said.

"Fair enough. But let's stay focused. You're right: this discovery may not tell us anything about who killed Hoppy, and it doesn't seem to help at all with Lizzie Renoir. I've gotta tell you, though— you homered this one, Gwen."

"Thanks. I'll hold off on any victory laps until we're done."

He said he would call with any other breaking developments.

I hung up, savoring the little croutons of joy in that big, big salad. I did that because Grant's attention was nice, Solly's pain was a delight, and who knew when I'd have the chance again. This was the Louisiana Purchase of information, and it was going to take a lot of time and mental energy to wade through it. Plus, I had a Cozy Foxes meeting to check up on.

Chapter 25

I called Lolo as soon as the hour was decent. For her, that was after noon.

"Everything's set," she said joyously. "The Foxes will convene at the deli at seven."

"Wonderful," I said, trying to match her gush-quotient.

"What will you be bringing to the party?" she asked.

I knew she didn't mean kosher pickles. She was telling me that in order for a plebian non-member to attend, I better have tribute for the queen.

"The Nashville Police file on Lizzie Renoir's murder," I said coldly.

"Poor Lizzie," she said. "We will find the assassin!"

I had to wonder if it was just spinsters and widows, or if every rich person in Nashville had an overwrought sense of theatrics.

Lolo asked if I would mind having sandwiches prepared, and I told her I would have Thom call to set it up. My manager would make sure she knew this was a paying gig, or they'd be eating candy bars and soda from the newsstand down the street.

I had assigned myself boiling oil duty during lunch: fries, onion rings, all things crisped in grease. It was hot and bad for the skin but it was mindless, robotic. I would go to the mini-freezer behind me, dump the pre-measured portions into the wire baskets, watch them bubble for two or three minutes depending on what they were, then pull them up when the timer went off. Then *Whap, whap, whap*— lightly bump the basket against the back of the fryer, below the fan, to knock off excess oil and then dump it in the tray to scoop, plate, and serve.

As I tried to organize the facts of the case, something my mother used to say popped into my brain: *The more you know, the more you realize you don't know.*

Too true. This case was like one of those paintings they used to show us in Art 101, like "The Murder of Crows" by Degas. The heart of the thing was defined by negative space. What we knew about the killings came from the things we could eliminate. That was progress, but it was a frustrating kind. Fortunately, whenever it threatened to drive me crazy, my brain went to the happy place of Solly's woes and the sun came out, a little.

After lunch, I told Thom about the after-hours gig and she asked if I wanted her to stick around.

"I can handle it," I said. "Let's just make sure the food is ready and the register isn't closed out."

"Will your other friend be attending?" she asked with a wink.

At first, I wasn't sure who she meant. When I did, I said, "Sugar!"

"You forgot to invite him?"

"Not him," I said, and scooted into the back. I put in a call to Rhonda Shays. She wasn't a member of the literary group but I thought it would be useful to have her there. She would keep the Foxes from becoming too cozy.

"*You* are inviting *me* to something social?" she said. Her tone was a cross between shock and be-musement.

"I am," I said. "On behalf of Lolo."

"Why doesn't she call me herself?"

"I'm afraid her outreach skills are a little brittle due to the murder of her housekeeper," I said.

I could hear Rhonda suck air through her teeth. "Oh, dear, of course. How thoughtless of me. Yes, yes, I'll be there. Anything we can do to help find the culprit must be done, must it not?"

"It must."

Excellent, I thought. Having one more crazy lady in the room would keep everyone off balance. If anyone were hiding something, there was a good chance they'd slip. If not, the agitation might help enflame their deductive skills.

Seven o'clock took forever to arrive.

After a day of chewing over the same-old

same-old, I was hungry for any fresh scraps I could find. Grant had stopped by at five. There was no peck this time, but that was fine; I knew, and he probably noticed, that Thom was watching. Also, I probably smelled like old, soggy funnel cake.

We stepped outside so I could air out. He said he had just been given a videoconference briefing by an agent from the Memphis field office of the FBI.

"Our attorney friend is doing things by the book," he told me. "Cooperating with the local Feds, giving them access to whatever information they are entitled to."

"Anne Miller's address?"

"Hasn't got that," Grant said. "As I suspected, all contact was limited to email. They're going to try and track that down. But if she was using a local cyber cafe in a big city, that may not help very much."

"Wouldn't she have had to pay with a credit card?"

"Some of them use access cards that you buy on-site. Those can be paid for with cash."

"Which is exactly what a terrorist would use. I'd've thought they would shut those kinds of anonymous Internet things down."

"BPOL says they're trying. Whatever the equivalent of the ACLU is in Germany, they're fighting it. Any intrusions on privacy and personal rights are not taken lightly by the children of their postwar, post-Soviet society."

"I prefer our balance of freedom and paranoia," I said.

Grant smirked. "You're a strange New Yorker."

"Come again?"

"I thought all you people were liberals."

"Okay, listen." I looked at him flush in his big blues. "First, when you say 'you people,' that is taken to mean Jews."

"It is?"

"It is. Trust me. It's perceived as a pejorative."

"Oh. I didn't know."

"I know you didn't," I said. "Second, not all New Yorkers are liberals. It only seems that way because they have the biggest mouths. Some of us are centrists and some are even conservatives."

"What are you?" he asked.

"That's fourth-date information," I said. "You'll just have to wait."

"Not too long, I hope."

"That's up to you," I said. I heard myself sounding unusually butch. *What's up with that?* I wondered. *Are you getting cold feet now that he's actually showing interest?*

That wasn't something I needed to consider at this time. He asked if the Cozy Foxes meeting was set, I told him it was a go, and then I gave him a little—okay, maybe a somewhat forceful— push toward his car with a fullabaloney story about having to get back to work. But it scared me. I wondered if the ghost of Phil were still hanging over me, ready to haunt any kind of man-happiness I might conceivably find.

Don't go there, I warned myself. *You're not in that relationship, you're not in the city, you're not anywhere near "that place."*

The pep talk barely got through the top layer of skull, so I went back and involved myself in the winding-down operations and started to organize my night-in with the ladies.

Chapter 26

Lolo arrived first.

Before leaving, Thom had explained—after assuring me that Lolo had agreed to pay for dinner—that, as far as anyone knew, that was a precedent established by the society queen herself when the Cozy Foxes began gathering.

"Nobody arrives on time, and the royalty is supposed to come last, right?" Thom said. "With the egos and vanity we got here, *somebody* would try to outlast Lolo . . . so she decided to show up first. That way, anyone who mattered would want to be there pretty early in order to enjoy the radiance of her company that much longer." It made the same kind of cockamamie sense as everything else pertaining to Nashville's elite.

Lolo was driven by her full-time chauffeur. Harold Jenkins lived on the grounds, in a guest house out back; he had been off the night of the murder, however, his presence at the local multiplex confirmed by several witnesses, a ticket stub, his son Gordon who attended a local trade school and went with him, and a summary of the Jason Statham film he'd gone to see. I had seen Jenkins drive her up before, but I had not yet had the pleasure of meeting him. He was—why was I not surprised?—an older African-American man. The whole setup was straight out of *Driving Miss Daisy*— which, as it happens, I had seen on Broadway with my Uncle Murray. He had come north for a visit and had gotten tickets by mail when he mistakenly thought it was a musical. He sat through it manfully if restlessly, trying to hide his disappointment that it was a drama. I loved it, though, and that made him glad. It was the last show we ever saw together, a string of tuners that began in 1988 with *Phantom of the Opera*. His sheer joy with musical theater led me to the natural assumption that he was gay, though my mother said no . . . he just liked music.

I felt a sudden twinge for the home town. I beat it back with a club. I did not want to backslide to where Helen Russell had left me.

As it happens, I still did not meet the chauffeur since he did not come in with Lolo. I offered but she declined.

"I fear the check is already made out in the correct amount," Lolo said rather snippily, I thought, as she handed it to me.

I offered to feed him for free.

She said that would demean Harold.

I got the ultra-clear impression that whatever I

offered, she'd have a reason to refuse. There was no way in hell a servant was going to dine with her.

God, I hope you killed Hoppy, I thought as she walked to her table, which was the biggest and roundest and most visible in the establishment. Next to Solly, there was no one here I wanted to see fry more.

Hildy Endicott, Mollie Baldwin, and Helen Russell arrived within two minutes of Lolo and within a minute of each other. They drove themselves. Rhonda obviously had not read the *How and Why Wonder Book of Lolo,* so she did not arrive until 7:20, by which time I had already served the sandwiches. I had also not informed Lolo she was invited until she walked through the door.

"I thought this was a members-only event," Lolo said to no one in particular, though, after glancing around, her eyes rested accusingly on me.

"My deli, my guest," I said, feeling a little persnickety myself. "I didn't think anyone would mind. She was at *your* party, after all."

"Of course we don't 'mind'!" Lolo beamed as Rhonda walked over, her handbag swinging low like an ax, her expression Amazonian, her high heels going click-clack as though she were wearing anklets of human teeth. "How *are* you, dear?"

"Carnivorous," Rhonda said. "I just took an hour spin class."

Taking her at her word, I gave her the same deluxe pastrami on rye platters I'd given everyone else. The Cozy Foxes always ate first and gossiped, and despite the murder of someone near to one of them, they did not change their routine. Rhonda ate her sandwich with mustard, actually aiming a kind of vulpine snarl at the squeeze bottle of mayonnaise I'd put on the table for Hildy. Rhonda finished eating at the same time as the others.

"Before we begin, I move that we offer membership to our guest Rhonda Shays," Lolo said.

The others rubber-stamped the motion by rapping the knuckles of their right hand on the table. I have no idea how that evolved; probably from some Perry Mason *Case of the Rapping Right Knuckles* story.

"Thanks," Rhonda said. "Do you have to have actually read a mystery to be a member?"

There was a snapshot of distress on the faces of the other women.

"Or does Nancy Drew count?" Rhonda asked quickly.

"She does," Lolo said, exhaling lightly. "Very much so."

I had been watching this drama from behind the counter, where I ate my own egg salad platter. While the other Cozies welcomed their new member—who, surprise-surprise, was loving the attention—I walked over with the folder and handed it to Lolo. She seemed surprised.

"Will Deputy Chief Whitman or the other one be joining us?" she inquired.

"No," I said. "This is—"

"An unofficial inquiry," Hildy offered. "A round-table without warrant."

"Exactly," I said.

Mollie and Helen nodded, obviously familiar with the phrases or the works from which she had plucked them. Rhonda looked at me as if to ask where the wine course was.

"I have a question before we begin," Hildy went on. "Do we know, or do we assume, that the murders of Hoppy Hopewell and Lizzie Renoir are related?"

"In fact, we do not know that," I said. "We assume it."

"Based solely on their close chronology and proximity?" Hildy asked.

"Sure, that and the fact that dear Lolo is common to both," Rhonda said with a smile so sweet, it caused her eyes to pinch.

"By association, we *all* have low cardinals of separation from the deceased," Mollie pointed out.

"Thank you, Mollie," Lolo said.

"I never met your housekeeper," Rhonda said.

"Can you prove that?" Hildy challenged.

"Ladies, come on—-have I met *any* of your housekeepers?"

"I'm sorry . . . did you say housekeepers or husbands?" Mollie asked.

"We have a crime to solve!" I interjected. "Bitch-slap not on the agenda."

Lolo cleared her throat at my language. I didn't mind when Thom objected; when Lolo did it, I felt like Belle Watling.

Lolo's reading glasses hung from her neck. She put them on and took a moment to study the official stamp and bar code, to feel the heft of it, then carefully slit the blue tab on the side, which I had fashioned from a Post-it to make it seem virginal and special.

I cleared away her plate and she laid the folder on its slim, accordion spine. She turned the pages carefully, from the top right corner, even though they all sat loosely. The other women looked on patiently.

"Perhaps if you passed them around?" I suggested.

"Yes, of course," Lolo said. She handed the first few pages to Hildy, who was on her left. Within a few minutes, the contents of the entire folder were circulating. There was only one photo of Lizzie's corpse in the batch, and Grant had cropped the printout in mid-chest. All the Cozies could see was a headless woman in a robe, her arms akimbo as though she were power-walking and her legs curled fetus-like into her belly. There were "tsks" and averted eyes and quick turnovers as that image made its way around. No one failed to react—save Lolo. Her demeanor throughout was one of composure. It was not serenity; her eyes were moving, her mind was obviously working, and her lips were a tight line. I couldn't tell whether it was her broad-net sense of noblesse oblige, or the sudden realization that this was the death scene of someone who had been close to her—physically, at least—for several years.

"See here," said Hildy with a hint of excitement. From the moment she walked in, she had seemed the most eager to engage this thing. "This isn't right."

"What isn't?" I asked, moving behind her.

She shuffled between two photographs then returned to the first. "This photo caption says the door was jimmied with a four-inch blade." I looked over her shoulder. It showed a close-up of the impression a knife had made in the soft wood. There was an overlaid dotted line with "4 inches" on top and an arrow showing the direction of the thrust. Hildy held up the photo so the others could see. "Why isn't the paint scratched?"

I moved around for a better look. She was correct.

"Because it's an old jimmy," Helen said.

"I knew one of those," Rhonda remarked.

"The intruder could have been very careful," Lolo said. Her role in this gathering was obviously that of Devil's Advocate.

Hildy went to the other photo she had been examining. "No, because—look. The abrasion on the outside of the strike plate is tarnished."

Bless her Foxy little eyes, she was right. The door had been jimmied once and the point of the blade had scratched the latch element. In which case the newly exposed brass should be shiny. This wasn't.

"The door has been opened and closed many, many times since it was illicitly pried," Hildy said.

"Most likely by the occupant who forgot their keys," Mollie suggested. "Otherwise, it would have been reported as a break-in and replaced. This"—she pointed to the first photograph—"was simply painted over."

"There's something else I noticed," Helen said. She pushed her plate aside—I quickly removed it and the others to another table to give her room— and spread out photographs of the living room and bedroom. "Do you see anything strange?"

The other women leaned forward as one.

"She was renting a furnished apartment?" Rhonda said, crinkling her nose at the decor.

"Cushions and pillows," Hildy said.

The others nodded.

"What about them?" I asked. I felt like I did as an undergraduate when I walked in on two of my professors debating the relative importance of micro- versus macroeconomics.

"They are undisturbed," Lolo explained. In addition to the devil, she was obviously the interpreter. "The report speculates that an intruder was looking for something. That may be. If so, it was not something Lizzie hid but something she *had*."

"Couldn't the thing have already been found so it wasn't necessary to—"

"Nonsense," Lolo interrupted me. "One finishes a room before moving to the next. The bedroom and living room were both disturbed but the fluffy contents were not."

"Look—the hem of the bedspread was not thrown up," Mollie said, laying out another photograph. "It was all shelves, drawers, and closets."

"Here's something," Rhonda said.

She was tapping a red nail on a photo of a throw rug in the bedroom. We all leaned over the image. There was a scrap of blue ribbon lying on it.

"From one of the overturned drawers?" I guessed, pointing to the chaos of clothes that began on the edge of the rug.

"Do you keep two-inch pieces of fabric with *your* panties?" Rhonda asked.

"A memento," Hildy said.

"Not from one of the drawers," Mollie said. "You keep scraps . . . in a scrapbook!"

We went back to the photos of the living room. There was a bookshelf with volumes of French poetry and books about Canadian history.

"Several books are missing," Lolo said.

"How can you tell?" I asked.

"Lizzie abhorred a vacuum," she said. "Look there." She pointed with a bony finger. "She filled an empty space on the lower shelf with a bust of Prime Minister Diefenbaker."

"I wondered who that was," Helen said.

I hadn't. And still didn't. "So books were removed," I said. "But if someone were looking for books, why wreck the rest of—"

"Not just books," Lolo said. "Photographs. Photographs too damning to leave behind."

"*And,*" Hildy said enthusiastically, "we now know the order in which the apartment was ransacked. The perpetrator went right to the bookshelf, took those volumes, then went to the bedroom to search for any other keepsakes."

"Then why tear up the kitchen?" Rhonda asked.

"The kitchen wasn't *searched,*" Lolo said. She pulled out one of the images that showed the floor with utensils strewn about. "They were thrown. In a rage."

"Honey, wouldn't someone have heard that?" Rhonda asked.

"Not necessarily," I said, making my first useful contribution. "Four college kids lived above her. Two were at their girlfriends' apartments that night and the other two were drunk. The police have their statements. And the liquor bottles."

There was a momentary lull in the discussion. Everyone was involved. No one seemed self-conscious or evasive. I had a feeling the killer was not in this room.

Lolo was still considering the kitchen photo. "Lizzie made her own Canadian bacon from pork belly. I've seen her do it in my kitchen. You see the bowls in the sink? They were probably for wet brine. The tenderizer was out to dry after she used it to add seasoning."

"Someone she knew was there," Helen said. "They talked in the kitchen. They argued. The individual grabbed the tenderizer in a sudden fury and killed her. Then he went through the house collecting evidence that may have linked him to the woman."

"Who did Lizzie know well enough to let them in at night?" I asked. "Was she dating?"

"She was a lesbian," Lolo said. The word did not come out effortlessly, the "L" hanging on like a drum roll. "Lizzie did not share, nor did I ask, that information."

Scratch that thought about the killer not being

in the room. Helen was a good actress, Poodle was man-crazy to a degree that suggested she was trying to not be like her mother, Rhonda looked like she could be game for anything, and Hildy liked tongue, which may not have meant anything at all.

"Lolo, what can you tell us about Lizzie?" I asked. "All I know is that she came from Canada."

Lolo removed her glasses. She looked out at the dark street and actually struck a pose. Once again, I had a sense that I was in the presence of Lady Macbeth—or at least someone playing the part of the queen whose every word was a little pearl.

"Lizzie came to the country in 1989," she said. "Her parents owned a liquor store and always dreamed of owning their own vineyard. It never happened. Lizzie immigrated because she got a job. I don't know what it was; she never shared that information."

"You didn't ask for references?" I said, rather incredulous.

"Young woman, I am an excellent judge of character. Should I have asked for papers from the man who wired my new television or repaired my *ceiling*?"

"You were letting someone in your home—"

"To work. If she failed to do so, or if she had proven light-fingered as one of my domestics once did—who, I might add, came festooned with documents—I should have dismissed her. As we all know, papers can be forged or extorted."

"She spoke with a French accent," Rhonda said. "That's why you hired her."

Lolo ignored her. "Do you have any other questions, or may I continue?" she asked me.

"Please," I said deferentially.

Lolo settled back into character with a shifting of her shoulders and a slight raising of her spine. "Lizzie's job ended and she heard that I was now in need of a housekeeper."

"How did she hear?" I asked.

Lolo did not answer. All eyes, save two, were on the statue she had become.

"I told her," Helen said, looking at her lap.

Four sets of eyes shifted to the speaker. There was a long silence. I broke it.

"So Lizzie went to work for you," I said. I didn't say anything more. I just wanted to get her back on track and break the embarrassment that had settled on the table like an upended wheelbarrow of sauerkraut.

"Lizzie was an excellent worker, very diligent," Lolo said. For the first time, a trace of emotion had crept into her voice. I couldn't tell whether it was for Lizzie or for the sacrifice Helen had just made. "We did not discuss her personal life but I cannot think of anyone *I* know who disliked her."

I looked around the table and there were general nods and murmurs of accord. The only exceptions were Helen, who was still looking down, and Rhonda, who was staring open-mouthed at Helen.

"What about Hoppy?" I asked.

The women all regarded me.

"What about him?" Hildy asked.

"Did he know Lizzie? Was there any connection?"

The women went silent with thought.

"I don't see how that matters," Mollie said after a time. "He obviously was not the one who went to her apartment."

"But they may have had someone in common," I said. I was desperate to ask if Poodle may have known Lizzie in any capacity, but I couldn't reveal what I knew about the young woman and Hoppy.

"Lolo, did Lizzie have any siblings?" Hildy asked.

"Not that I'm aware," the society matron replied.

"So—no nieces and nephews."

"She never mentioned any."

"Then why would she have saved a blue ribbon?"

"Holy crap yeah," I said.

Lolo was too intrigued with that to chastise me with her eyes. "I don't know," she admitted.

"Is there any way she could have had a child out of wedlock?" Helen asked, emerging from her little cocoon.

"I suppose it's possible, but what would that have to do with her murder?" Lolo asked.

"I've only known one adoptive child who sought out his birth mother to tell her how being given away left him all scarred and rejected," Rhonda said. "That was my cousin Stymie, and he only found her so he could yell at her. He didn't kill her."

"You had a cousin named Stymie?" Mollie said.

"Hey, I *said* he was adopted. He came already named."

"I don't mean to defame the dead," Hildy said, "but if we're looking for a connection, is it *possible*—and I'm just putting this out there—that Lizzie had a child with Hoppy?"

Lolo and Mollie both made faces.

"He would have to have known her in Canada," Lolo said. "How many nine- or ten-year-olds want to kill their mothers?"

"Well, there was that Jim Grand story *What's the Matter With Oedipus?*" Hildy said unhelpfully.

"That was fiction and it was the only one," Lolo said.

"Besides, she didn't—well, what interest would Lizzie have had in Hoppy?" Mollie asked, changing course in deference to Helen.

"He could have raped her," Hildy suggested.

"I would put that in the 'very remote possibility' pile," I said. "Lizzie would hardly have saved a memento of that . . . event."

Silence once again descended.

"I wonder if she wasn't a housekeeper when she first came here," Hildy said. She was just a bundle of ideas.

The group waited.

"She might have been a nanny," Hildy said. "Not like Fran Drescher, but maybe a mentally unstable one, like in that old Bette Davis movie."

The group thought. Except for myself and Rhonda, they seemed like a single organism. It was pretty impressive, though. Their brainstorming had produced some useful results.

"Lizzie could be severe, but she was not cruel. I will attest to that," Lolo said, effectively ending the debate.

"Which doesn't rule out that she may have been a nanny," I said, still chewing on that. "Nannies pose with babies and photos are apparently missing."

"They pose at Disney World too," Rhonda said. "Maybe Mickey did it."

The remark was ignored. Rhonda went to the glass-fronted refrigerator behind the counter and got herself an Amstel Light. The rest of us just sat. We seemed to have hit a wall.

My mind was still working, though. I knew things about Hoppy that the rest of them did not. I was sifting through the dates and places and dramatis personae, looking for anything that fit with the Lizzie hypotheses.

And then something started scratching at my brain.

"Let me see that file," I said. "Not the photos, just the pages. The background report."

Hildy fished it from the pile and handed it over. I flipped back to the bank records Grant had obtained. They went back eighteen years, the entire time Lizzie had been in Nashville. Since there was no attorney to prevent it, that was pro forma research to find out if someone had been extorting money. There were no withdrawals to suggest that was the case.

"Lolo, how much did you pay her?" I asked.

"What a question!" she said indignantly. "I don't see how that is relevant."

"It is, but—fine, fine." I did the mental math. I was good at that. "Was it less than a thousand bucks a week?"

"It was. Really!"

"Less than five hundred?"

She didn't answer. She didn't have to.

"*Cheep!*" Rhonda imitated a bird as she returned to the table. The bottle was already half-empty. The harsh looks suggested her impulsively launched career with the Foxes was on life support.

Lolo's answer was close enough to a figure that fit. I checked another page. "Lizzie's rent was three-fifty a month."

"What does all that mean?" Hildy asked eagerly.

"Thinking," I said. "If we knock out what she managed to save during her years of working for Lolo and what she spent, the woman managed to save—not earned, mind you—seventy thousand dollars."

"I still don't understand," Hildy said impatiently.

"She's saying that's a lot of bread," Rhonda said.

"It *is* a lot," I said, "but that's not what's interesting." I was still working the numbers as I went through the bank statements. "She deposited decent-sized checks every June for the last ten years."

"That's how long she worked for me," Lolo said, trying to reclaim control of the discussion.

"Did you give her summer solstice bonuses?" Rhonda taunted.

"Not for $1,023.11," I said, looking at the last one. "That's a tax refund."

"So?" Mollie asked.

"There were no rebates before she went to work for Lolo. And the deposits weren't weekly, they were sporadic. Once every three months . . . six months. . . ."

"What am I missing?" Rhonda said. "Someone was paying her off the books. That's how I pay my gardener."

"Someone was paying her when they had the money," I said.

I didn't have to say anything more. They all knew someone who was constantly looking for revenue. They didn't necessarily know who else among them had been tapped by Hoppy or how, so no one said a word.

"I think this session is over," Lolo said.

I agreed, and the ladies made a very subdued and hasty end to it. Even Rhonda was unusually quiet, albeit for a different reason.

"I'm confused," she said, grabbing another beer as the others left.

"Me too," I admitted.

She chugged half the bottle. "Do we think Hoppy was paying Lizzie for something? For being a nanny?"

I looked at her. From the mouths of boozers—

"Did Hoppy have a kid?" I asked.

She shrugged. "Who knows? I didn't know Lizzie was a carpet cleaner until tonight."

I had to call Grant. We may have gotten some things wrong.

I thanked Rhonda for coming and all but pushed her out the door after taking the empty bottle from her hand.

"What's the hurry?" she asked.

"You're driving," I said. "No more drinkee."

"Oh, balls! You got a date? Is that it?"

"Yeah."

"Not with my ex-husband. . . ." she said threateningly.

"Not with Royce, God, no!"

"Hey, watch your mouth! What's wrong with Royce?"

A lot, I thought, but I didn't have time to go into that now. I managed to get her outside, locked the door, and called Grant.

Chapter 27

I scooped up the file and let myself out. Helen was still parked down the street. I could see her head was bent, her shoulders moving lightly. I didn't know whether she was relieved because she'd wanted to come out, or whether she was afraid of social consequences for an impulsive act. In any case, I decided to let her be. She was, however, a little less intimidating than she'd been the day before: despite that big play of setting me up and knocking me down, she had the same insecurities and tender spots as li'l ole me.

I had told Grant to meet me at Lizzie's place. We had stuff to go over.

The apartment was still a crime scene with a patrol car parked out front. I waited in my car until Grant arrived. He walked me in.

"Productive night?" he asked—a little condescendingly, I thought.

I gave it to him between the eyes, told him what

the Foxes had figured out. He was impressed and, I think, a little embarrassed. His mouth definitely assumed a scrunching posture when he glanced at the door.

"We've been circling some of that ourselves," he said, a tad defensively. "We've got requests out with the RCMP, checking into any reason she might have left Canada. The IRS is looking into her tax records. We also found out that Lizzie occasionally frequented a girls-only bar in—"

"All useful but none of that gives us Hoppy Hopewell."

"Gwen, we can't assume a serial killer based on Lolo as a common link. I'll grant you there *may* be a connection—"

"I'm not the press, Grant. You *will* admit it would be a humungous coincidence if these killings are unrelated."

"Yes."

"Then we need to fit them together somehow. Starting, maybe, here."

I took him to the bedroom, showed him the blue ribbon on the edge of the carpet.

"Yeah, we saw that," Grant told me. His hands went defiantly to his hips. "Let me explain something. We have a methodology, the way we remove and categorize evidence. That goes from event-related—the body, the murder weapon, the blood, hair and fingerprints from the immediate murder vicinity—"

I cut him off. "Can I borrow your pen?"

"Sure." He lifted his lapel and I lifted his ballpoint. It was imprinted with the name of a local realtor, Stacey Paul. I knew her. I frowned.

"What?" he asked.

"She's a walking advertisement for breast enhancement."

"Oh, please. It's a good time to buy."

"Homes or implants?" I asked.

I couldn't help myself. He put on a give-me-a-break look and I went back to work. I squatted and touched the top of the pen to the ribbon. Nothing happened. I used the plunger to flip the ribbon over. I touched the top to the ribbon. It stuck. I lightly shook it free and rose. I handed him back his pen.

"There was a baby at some point," I said. "This was taped in an album, an album it obviously slipped from, an album that was taken." I looked at the bed and the trail of scattered clothes. I took a rain boot from the corner, weighed it with my hand, and tossed it on the bed. It bounced off. "Our killer walked in here, flopped the album on the bed, didn't count on it flying to the floor, and scooped it up quickly as he went to check the dresser."

"The perp didn't see it fall out," Grant said.

I ignored his obvious conclusion. "Racy" Stacey had gotten under my skin.

"Let's assume, for the purpose of this discussion, that Hoppy fits in this scenario some way," I said. "How?"

"Well, if there is a baby and Lizzie didn't have it—"

We looked at each other. I tried to speak but my brain was frozen with the realization:

"Hoppy had a kid with Anne," Grant said. "*She* may not have been the one he was supporting."

Thanks, brain, I thought. *Now he gets the points for that.*

My brain didn't care. It had a gender and an age range and was compiling a list. There was Gary Gold. My own Luke. Lolo had said the electrician was a boy—did he know the back way in? Most likely, since that was how servants entered in Lolo's world. And what about the chauffeur's son Gordon. Maybe his father was covering for *him.*

Idiot! Hoppy and Anne wouldn't have had an African-American baby.

How do you know he's African-American? Maybe Gordon adopted a white child!

Stop! I yelled at myself.

"But let's put 'er in reverse," Grant went on. "Even if there is a child, we don't know where he lives or whether he killed either of them. Or whether someone else knows what we know and is trying to frame said hypothetical child. This is a town full of—what's your word?"

"*Yentas,*" I said. There was the annoying "you people" again.

"That's the one. Hell, Gwen, we don't have anything *approaching* a motive, other than that Hoppy was a tomcatting swindler."

"What about insurance?"

"That's a negative," he said.

"Huh?"

"I called in a favor from Clancy at Ryan & Clancy Insurance, had him make some calls. Hoppy had a policy that expired two years ago. He terminated it for the cash value, about twenty-five grand."

Ouch. So Grant was holding back from me the same way I held info from the Foxes. He seemed to read my mind.

"I received that call during your tête-à-tête with the Foxes."

We stood there again in silence. Standing in the bedroom, her clothes strewn around us, I couldn't help but think about poor Lizzie. The only thing we knew for sure was that the butler didn't do it. *But why was she involved? Who did she let in?*

"Two years ago, you say?"

He took out his notebook. "January 2009."

"A little over two years," I thought aloud. "You know, there is one thing the killings have in common."

"What's that?"

"The tenderizer to the head, the drill to the brain—in both cases the murder weapons were handy."

"Okay—the crimes weren't planned. I agree with that."

"They're also different," I said. "The first one may have been a crime of passion, the second one of reluctant necessity."

"Possible," Grant said. "What has that got to do with the two-year thing?"

"Hold on." Something else hit me. I turned and ran to the living room.

"They're not here," I said.

Grant had followed me in "What's not here?"

Heart and brain were together on this one: they did not feel like sharing. "I'll tell you when I check something."

"Gwen, this is a killer we're dealing with!"

"I know," I said.

"I'm coming with," he said. "Where are we going?"

"To see a writer about a newspaper article."

Chapter 28

We took separate cars, not because it made logistic sense—we had to pass Lizzie's on the way back to town—but because I didn't want to be with Grant any more than I had to.

It made a sick, sad sort of sense, I thought as I drove.

I want him, I don't want him. He's being too familiar and personal, he's being too disinterested and professional. I had to blame my delicate gyroscope on the ex. I wanted a man, a good man, to be around me, but I didn't want him to be too close. Or stay close. Or be in the same zip code. I don't know. Phil failed at the first and corrupted the second with his presence. I was a victim of need versus fight-or-flight.

Or I was being a *kvetch*. Maybe my mixed signals were destabilizing *his* gyro.

Fortunately, there wasn't time to contemplate any of this; the ride to Confederate Hill was a short one. I parked in front of Gary Gold's house and was at the door before Grant arrived. He got there as I rang the bell.

There was no answer. But I would have bet dollars to Hamantashen he was home. Gary felt safe there. It was probably the only place the poor kid—and possible multiple killer—felt safe.

I knocked. "Gary, it's Gwen Katz. I need to talk to you."

"Go away!" he wailed.

"He did this last time," I said to Grant.

"What last time?"

"Someone close to him died," I said. "He cocooned."

"What's going on?" Grant asked quietly. "Do you think this man is our killer?"

"It's possible," I said.

"You'd better stand aside."

"If he's our man, I don't think you have to worry about him shooting," I said. "Otherwise, we would probably have two gunshot victims."

Grant considered that, then leaned past me and hit the door several times with his fist. "Mr. Gold, it's Grant Daniels of the Nashville PD. Please come to the door."

"I don't want to!"

"You don't have to admit us," he said. "But I do need to speak with you. If necessary, I will come back with a warrant for your arrest."

"I know police procedurals!" he said defiantly. "You need cause to subpoena a person of interest—"

"Not when that individual has concealed the

fact Hoppy Hopewell was his father and Lizzie Renoir was his nanny," I said.

The silence from inside the house was thick as *latke* batter. Grant's face was a black silhouette against the city-light glow in the nighttime sky, but I did not have to see it to know he was surprised by my certainty.

"So much for drawing him out," Grant said. "While we're out here, why don't you just ask if he killed them?"

"He'll come."

"What makes you so sure."

I knocked again. "Gary, I'm your friend, remember? You've been to my house."

"What, you're backtracking now?"

I ignored Grant. He was being anal, didn't like that I was treating his by-the-book like an e-edition, skipping here and there. *Tough nuggies,* as they used to say in my hood.

"I know about your mother, Anne," I said. "Please, Gary. Let us in. No one's going to hurt you, I promise."

There was a shuffling sound on the other side of the door. I took some consolation in the fact that if it was followed by a shotgun blast, I wouldn't be around to hear Grant's told-you-so. A chain was slid from its track. A lock clicked. The squeaky door opened slowly on darkness. Framed within it was a wide man. The man-shape moved back into the shadows. Peripherally, I could see Grant looking him over for weapons—if not a gun, then a power tool or kitchen utensil.

"May I—we—come in?" I asked.

He just hovered there, like those pictures of the Hindenburg in Lakehurst.

"Is there a light?" I asked.

"Insuhtoor," he said. It took me a moment to pluck "Inside the door" from the slurred, unhappy words.

I snaked my arm around the jamb, found a pole lamp, switched it on. Gary recoiled like Dracula, his arms crossed in front of his face. He didn't look like Dracula, however, in his white jockey shorts and a white terry-cloth bathrobe, the kind they have in hotel rooms. There were no bulges in the deep pockets.

I moved in. I couldn't tell if it was just the sudden brightness that bothered him, or whether he was hiding eyes that were bloated from crying. I thought I saw moisture on his cheeks. Grant shut the door and moved to the right so that we formed the points of an equilateral triangle. He obviously didn't want Gary to be able to watch us both. It was pure police and I have to admit it turned me on a little.

I know. A *kvetch* and *meshuge.*

I approached Gary with my hands out slightly, like I was dealing with a drunk at the deli.

"Let me look at you," I said.

"No."

"Gary, come on. I don't want to talk to your sleeves."

That did the trick. He dragged his arms across his eyes, then pulled at his hair for a moment before lowering them. His face was a mess. It wasn't just tears, it was agony.

"Thank you," I said. I was closing the gap.

"Nnnn," he grunted.

I could see Grant moving more cautiously. He was keeping his distance like an orbiting satellite. "Gary, would you answer a few questions for me. About one of your books?"

That seemed to raise the tiniest spark in his eyes. "My books?"

"Yes. *Carl Is Afraid of the Closet.*"

"All right," he said.

"Great. First, I assume the main character was named after your mother's older brother, Karl?"

He hesitated as if considering whether this were a trick question. Then he nodded.

"And your other book—"

"Novel," he said, finding his emotional footing. "It's a young adult *novel*, not a book. A telephone book is also a book."

This was what I wanted: to get him somewhere closer to lucid than *Insuhtoo* and *Nnnn*. "So sorry. You're right," I said. "The other novel—who is Wagner?"

"A 19th-century German composer," he replied.

"Of course," I said. "When your first novel was published, you had a book signing at Lolo's."

"Yes. It was in the newspapers."

"I know. You must have been very happy. I saw a photo of you signing copies."

"Twenty-nine of them," he said.

"Good number. Do you remember signing a copy for Lizzie?"

The name rocked him back a little.

"Gary, don't go away from me—this is important."

He started to raise his arms, seemed to fight the urge to rake his face, then dropped them.

"She's in the photograph," I said.

"I signed it with just my name," he said. "Later, I went to her home and added an inscription."

"What did it say?"

I noticed Grant looking around. He had picked up on the fact that Gold's books were missing from her bookshelf.

"It said, 'To Lizzie,' and then I added with the same pen, 'Who saved my life.'"

Gary started to cry. He stood there heaving like a big baby. I don't mean that as a judgment; he literally looked like a big, swaddled infant.

"Tell me about her," I said. "What did she do for you?"

Through the awful, heartbroken sobs he said, "My father . . . found out . . . about my mother."

"Found out what? That she was pregnant?"

"That . . . of course. But then . . . about . . . the group."

"Baader-Meinhof," I said. "The Red Army Faction."

Gary nodded. The weeping waned; he was tapped out. He looked around and Grant's hand went for his lapel; the detective relaxed when Gray reached for the arm of his tattered old couch and fell onto the seat. I circled to the other side and sat slowly with an extra Gary of space between us.

"Go on," I said. "Tell me about Lizzie and your dad."

"My father . . . Lizzie only knew him from the time he engaged her . . . to care for me," he said.

"Was that in Canada?"

"Yes. My mother was pregnant. She called and told him about that, then told him everything about her connection with the terrorists. She wanted him to take her baby—me—out of the country. She was afraid the police were looking for her, that maybe they knew about my dad, so he found and engaged Lizzie to go and get me."

"Why Lizzie?"

"He figured I'd have an easier time getting into Canada than the U.S.," Gary said. "Even though I had a passport with a different name, customs officials were scrutinizing every first-timer who came from Germany."

"Even babies?"

"Of course," he said. "What better hostage to get a terrorist mom to surrender?"

Good point, I thought. "How did he get the passport?"

Gary smiled. "Dad was pretty resourceful. He had scored a connection to the State Department through a connection in government. Cash in a brown paper bag put him in touch with something called the Dead Passport Office—the graveyard where our old passports go when we renew. He bought one that belonged to a baby—"

"But what if the real person—"

"Showed up? It would be a miracle. Gary Gold was dead. Long live Gary Gold."

It was pretty clever, I had to admit. A victimless

crime that would be a lot tougher to get away with in the post-9/11 world.

"So you came here," I said.

Gary nodded.

"You didn't live with your father, did you?"

"No. When he found out about the RAF, he was afraid he was on some kind of watch list. He set me and Lizzie up in this house. He came by when he could, at night."

"Did you go to school?"

"She tutored me," he said. "She had a teaching degree in Canada."

"How was that?"

He smiled warmly. "She was a hard teacher, but she taught me a lot about words and books and life."

"And—your mother?" I asked. I hated to jerk him from here to there, but I wanted to get him while he was lucid.

"I have not seen her since the day she bore me," he said. "I couldn't exactly renew my passport and Dad didn't have enough money for another."

"Do you know he left her the chocolate shop?"

"I do," Gary said. "He always thought—no, he hoped that with the right encouragement and the passage of time, she might risk coming to America. I understand, from my father's attorney, that that time is not now."

He was fighting tears again. I was fascinated by the story, but at the same time I was increasingly concerned. I could tell, by his expression, that Grant felt the same. Either this young man was severely unstable and had off'd those close to him for reasons as yet unfathomed, or we did not have our killer. I had to start directing the conversation.

"Gary, would you mind sharing something else? How did you feel about your father?"

His smile collected tears in the corner, then respilled them. It was not the smile of a murderer.

"I loved him," he said. "Hoppy Hopewell was a good, good father."

"How so?"

"For one thing, he published my books."

Big, damn duh, I thought. P.O. box for an address and paid for by the cashing-in of his insurance—whence "Policy" Press.

"For another, he paid for this house and put me in touch with his friends, like Lolo, who needed writers. He was always looking out for me."

Gary broke down again and put his face in both hands.

"I . . . miss . . . him . . ." he cried. "That's why . . . I . . . couldn't . . . come to . . . the door . . . that day. . . ."

"I understand," I said, moving closer.

I saw Grant shake his head, but I backed him off with a frown. I laid a hand on Gary's elbow and, like an octopus, he threw his arms around me and hugged me close and bawled into my shoulder. Grant started toward us to rescue me; I shook my head and shifted my eyes back and forth, telling him I was okay and to search the damn house. Grant gave me a look, but I made an exasperated face that I hoped said, "I know it's not admissible but search anyway," and he did. He came back about two minutes later and shook his head. By that time, Gary's hysterics had subsided again. I eased away from him.

"Would you like some water?" I asked.

"Why . . . does everyone think . . . upset people need water?" he asked.

"Maybe because you just cried me a river?" I smiled.

He considered that. "Okay. Thank you."

I went to get it while Grant kept an eye on him. I looked around as I filled a glass at the sink. The place wasn't the dump I'd imagined on my first visit. It was neat, with photographs of a young Hoppy, Anne, and what I assumed to be other family members on the wall. I got a little choked up myself when I saw a tiny black bow tied to a wall frame of what looked like a pretty recent photo of Hoppy at the store. I couldn't forget that he had a sordid side and had preyed on young women. But that had no coin here. As far as Gary was concerned, Hoppy Hopewell and Lizzie Renoir were saints.

I returned with the water and Gary slurped it down. I remained standing. I felt bad for the young man. His lack of social skills was not his fault; Lizzie obviously had done the best she could. But that had been years ago and there had been very little social interaction since then. Gary Gold was effectively a hermit.

Before we left him to his solitude, however, there was one more place I had to go with him.

"Hey, I want to thank you for being so honest and open with me," I said to him.

"You're welcome." He searched for something more to say. "Thanks for the water."

"My pleasure. I have one more question for you, if you're up for it."

He gave me a look that I would describe as borderline wary—not because I thought he had anything to hide but because after he answered he was going to be alone again.

"Do you have any idea who could have done this?"

His chest heaved slightly and his lower lip quivered. But he really didn't have anything left.

"I don't," he said. "I still can't believe any of it." He looked into my eyes. "I'm sorry," he said.

"That's okay," I told him. "I didn't really—"

"No," he cut me off. "About scaring you at your house. This whole thing has left me in a little bit of a daze."

"You don't need to apologize," I told him. "I understand."

I thanked him for his time, but most importantly for his trust. He didn't rise when we left; he continued to sit in his corner of the couch, looking at the spot where I'd been sitting, but probably seeing happier times and people he could only visit in his memory.

Grant followed me out and shut the door.

"Well done," he said.

"Thanks."

"So Hoppy canceling his insurance policy—"

"Yeah. To pay print bills. Nice gesture, but they really didn't help him."

"How so?"

"The only editors he had were a chocolatier and a woman whose first language wasn't English," I said. "Everyone needs a critic."

"That is a fact," he said.

There was an uncharacteristic humility in his answer. I think it was a compliment.

"What's really sad," I went on, "is that never mind the writing. Between Lizzie and Hoppy, they scared the crap out of that kid. He hasn't had a chance to experience much of life himself."

"He's going to have to now," Grant said.

That was a fact too. But it wasn't something I could afford to think about right now. There was still a killer out there, and we were no closer to finding that person than we were an hour ago.

"Someone tried to frame that kid," Grant said.

"I was just thinking that," I told him. That was why they had taken the books signed to Lizzie. And the photo albums. And maybe even planted the blue ribbon for us to find and draw the conclusion we did. The killer was no dope.

"What are you going to do now?" Grant asked when we reached the curb.

"Go back home and go through the Lizzie file," I said. "I want to think about some of the points the Foxes raised. You?"

It was a loaded question. He probably felt like I did the other day when I'd left the door open and didn't know whether or how to close it. Except that in his case, he probably realized that whatever answer he gave was probably the wrong one.

"What do you think I should do?" he asked.

I hadn't anticipated that. He was learning to defer.

"I think you should probably get some sleep," I said. That showed concern, I thought; it was kind of a chickeny bookmark move. I wanted time alone to think.

"That's probably a good idea," he said. "Maybe I'll check in later?"

That was a good, oh-so-mildly pushy response.

"Perfect," I said.

I avoided a kiss but gave his hand a squeeze as I went around to the driver's side and headed into the night.

I did, however, succumb and snagged a glance in the rearview mirror as I pulled away. The boy *was* standing there watching me go.

Whatever other *tsuris* was poking and driving me, that made me grin.

Chapter 29

I got home feeling beat. Not just physically but emotionally; the visit with Gary had not been the walk to the scaffold I had been expecting.

I flopped into the sofa with a Diet Coke, pushed the cats away—they knew when I meant business—and set my laptop on the coffee table. I had the edited Lizzie folder beside me with the notes I'd taken during the Cozy Foxes dinner.

The Hoppy-Anne-Lizzie-Gary pieces all fit now. They formed a nice little tray puzzle that seemed to have absolutely nothing to do with the two murders. I was starting over.

I went back through my favorite places hoping something would stand out, trigger a new direction. The only thing new we had was that whoever tried to frame Gary knew more about him than the rest of us had. They knew about Lizzie and probably about Hoppy. That left a lot of gossipy rich people on the table.

But why? What started this?

I was going through my files and stopped on the old newspaper article. I wished the photographer had taken a reverse angle so I could see Gary's face. It would have been nice to see him happy—

"Hello!"

I was looking at the fuzzy photo of autograph seekers at Lolo's house. There was a face in the crowd—

A tumbler clicked into place.

It reminded me of something someone had said. Another tumbler.

That reminded me of something *that* person had said.

Tumbler number three. I reached for my cell phone and remembered I left it in my coat, which was on the coat rack by the door. I had to call Grant, tell him—

The doorbell rang as I reached into my pocket. I opened it. "You saved me a call—"

It wasn't Grant.

Poodle Baldwin stood at the threshold. "Can I come in?" she asked.

I tasted the egg salad I'd had for dinner. "Sure," I smiled and stepped aside, the phone in my palm.

Poodle entered. She shut the door behind her. She was wearing a duster. Her other hand was in her pocket. We stood two feet apart staring at each other.

"Hi," she said belatedly.

"Hi," I replied awkwardly.

"You were at Lizzie's tonight."

"I was," I said. "How did you know?"

"I dated that cop," she said, then frowned. "Not yours," she added quickly. "The one in the car. The one who was on his cell when you left."

"Nice guy?" I asked.

"A peach," she replied.

"So he just happened to mention—"

"No. I asked." She looked down at her feet. I couldn't tell if she was ashamed or marshaling her energies or thinking or all of that. I had my eye on the hallway to my right, beside the sofa. If I needed to make a run for the bathroom or bedroom—

"You were at Lizzie's too, weren't you?" I asked boldly. No sense dragging this out. "Not today, but—"

"I killed her," Poodle said without a hint of remorse. "Also that shit Hoppy. I tried to tell you the other day, before I went to Lizzie's. But you weren't hearing me. I thought you would. I thought you would understand."

"I did!" I insisted. "My God, you think I don't know what a man like Hoppy could do?"

"He wasn't a man," Poodle said. "He was a creature. An it. A dog who used young girls the way a stud uses bitches. Him and that sick beast he procured for. The thing that made Hoppy worse is that he made you think he cared."

"He may have," I said.

"Only for *one* woman!" Poodle said with anguish. "The German girl. I was just a substitute for her. He took my heart and my body and he broke them all up because he had fallen for his little tart girlfriend and couldn't have her! We all became little Annes. You know why?"

"No," I said.

"I think because it was right before the fall," she said. She was starting to lose it now. She began to approach me. I backed away, toward the hall. "When he met her, he was still a poor little rich kid, free to roam the world and pluck whatever young petals he wished. Then he found out he was broke. It was the last time he was happy Hoppy!"

I didn't know how on-target her pop psychology was, but there was probably some truth there. That, plus the fact that he struck me as an arrested adolescent who couldn't relate to any woman over fifteen.

"I hated him and I promised myself he wouldn't get away with what he'd done," Poodle said. "I vowed to stop him from damaging other girls."

"Yet you waited all this time—"

"For a plan!" she said. "Oh, and to get through years of therapy *because of what he'd done to me!*"

"But why Lizzie?"

"I went to her because—Jesus."

"What?"

"You know, I didn't plan to kill Hoppy."

"Excuse me?"

She started to weep. "I didn't plan to kill him! I phoned him. I told him I had to talk to him. He said he thought that was a bad idea. I said I'd be at the party and would meet him there, that I only wanted to see him for a few minutes."

"Why?" I asked.

"I wanted an apology," Poodle said. "That's all. Just—you know, a 'Sorry for what I did. It was wrong. *I* was wrong.'"

"I didn't see you there that night. The police didn't know—"

"I told my mother I'd meet her inside. I said I wanted to have a walk around. I knew the grounds. I've been there. I even went with my mom to one of their stupid meetings so I could check the place out."

"So you went up the back where you'd arranged to meet Hoppy."

She nodded.

"And he didn't apologize."

Poodle laughed through her tears. "Apologize? That twisted shit tried to *kiss* me! He said he still had feelings! I mean, Christ! He backed me against the cabinet and the table with the tool chest and—"

She removed her hand from her pocket. She was holding . . . her car keys. I relaxed slightly as, almost trance-like, she reenacted what she'd done.

"The box was open," she said. "My hand was on the drill. I had nowhere to go and started to push him back with one hand while I happened to press the trigger with the other. It came on. I remember thinking, *'Batteries!'* A silly thought at a time like that, right?"

I didn't know. I couldn't imagine what was going through her tortured little mind.

"The next thing I remember was Hoppy sort of—gurgling, I guess. There was blood in his mouth. He fell backward. I looked at the drill as he disappeared. I tried to wipe the blood away with my shirt, I just scrubbed the whole thing. Then I ran."

"Out the back again?"

"Out the back and into the night and back to the car. I drove home and called my mom and told her I hadn't felt so good. She had someone bring her home."

"Poodle, I understand all of that—but Lizzie? And why try to frame Gary?"

"When I realized what I had done . . . I'm sorry, I really did try to tell you. But when that didn't work, I went to Lizzie. I figured if anyone would understand, it would be her."

"You knew about her and Hoppy and also Gary because he tutored you and told you about himself."

"Tutored me?" She laughed. "He knows as much about writing as he does about pedigreed dogs, which is minus-nothing! I went there to find out all I could about Father Shit. I thought about blackmailing him, and—"

She stopped. Now *she* was crying. Hoppy's legacy: tears all around.

"I told Lizzie what I had done and that I wanted to turn myself in," Poodle said. "I said I'd do that *if* she would tell the court or the police or whoever that Hoppy was a cradle robber. She refused. She was going to call the police. I—I. . . ."

Hit her, I thought. And then got scared. And felt okay framing Gary, not because he was a bad writer and worse tutor, but because of the unfinished business with Hoppy. *The sins of the father . . .*

"So what do we do now?" I asked.

Poodle looked at me with her big eyes. She returned the keys to her pocket with a kind of snake-charmery move. She was gliding forward again. I resumed my own retreat just in case she had something else in there, like a knife or a gun.

The hand came out empty. I stopped. So did she.

Beside the DVD player. Where I'd left the nine-inch kitchen knife when Gary came calling. She picked it up and held it in front of her.

"Everyone deserved what they got," she said. "You see that, don't you?"

This was another Grant situation where there was no good answer. Except that the payoff was death, not sex or abstinence.

"I think we need to have some tea," I said.

"You're going to turn me in to that cop," she said.

"I won't have to," I said. "He's going to be here any moment—he'll figure it out when he sees you with the knife."

She scowled. "You and my mother—you both think I've got my head up my ass. I called my cop friend again before I came in. Said I'd come visit if he was alone. He said he was. Your loverboy went back to Lizzie's to look around, then said he was going home."

"He's not. He's coming here."

"He's not. At least, not until they find you dead."

"Poodle, think about this—"

"Why!?"

I was almost at a point where I could make a break for the bathroom and hope to beat her. But then I'd be trapped with nothing to defend myself except a toothbrush and a Lady Schick.

"I am not going to spend my life in prison because of something a corrupt and evil man *did to me*!"

"There are other options," I said.

"Oh, you mean like *insanity*? A straightjacket and padded room? *This is self-defense!* You people all want to punish me for something I had every right to do, that I had an *obligation* to do! No! I'm not going to suffer anymore!"

She ran at me then and I had no choice but to meet her. The knife cut diagonally across the back of my forearm. It hurt, but not that fine intense pain of a paper cut; it burned like hell. I fell back over the coffee table, which probably saved my life, since I had grabbed my cut arm and my chest was exposed and her return upward slash would have slit me from waist to shoulder. I screamed as I fell and kicked back with my feet to get away, then kicked at her as she threw the table aside, tossing my laptop and Uncle Murray's keyboard across the room.

They landed at Grant's feet as he crashed through the door.

"Hold it, Poodle!" he shouted from behind his beautiful blackened alloy compact police-issue handgun.

She turned on him, snarling.

"Drop the knife and raise your hands!" he said,

both hands tight around the weapon. "I will shoot you!"

I hugged the carpet thinking, ridiculously, how much I really hated it. It's strange where a brain goes in times of danger.

Poodle hesitated.

"Do it!" he yelled.

The knife clattered to the ground. Poodle followed it, falling to her knees and then her side. Grant sidled over and kicked the blade away.

"How bad?" he asked me, nodding to my arm with his chin.

"I think I'm gonna need some sewing up," I said.

He approached Poodle cautiously but quickly. He told her to put her hands behind her back. She was alternately screaming and crying into the floor and didn't seem to hear him. Holding the gun in his right hand, he took the little plasticuffs from a belt loop with his left and managed to get them around her wrists. He put the gun in his shoulder holster, called for backup and an ambulance, and went to the kitchen to get a dish cloth.

"I am really, really glad to see you," I said, choking. The whole thing was catching up to me now.

"I'm glad I'm here," he said as he put a makeshift tourniquet around my arm, just above the elbow. "I'm glad about something else, too."

I looked at him inquiringly.

"That you didn't say *where* I should get some sleep."

Chapter 30

I belonged.

For the first time since coming to Nashville I felt like it—the house, the deli, the city—was home.

That wasn't the result of being part of the murder-solving, though that had its own rewards. It was forcing myself to know the people, to overcome doubt and hard-wiring and to let Gwen Katz through. I had mistakenly seen Nashville as the enemy; it wasn't. It was my past life that held me prisoner.

Not anymore.

I slept soundly that night, partly from a draining of the adrenaline rush, partly from the painkillers they gave me at the hospital. I was able to drive myself to the deli, but I wasn't much good there . . . except to delight and worry the staff.

"You tigress you," Newt said when I told him what had happened.

Luke started singing the theme from TV's *Wonder Woman*.

Thomasina just kept tsking and casting looks heavenward, alternating praying for God to watch over me and thanking Him for my deliverance.

Grant had called around ten to find out how I was, and tell me he was kind of crushed with paperwork and briefing Deputy Chief Whitman, but would stop by after lunch. He arrived a little after one with a look of concern for me that offset the spring in his step.

I was standing behind the counter, *shmoozing* with the customers who came by to ask about my wound; the newspaper had carried word of my adventure, which would also explain why we were unusually busy with diners and pointers.

Grant walked to the far end of the counter, to the swinging door. "How are you?" he asked.

"Sensationalism is good for business," I said. "How are you?"

"Tired but getting things sewn up," he said—immediately regretting his choice of words as he looked at the sling I was wearing. "I just got finished briefing Deputy Chief Whitman so he can finish his investigation."

"How's Mollie?" I asked. "Apart from the obvious."

"Distraught, of course, and trying to figure out what to do next. They've got Poodle in a psych ward at Vanderbilt. Her involvement with Hoppy was obviously quite a shock to her mother, but she confided that it did help to explain a lot of her behavior."

"What kind of charges do you think Poodle's facing?"

"Too early to say. She's probably looking at manslaughter on Hoppy but it's Lizzie that may put her away for life—if not in jail, then in an institution. I don't think anyone would argue that she was in her right mind after the party. Your testimony may be crucial there, since you're the only one she really talked to."

"Before she came to the house and tried to kill me, you mean."

"Yeah."

"I guess the real casualty is Gary," Grant said. "Solly was pretty forthcoming this morning. He said that Anne Miller's intention is to give all the money from the sale of the shop to Gary. Could net him two or three hundred thousand, maybe more."

"That'll be a good start."

"As long as he doesn't use it to self-publish," Grant said.

"I was thinking. I know some book publishers in New York, some professionally, a few socially. I wonder if they'd be interested in a memoir about this whole affair. Could make Gary a lot of money if someone worked with him on it."

"That's awfully nice of you," Grant said. "I got the feeling a little of the mist cleared from his mountaintop yesterday. Sounds like all of this was something he had to work through."

"He definitely didn't have things easy emotionally. It's too bad his mother's not going to try and come to the U.S. to run the chocolate shop," I said. "That would be good for them both."

"Maybe, but the BPOL still wants her. If she came here, I'd be obligated to report it. No way around that."

"Even if you sort of didn't 'know' she was here?"

"I couldn't. Women should think about stuff like that before they start kidnapping, bombing, and having kids."

The absurd juxtaposition sounded almost Yiddish. Maybe one day I'd be able to explain the concept to him.

Grant gave me a lingering look. "You did great," he said. "You're really something."

"Thanks. You didn't do so bad yourself." I replayed that quickly in my head. Added, "*Aren't* so bad yourself."

"It's gonna be like this, isn't it?" he said. "A dance."

"Pretty much, at least for now," I said. "Can you handle it?"

"Watch me," he grinned. "Oh, yeah." He reached into his shirt pocket. "Remember I told you Clancy owed me a favor? The insurance guy?"

"I do."

"It's because I told him I could get the Tennessee Insurance Providers League a way better deal for food than those crooks that catered their last convention," Grant said. He put a business card on the table. "Call him."

I smiled. "Gee. Thanks!"

"My pleasure." He turned to go.

"And by the way, they're not crooks," I said.

"How do you know? I didn't tell you who they were."

"Doesn't matter," I said. "What they are is *gonefs*."

"Gawnuffs," he said. I didn't correct him. "I'll remember that."

"Do that, and if you come around later I'll teach you some more."

"I'll remember that too," he said with a non-committal wink that made me burn . . . but just a little.

What was it my grandmother used to say? "A lung un leber oyf der noz." Literally, don't imagine there's a lung and liver on your nose.

Sound advice. Don't talk yourself into an illness.

I'd take it all as it came. Life, like the menu at Murray's, would always be an evolving work-in-progress.

Note: When Murray the Pastrami Swami passed away, hundreds of delectable recipes passed away with him. However, his Uncle Moonish from Romania, who ran his own delicatessen on Manhattan's Lower East Side (where he hung a sign that said, "Our tongue sandwiches are so delicious, they speak for themselves") and taught Murray everything he knew, did in fact write down some of his recipes, which we, the authors, found among his other possessions (including a stringless ukulele and a signed photo of Alice Faye) that were stored in his daughter's attic in Long Island.

We've updated the recipes where necessary but here they are, in Uncle Moonish's own words.

Moonish's Delancey Street Cole Slaw

Ingredients

3 cups green cabbage, nicely shredded
⅓ cup mayonnaise
1 tablespoon white wine vinegar
2 teaspoons granulated white sugar
(skip the sugar if you got the diabetes, it's OK.)
½ teaspoon kosher salt (regular salt if you don't
have access to kosher salt. I know it's hard to
find kosher salt at gentile stores.)
½ teaspoon celery seed
2 tablespoons prepared horseradish (Gold's
Horseradish is best, but get the white one, not
the red one, because the red one has beets in it.)

Directions

Put the shredded cabbage in a big bowl. What, do
I have to do everything?

In a smaller bowl you should blend mayonnaise,
white wine vinegar, sugar, kosher salt, celery seed
and your horseradish until it's nice and smooth.
Pour the whole thing over your shredded cabbage.
Mix it nice and you'll put a smile on your face with
my coleslaw. Hey, Lucky Luciano, the racketeer,
loved my coleslaw. And if it was good enough for
Lucky Luciano, who are you to complain? The
man killed people for a living. Come to think of it,
as a deli owner, so did I.

Serves six.

Deli-Style Kosher Dill Pickles

Per gallon jar:
8-10 cucumbers Kirby cukes are best
1 large handful fresh dill with flower heads (or
add ¼ teaspoon dill seed if flower heads are missing)
4-6 large cloves of garlic, and make them flat.
Water (what, you were maybe expecting beer?)
½-cup kosher salt or pickling salt
4 teaspoons pickling spice
1-2 large bay leaves

You're probably wondering why there's no vinegar in this recipe. For one, did I say to use vinegar? I did not, so don't. Second, these kinds of pickles get their pickleness from fermenting them, like back in the old country. Who had money for vinegar?

Pack each gallon jar with cucumbers, sprinkling salt between each layer.

Add pickling spice, salt, dill, garlic, and bay leaves.

Fill jar with water but leave two inches of room for brine to form.

Make sure the cucumbers are all under the water. Then cover.

After two or three days, skim off the scummy mishagoss on top. If there isn't any, not to worry.

Let them ferment for three more days (and nights) and check for doneness by cutting off a slice of one cucumber. (Try not to slice a finger in the process.)

Once they are fermented to the right stage—they should still be green—transfer the little bubalehs to a glass jar and put them in the refrigerator.

If you like them more sour, leave them out for a couple of days uncapped, and they'll ferment even more. But not too long—you don't want they should get soggy. A good pickle should squirt your husband or wife from across the table. And mushy pickles don't squirt.

Romanian Potato Salad

First, steal 5-6 pounds of potatoes
1 medium yellow onion, finely chopped
3½ cups of water
¾ cup white vinegar
1¼ cps sugar (A little less sugar
if you got the diabetes. In fact, if you do,
don't use any sugar.)
¼ cup salt (A little more salt
if you like it saltier, a little less
if you're watching your blood pressure.)
2 cups mayonnaise

Boil potatoes with skins on until they're soft. Do not overcook, *shmendrick*. Poke frequently with a knife because a spoon makes a mess. When fully cooked, place in cold water for about an hour. Peel potatoes and refrigerate for one hour. Cut potatoes into cubes (not too small, not too large. Somewhere in between is nice) and place in large bowl, sprinkle with chopped onion. Set aside.

To prepare brine, in a saucepan, mix together:
3½ cups water
¾ cup white vinegar
1¼ cups sugar (see above)
¼ cup salt

Bring this mixture just to the boil, and immediately pour over the potato/onion mixture in bowl. Let the whole shmear soak for an hour.

Drain brine from potato/onion mixture (large strainer is best for this).
Carefully stir in:
2 cups of mayonnaise
Chill overnight. Or, if you're hungry, don't chill overnight. We won't tell.

Serves six, unless fat cousin Irving drops in unannounced, in which case it'll serve three.